LOST CAUSES
Silent Scream

LOST CAUSES: Silent Scream
Copyright © 2022 by Donna J. Thompson

Published in the United States of America
ISBN	Paperback:	978-1-959761-34-1
ISBN	eBook:	978-1-959761-35-8

All rights reserved. No part of this publication may be reproduced, stored in a retrieval system or transmitted in any way by any means, electronic, mechanical, photocopy, recording or otherwise without the prior permission of the author except as provided by USA copyright law.

The opinions expressed by the author are not necessarily those of ReadersMagnet, LLC.

ReadersMagnet, LLC
10620 Treena Street, Suite 230 | San Diego, California, 92131 USA
1.619. 354. 2643 | www.readersmagnet.com

Book design copyright © 2022 by ReadersMagnet, LLC. All rights reserved.

Cover design by Kent Gabutin
Interior design by Daniel Lopez

LOST CAUSES
Silent Scream

DONNA J. THOMPSON

ReadersMagnet, LLC

This novel is dedicated to my Grandson Arron Andrew Thompson who was one of my main characters. It makes me happy to know you have inherited some of your grandmother's talent for creative writing.

Whatever you do in life, I wish you the best.

Lost Causes

Casey West received the same attention at the 17th Precinct, in the Springfield police department, as she did everywhere else she went. The young officers ran into each other trying to be helpful, and the older men huddled in the corner, punching each other and giggling like schoolgirls.

Officer Tim Kelly led her to, Homicide Detective, Karl Larkin's, door, knocked, and was asked to enter.

Karl Larkin looked up from the stack of papers on his desk taking in the young officer and the attractive young woman with him. Her long caramel colored hair fell around her oval face as she turned to face Larkin. Now, he understood what the commotion out front was all about.

"What's her story?" Larkin let his breath out in a sigh. After a long night of going over cold cases and finding nothing new, he wasn't in the mood for this. Their department had few unsolved cases, but Larkin had trouble with having even one. When he was off duty, he spent his time looking through the unsolved cases. He laid the files in question aside.

"This is Ms. West… Her problem is kind of complicated…" Tim informed him. "I'd better let her tell you."

"Where's Cramer?" His partner, Ted Cramer, usually dealt with people first and only allowed the ones who truly had a problem to see him.

"Does she have a murder to report?" After all, this was homicide.

"Cramer's in court today, don't you remember?"

Ever since he'd turned fifty, Larkin felt as though the younger guys treated him as if he suffered from dementia. Because of lack of sleep, it had slipped his mind about his partner having to testify today in the Tibbs case.

Larkin felt a pang of regret remembering the drive-by shooting that left a widowed mother devastated. Her nineteen-year-old son was shot in the head and left to die in the street. It turned out that he was only brain dead and Mrs. Tibbs had to make the decision to pull the plug. Cramer was the lead detective in that awful case.

"I told Ms. West that if anyone could help her, you could, sir," Tim said.

Larkin raised his eyebrows. He was two weeks past his fiftieth birthday, two years past a broken heart, and born immune to flattery.

"She would make a great cure for a broken heart, wouldn't she, sir?" Tim lowered his voice to a whisper and gave Larkin a wink as if reading his mind. Everyone in his precinct knew Larkin had gotten involved with a woman in a previous case and it left him wide open to pain.

"A little young—don't you think? What is she? Twenty-five...?"

Casey had had enough. She was standing right there, for heaven's sakes, and she could speak for herself. Just because she had blonde highlights didn't mean she was stupid.

Tim introduced Casey to Karl Larkin and left the room.

"Sit down, Ms. West." Larkin indicated the chair in front of his desk.

"Call me Casey," she said, sitting down and taking inventory of his appearance at the same time.

He was clean-cut, no beard or mustache, no potbelly, pretty decent shape, probably between forty-five and fifty. He was dressed in gray slacks and a gray and white pullover shirt. He wasn't her type, but he was an attractive man.

"I hope I'm not keeping you from anything," she said, crossing a pair of extremely long legs and turning to face him.

"What is it you wanted to see me about, Ms. West? I'm sorry—Casey."

The man got right to the point. She was happy about that. What she had to say was too important for the detective to be distracted.

She took a deep breath. "I don't really know where to start."

"How about the beginning…?"

"I'm an adopted child, Mr. Larkin. I didn't know that until my parents died, or at least the people who I thought were my parents. They were in an auto accident about a year ago. I was sorting through my dad's papers and found a file about my adoption. There were pictures of my real parents, the Franklins, and a sister I didn't know existed. The file also contained their last known addresses."

Larkin stifled a yawn and shifted in his seat. Another lost relative… He was really not in the mood for this.

"As soon as I found out I had another family, I hired a private detective to locate them for me."

"And was he successful?"

"Yes—and no…The PI gave me some disturbing news." She seemed embarrassed. "I found out my mother suffered from mental problems. I assume that is why our real parents gave us away. My mother was in the hospital more than out, and my father couldn't cope alone with two little girls."

"I'm sorry," Larkin said and meant it.

"Oh, it was fine for me," she assured him. "The Wests provided me with a good life. My sister wasn't as lucky. She ended up in foster care. The information in the file indicated that she suffered from emotional and mental problems just like my mother.

My guess is that she was already showing signs of schizophrenia when my dad abandoned us."

"My real father was a brilliant artist and, having to deal with my mother for years he didn't want to go through the same thing with my sister. As it turned out, neither did my adopted family. At first, the Wests were interested in adopting both of us, but they found out about my sister's problems, and they refused to take her."

"My PI said that at one time, my sister lived right here in Springfield with her husband and child"

"What about your real parents? Did you find them as well?"

"My mother took her own life several years ago. Soon after that, my dad died of cancer."

"I'm sorry."

"It's all right. I never really knew them."

"What's your sister's name?" Larkin thought he may have dealt with her in a professional capacity.

"She married a Thompson, but the marriage never lasted. The way I understand it, the responsibility of raising a child was too much for her. You see, the boy also has problems. He's a patient in the hospital where I work. Lakeview, do you know the place?"

"I was born and raised in this town. I know it well." And heard all the jokes about Lakeview where they served soup to nuts.

"Seems ironic that I would choose psychology as my profession, doesn't it?" Her eyes clouded with pain.

"Are you a nurse?"

"I'm a psychologist. I'm doing my internship there."

"You seem awfully young."

"I'm thirty."

"Like I said—you're awfully young."

"I found out that my sister, Ruth, was once a patient at Lakeview, and that her son, Arron, is still there. I wanted to be his doctor, so I asked for the job."

"I've heard that it's difficult to get a position there," Larkin said. "You must be very good."

"Actually, I had help getting the position. A family friend runs the place. He and my adoptive father were very close. In fact, when I was small, he spent so much time with our family, I started calling him Uncle Jerry."

"I wasn't implying you weren't qualified," Larkin assured her.

"I found out where my sister lives and paid her a visit. She wasn't happy to see me like I'd hoped she'd be." She hung her head but not before Larkin could see the pain in her eyes.

He cleared his throat. "Unfortunately, a lot of times, that is the case."

"But that really isn't the problem. The woman who claims to be Ruth Thompson is an impostor. She's not the same person as in the photo I found in the file."

Larkin shifted in his seat again and shook his head. "It's hard to get a good likeness from most pictures. I'm assuming the photo was taken some time ago. The same person can look entirely different depending on the lighting and the shadows."

"But the woman in the photo has dark hair—the woman who claims to be Ruth Thompson is a blonde."

"Women never leave their hair the natural color." He stared at top of her head.

"It's highlighted," she said defensively. "But the woman who claims to be Ruth Thompson is a true blonde. A woman can tell."

Larkin shook his head and smiled. "Is it a black and white picture?"

"Yes… but it's not just the hair. The two women look nothing alike. Someone had written on the back of the photo that she was twenty-five when the picture was taken in 1987. I was only fifteen that year so it makes her ten years older than I am. She would be forty now."

"Like I said… the lighting or the shadows—anything can cause the same person to look completely different." Larkin said.

Casey gave him a hard stare. He knew, she wasn't happy with the way things were proceeding.

"I asked the director at Lakeview, Kathryn Bailey, if I could have my nephew's case. At first, she refused, saying that I was too inexperienced, but I went to Jerald Connors, my adopted father's friend— he's the one I told you about. He had the boy's case assigned to me."

Larkin stared at her. Not only was she beautiful, she was determined.

"I didn't tell him about my relationship to the boy."

"Do you think it would have blocked your chances of getting the job?"

She hung her head. "I don't know—but the boy's case is too important for me to take the chance. I'd rather this information be kept confidential."

Larkin shook his head. "Casey, are you here to report a crime?"

"I'm coming to my point, Detective Larkin—I really am. It's just important that you hear my entire story. A nurse by the name of Trudy Madison works with me. Most of the doctors and nurses are not allowed in the South Wing. It's where patients are kept, who are a threat to themselves or to others."

"You mean the ones who're considered dangerous?"

"Exactly… they hire and train special people to work that floor, and the rest of us aren't allowed back there. Anyway, Trudy went there to take pictures. She thinks they mistreat their patients, so she went there hoping to get evidence. She knows I have a heart for these lost souls as well, so she showed me the photos. One of the women she snapped a shot of looks just like the picture I found of my sister, Ruth. I believe that woman is truly my relative, not the lady they released to live on her own." She stared at Larkin, trying to gauge his reaction. "You don't believe me, do you?"

"I believe you want very much to find your family…"

"That's not all. Later that day, I met with the boy."

"What's wrong with him?"

"Kathryn Bailey, the supervisor, said he hadn't spoken since they brought him and his mother to the hospital the last time. Bailey claims he's delusional."

"I'm sorry to hear that."

Casey could hear his impatience but also the sincerity that echoed in his voice.

"When I first met with the boy, I'd forgotten that I'd left a large copy of the pictures Trudy gave me, lying on my desk. My sister's photo was on the top. When Arron walked into the room his eyes went straight to it. "You recognize her, don't you?" I asked. Never taking his eyes off the snapshot, he said, "That's my mother.""

"I thought he didn't speak?"

"I didn't think so either. I quickly closed my door and began to question him. At first, he didn't respond. I told him he might as well talk to me because I was on to him. He finally admitted to throwing his pills away. He said he didn't take them because they made him feel weird."

"I've heard that these people don't like taking their medication," Larkin said.

"These people, as you call them, are just like anyone else. The only difference is they have an illness of the mind instead of a physical condition, Mr. Larkin."

"I meant no offense, Miss West…Believe me."

"Anyway, I could tell he didn't trust me, and it broke my heart. I don't know what's going on at Lakeview, Mr. Larkin, but something is. I told him I would go along with him pretending to take his medicine, for a while until I found out if he really needed it."

"Couldn't that be dangerous—him not taking his medicine?"

"I'm beginning to believe there's nothing wrong with the boy."

"Are you allowed to prescribe medication or take it away?"

"No, not really… But, Mr. Larkin, please don't make this about me."

Larkin was reluctant to point out the fact that she was young, inexperienced, and personally involved. He'd seen it all before. The young kids who'd studied to become detectives came out gung-ho ready to catch bad guys. They didn't have a clue how to go about solving a crime. It took years on the job, dealing with criminals to do that.

"Arron also told me they try to make him believe the blonde woman is his mother."

"Didn't you say the boy is delusional?"

"What about me, Detective Larkin? Do you think I'm delusional?" she asked.

"Of course not…"

"But you don't believe me?"

"I think, you're a young lady who is desperate to find her real family. You've run into some problems, and you're feeling frustrated. Lakeview has never had a complaint lodged against them in all the years I've worked for the department."

"So, what you're telling me is that I'm wasting my time here," she said as she stood to leave.

"I'm sorry," he said. "But this is the homicide department. So unless you're reporting a murder…?"

"Let me get this straight. There has to be a murder before you take me seriously? I'm here because people are trying to say an impostor is my sister and a normal child is insane. Isn't that worse than killing them?"

"I know you're upset, but I haven't heard any proof of a crime," Larkin said. "Suspicion and proof are two different things…"

"I'm sorry to have bothered you, Detective Larkin. I'll find my own way out," she said, rising and walking toward the door.

She met Cramer in the doorway, and he had to step aside to let her pass.

"Don't step on your tongue," Larkin snapped, as Ted Cramer, his partner, came into the room.

8

"Wow! What was that?" he asked, stepping back to the doorway and continued to watch her swinging hips as she retreated.

Larkin quickly filled his partner in on the short version of her story.

"Sounds like the whole family's crazy," Cramer said.

"She's a psychiatrist or psychologist at Lakeview."

"I rest my case," Cramer quipped.

Chapter 2

Jerry Connors was a gentleman; everyone who knew him said so. At sixty-five, he had the body of a forty-year-old. He lifted free weights and ran a couple of miles every other day. He had gotten to the supervisor's office early and listened to the tape. Afterward, he sat for a time before speaking. Finally, he turned to the woman who had delivered the recording to him the first thing this morning.

"Kathryn, I thought you could handle this project," he said, a troubled frown marring his handsome features. "Let's face it. You're no beauty, and you'd think a woman built like an ironing board, would have learned to use the few brains the good Lord gave her," he said, running his fingers through the thickness of his white hair. "Turns out you've been outsmarted by a eighteen-year-old kid."

"That boy is sneaky," she said, gritting her teeth. "How was I supposed to know he was throwing his pills away? I feel like giving him a good beating."

"That would draw some unwanted attention, now, wouldn't it?" he said, walking over to the window that overlooked a man-made lake.

"What do I do—pry the jerk's mouth open and check to make sure the pill goes down?" Kathryn asked, walking up to him.

"You need to stay on top of things, Kathryn, that's why I have you here."

"At least I had the idea to bug the new woman's office. If it wasn't for me, we wouldn't have a clue as to what was going on."

"Just make sure the boy stays alive. I don't care if his brain is addled, but you understand why we don't need anything calling attention to Lakeview."

"It's easy to see that Casey has already bonded with the kid," he said. "It seems ironic; I know…"

"Why did you hire that little bitch in the first place?"

"I told you, I need to keep an eye on her. Do you think she believed him?" Jerry asked.

"I don't know, but I think she should never be allowed to see him again."

"You leave her to me. I can handle her. She sees me as a father figure, especially since hers passed away." He laughed at the idea.

Kathryn Bailey chuckled with him as she poured two shots of bourbon and handed him one.

"Make sure you get the pills in him before she sees him again," he said, taking the drink she offered.

"So, you're not going to stop her from seeing him?"

"Use your head, Kathryn. She'll get even more suspicious if we start changing things. I told you… I will handle her. You have one job. See to it he has his medication before their next session."

"I don't like it, but it's your call," she said, shaking her head.

"Now, let's talk about the nurse who took the pictures," Jerry said.

"Her name is Trudy Madison. She's a bleeding heart—always touting some cause or other." Kathryn Bailey spread her hands as she spoke and gave him a sarcastic smile. "For some reason, she thinks we're inhumane to our patients in the South Wing."

"She's expendable. Get rid of her!" He turned his frown on Kathryn.

She knew by his fierce stare he wasn't talking about firing the girl.

"She's no more dangerous than your new employee" Kathryn gulped the rest of her drink and set the shot glass on her desk.

His eyes narrowed in a warning as he stared at her. "She's young and impressionable. We need her to recommend keeping the boy and his mother indefinitely. I'll second it, of course. She must never know that she's related to them, however. That's why the nurse has to go,'" he stressed again. "She's giving our young doctor too much information and we can't have her getting suspicious."

"Are you sure that's the reason you want to keep her around?" Kathryn stared directly at him.

"What other reason would I have?"

"Oh, I don't know. Maybe you think you might get lucky."

"It's a thought, but this project means more to me than a piece of ass, Kathryn. That's why I'm warning you to be careful."

"Don't be mad." Kathryn raised her mouth for his kiss. He turned his head away.

"I must punish you for this slip-up. There will be no sex for two weeks. You get rid of the girl and come by my place on Friday, and then we'll talk."

Kathryn poured herself another drink and walked to stand beside of him at the window, taking in the beautiful view of the grounds. Her life had been less complicated before she became involved with him. She hated this place, but it paid the bills and kept a roof over her head. In less than five years she could retire. She could leave much sooner if the scheme they were working on came through. She wasn't going to allow her hopes to get too high. Jerry left too much to chance as far as she was concerned. She was the type of woman who always had a back-up plan. There was one hitch in hers. She knew that Jerry Connors was scum, but he had a hold on her she couldn't seem to break.

"A penny for your thoughts…" Jerry walked up behind her, so close she could feel his hot breath on the back of her neck. His hand cupped her right buttock. He let his lips trail across the back of her neck. She spun around to face him, pressing her body against his, kissing him hungrily. He allowed the kiss to become heated, and then shoved out of her arms. He grabbed her roughly between the legs and squeezed.

"You take care of our little problem, and I'll take care of yours," he hissed, his mouth close to hers. He pushed her away and walked to the door. "I'll see you soon," he said before leaving the room.

Kathryn stood shaking uncontrollably. Not only was she sexually aroused, she was angry. The man knew she had plenty of weaknesses. She wished she'd told him to go screw himself the second he had mentioned the scheme.

What he didn't know was that she had a plan of her own, and she called him the minute her lover left the building. She smiled smugly as she watched Jerry Connors through the window as he slid into the driver's seat of his Lexus and pulled away from the curb.

Within minutes, there was a knock, and a satisfied smile crossed her face. She opened the door to a big bruiser named Sam Talbot.

"You called me, Mrs. Bailey," he asked.

"Yes. Come in and close the door. I have a job for you."

The man was young with a huge physique. He worked exclusively on the South Wing with the criminally insane.

"What do you want me to do?"

"There's a girl who works here who is causing us problems. She's saying things about us that aren't true. She's trying to get us closed down, Sam. If she does, then we'll all lose our jobs."

"What's her name?" His eyes burned with unsuppressed rage.

"Her name is Trudy Madison. She's young and blonde. You might have seen her snooping around, taking pictures. She's trying to make us all look bad, Sam. She's even been to the South Wing… your wing… You shouldn't let her get away with that."

"Do you want me to kill her?"

She approached him and began to fondle him through his white pants. His erection was large and immediate. She stripped off her underpants and sat on the edge of her desk, her legs wide apart. "This is your pay, Sam, for getting rid of her."

Jerking his pants down to his knees, he went to her. She wasn't the best-looking woman he had ever met, but he didn't get many dates, and anything beat the old hand jive.

Sam left the office awhile later zipping his pants. He looked both ways to see that he wasn't watched and then he headed back to his patients. It was the second time Mrs. Bailey had called him to her office and both times had served him well. The first time, she hadn't asked him for anything but sex. This time, she had given him a plan. If the bitch was as nosy as Bailey said she was, the plan should work great.

Kathryn Bailey smiled in contentment. The big stud serviced her well. That would teach Jerry to leave her hot and bothered. If all went well, Sam would get rid of their biggest problem. Who knows? She might get lucky twice in one week. Her loins quivered in anticipation.

Chapter 3

Trudy Madison was ready to go home after her long tiring day. A storm raged outside. While she was standing by the time clock waiting for it to hit 11:00 P.M, a male nurse came up to a pegboard next to the receptionist desk.

He glared at Trudy before hanging up a set of keys and hurrying away. Most employees had left already, and he was probably anxious to leave as well.

Trudy had seen him before and knew he worked in the South Wing. When they had occasion to run into each other, he always frightened her a little. There was something about him that gave her the creeps.

Over the top of the key ring, beckoning like a neon sign, was a label reading South Wing. She and Casey West had talked several times about how they would like to go through the files that were kept there. They felt the management was hiding something and they both were sure the answer was down that the long hallway. Normally, Mrs. Bailey was very protective of those keys and that made Trudy and her doctor friend more suspicious.

Trudy greatly admired Casey West. The young woman was only two years older than her, and she was a full-fledged doctor. What made Casey even more remarkable for Trudy was knowing that she cared about helping people, especially the ones shut away in the South Wing.

Trudy felt sorry for Arron Thompson and the woman she believed to be his mother.

The helpless woman truly loved her son, and now she was locked away from him in a place where no one should have to live. It was sad. She had almost cried when Casey told her the reason her sister had given him the unusual spelling of his name. She said that Ruth wanted him to be different from the other Aarons of the world and different from her as well.

This was something Casey learned from reading an interview a doctor did on Ruth Thompson when she first entered Lakeview. It was all in a report Ruth's first doctor filled out, and he had found it important enough to record it in her file. Trudy knew that when Casey first came to Lakeview, she had gone over the patient's recorded sessions, especially the ones housed in the South Wing.

Casey had pointed out the fact that the woman, she thought was her sister, was able to write out her son's name when she first was committed. That was ten years before Trudy was hired. By all accounts, this Dr. Allen saw nothing but improvement in Ruth. She supposed this was the reason Jerry Connors had recently released her to live on her own. But, in reality, it wasn't Ruth who'd been released. It was all so confusing. Trying to sort through it was giving Trudy a headache.

Casey said the woman living in the South Wing, was supposed to be Dana Collins. The woman's toilet training began to suffer, and she stopped going to the bathroom on her own. She would mess herself and when the nurses tried to change her, she would become violent. She stopped cooperating with the help and that was when she was placed in the South Wing.

Studying her family's detailed records had left Casey more and more troubled.

There was mention in her adoptive father's folder of Ruth's schizophrenia. It caused her real father to give her away and Casey's adoptive parents not to want her. That made Trudy sad. She knew that

Casey didn't believed Arron suffered from the same disease that plagued his mother. So why was the staff at Lakeview convinced that he did?

Trudy sure hoped Casey was right.

It had been the way Ruth had spelled the boy's name that caught Casey's attention. She was all about knowing everything about her real family, and Trudy could understand that.

Trudy's own father had walked out on her and her mom when she was just a baby. She fantasized about finding him one day, but she probably never would. She needed to take care of her mom and that was a full-time job.

Casey told her she never felt like she belonged with her adopted family and now they both knew why. If Casey's suspicions were true, she had a real family, and Trudy wanted to help her find out the truth. Why were the people in charge of Lakeview lying about the woman Casey believed to be her sister? The one locked away like an animal in the South Wing.

Trudy noticed from the start that the blonde woman the staff claimed was Arron's mother never visited him before she was released or after she left the hospital. What really made her and Casey know they weren't imagining the whole thing is when the boy recognized the woman in the picture—the very photo she herself had taken. The boy knew the woman was his mother. It was all very suspicious. Casey had even gone to the police, but they said they needed more evidence. The two of them had discussed the situation and she remembered, Casey saying the proof they needed was probably in the locked room in the dreaded South Wing. Everyone who worked there knew where they kept the files for that floor.

Trudy looked in all directions; there was no one around. All she would have to do is grab the keys and go. The patients were all down for the night, and most of the employees had gone home. Only a skeleton crew stayed the night in case of a problem. Visiting hours had been over since 8:00; the doors locked automatically at 9:00. Employees could leave the building, but no one could enter.

She looked around once more to make sure no one was watching before she hurried to the big double doors. The huge lettering screamed at her: "Authorized Personnel Only." It caused her to stop in her tracks. She considered a moment before boldly pushing the swinging doors open and looking inside. She waited to see if there was any motion from someone working the floor. No one was stirring.

As Trudy surveyed the dim hallway, misgivings flooded through her. The file room was at the very end of the hall, which seemed extra-long tonight. She breathed in slowly and deeply, bolstering her courage.

Co—splat. The wind slammed a wet tree branch against the glass doors in the reception area behind her. She whirled around. The storm outside matched the turmoil she felt inside, but she knew where she had to go. The things happening here were affecting Casey's life and her family's as well. Trudy owed it to her friend to find out the truth.

Swallowing the lump of dread in her throat, she hurried back to the time clock. The keys still beckoned. Coward, her conscience accused. All she would have to do is reach over, slip the ring off the pegboard, and put it into her pocket.

She had tried telling her mother about what was going on, but her mother cautioned her to leave things alone She said Trudy needed to keep her job and accused her of being an ungrateful daughter. After all, she had taken care of Trudy all those years after her dad had left. Now it was her turn to take care of her mother through her sickness. By sickness, she meant her drinking, but Trudy guessed it might be the same thing. Everyone said alcoholism was a disease. Funny though, it was the only disease that involved putting your own mouth to the bottle. She sighed heavily. She'd put her life on hold and had been taking care of her mother as long as she could remember.

She thought about it a few seconds before snatching the keys from the hanger board. She stood there for a few seconds more, pushing them back and forth on the ring. Maybe she should just put them back and go on home. A chill raced down her spine. She felt someone watching her. Again, she wondered if she should return the ring to its holder and just get out of here. There will never be a better time to go, a little voice in her head whispered. There wasn't anyone around. Trudy guessed most everyone wanted to get home before the storm raging outside got any worse. You may never get another chance, the voice whispered.

She moved quickly before she lost her nerve. She slipped the keys in the pocket of her smock to hide them in case she ran into a coworker. She wondered if old battle-ax Bailey had gone home. She usually left by nine, but sometimes she stayed later doing paperwork.

Mrs. Bailey's office was to the left of the reception area, two doors down. Trudy paused by her door. There was no light underneath. She sighed with relief but placed her ear to the door to be sure. The telephone inside Bailey's office shrilled.

"Gee-zee." Trudy jumped. Her heart lurched crazily. She was a nervous wreck, and she hadn't even made it back to the dangerous hallway yet.

Think Trudy, before you go off half-cocked, she said to herself. I'll need a flashlight. She couldn't very well turn on the overheads lights.

She hurried to the pantry where the emergency flashlights were kept and slid the doors open. A mouse scampered over her foot. She screamed so loudly it echoed down the hall. There was nothing like calling attention to herself. She willed her nerves to settle down. When she lifted her head to look behind her, she thought she saw a flash of white at the end of the North hallway. She waited a few minutes, staring at the place in question. She was getting paranoid. So what if someone saw her? No one knew when her shift ended. She had every right to be in the supply closet.

Trudy took a deep breath and closed the folding doors with a soft click.

A sudden crash of thunder shook the windows. A streak of jagged lightning showed through the reception doors. She wasn't in a hurry to go out in this mess, anyway.

Again, she looked around, waited, then moved slowly toward the South Wing, pausing as she neared the closed double doors. She scanned the area one last time before she pushed her way into the hall.

There was only subdued lighting in the area. Mrs. Bailey claimed that bright light agitated the patients. It was plain, bare, and depressing. How did they expect someone to get better living in a place like this? Her guess was, they didn't. This was just a holding place to put them so the world could forget they existed.

She slid along the wall, hoping none of the patients would peer out at her from the tiny window in their doors. She wondered about the woman whom young Arron called his mother. She was somewhere in the middle. Was it room 10 or 12? She couldn't remember. The door had been open that day, and she had heard the screams. She followed the big guys in the white suits and while they were busy trying to restrain the woman, she had snapped her picture. The men had never known she was there. No one had, except Casey, and that was because Trudy had shown her the photographs. Oh, the boy knew, but he wasn't going to tell anyone.

The furnace rumbled on with a jerk. Her heart pounded. The breeze from the ceiling vents caused the little hairs on the back of her neck to rise. Apprehension traveled up her spine. She shivered. She couldn't tell if she was cold, nervous, or both.

The heating system shuddered once more, then stopped. A board creaked beneath her feet. She swallowed the lump of fear that moved to her throat and turned around quickly. She felt there was someone behind her. The door to the file room was closer than the entry doors. There was no turning back; she was too near her destination.

Her hands shook, but the key worked smoothly and she slipped inside. She hadn't really thought about how dark it was going to be. She stood for a minute letting her eyes adjust to the darkness. There were windows on the outside wall, but there were no outside lights. The occasional bolt of lightning was the only illumination. The wind slammed the rain and tree limbs against the glass.

Holding the flashlight down toward the floor, she made her way to the first drawer of files. Leafing through them, she soon recognized the system. They were not alphabetical like most files; but went by the room number for each patient on the South Wing. She quickly found room ten, but the patient was a man. The next file was room 12. Ruth Ann Thompson! There was also a picture of the woman. Trudy gasped. Arron's mother wasn't the blonde woman they had just released from the hospital. The woman, still in room 12, was Casey's sister. It was just as she and Casey figured.

Trudy searched on, not really knowing what she was looking for. Suddenly, she stopped. "Oh my God!" she exclaimed aloud. "Wait until Casey hears about this!"

It was just a swish at first, but she had definitely heard a noise. She switched off the flashlight. She had to get out of here because there was someone else with her in the room. White-hot panic flooded over her. She knew someone would kill to keep her from telling what she had learned. If there were only someplace she could hide. Her eyes fastened on a tall file cabinet to her left. As quickly as she could, she flattened herself beside it and waited for her stalker to make the next move. The footsteps approached her, loud and menacing. She needed to leave Casey a clue in case she didn't make it out of here. She had a pencil in her pocket, but no paper. Then her fingers closed around the tiny business card Casey had given her the day they had lunch together. It was too dark to see what she was writing, but she would do her best. Running her fingers across the card, she felt the slightly raised surface. She flipped the card over and quickly wrote down the clue. Just then, a bolt of lightning exposed her attacker, and Trudy decided to make a run for it.

She sprinted. Her fingers were on the door knob. She was going to make it—then a ham like arm circled her neck. She choked, her lungs begged for oxygen. Her neck snapped like a dead twig! Her flashlight fell to the floor, along with her pencil, and the lights went out for Trudy forever.

Chapter 4

Mrs. Bailey met Karl Larkin and Ted Cramer as soon as they arrived at Lakeview. She was nervously wringing her hands and chewing her bottom lip. "Oh, dear, dear, dear," she said. "I tried to warn that girl not to go snooping around over here. I told her it was dangerous."

"What happened?" Larkin asked.

"An orderly named Sam Talbot found her this morning when he started his shift," Mrs. Bailey said. "He was making his rounds and found her inside Carl Johnston's room, her body crumpled on the floor with Carl's room key clutched in her hand. The patient was once a bouncer at a local club until he went berserk five years ago. He left four men dead. He thought they were fooling around with his wife. He pleaded insanity and was sentenced to the hospital here. We housed him in the South Wing. I tried to warn her that these patients are unpredictable."

"Do you have any idea why she would go to this particular patient's room?" Larkin stopped her tirade.

"Who knows? She was always snooping around. Always complaining about how we're inhumane to our patients. She didn't understand that we had to use force to subdue them sometimes."

"You're saying, she just didn't care how dangerous the patients on this floor are?"

"She must not have, considering what happened to her. We tell our employees in orientation that they're not to be on this wing for any reason. We let them know that the patients on this floor are extremely violent. We hire and train special people to handle them. They're the only authorized personnel allowed back here. You have to be a big man to work on this floor. I never come here, myself, without an escort."

Cramer hesitated, looking around as they walked to the crime scene. "Where are these big guys now?" he asked, making quotation marks with his fingers.

"Don't worry. I've made sure all the patients are locked in, and we have Johnston secured in another room."

"I'll need a statement from everyone who works on this floor," Larkin said.

"I've sent them all to the break room. They were pretty shaken up," she said. "You can take their statements, if you need to."

"Cramer, how about you doing that?" It was the first time Larkin had acknowledged his partner since they arrived. "Send Sam Talbot to me. I need to talk to him personally."

"Sure thing," he said, going quickly before his boss changed his mind. Ted Cramer hated crime scenes. He just never got used to them.

"You'll have our full cooperation. I have briefed all of our employees about that. If it's all right with you, I'll go also. I just don't think I can go back into that room."

"No problem. If I need you, will you be in your office?"

She nodded and hurried away.

Cramer came back a few minutes later with Sam Talbot in tow, embarrassment reddening his cheeks. "I left my notebook at the precinct."

Larkin wondered why his partner had been so distracted lately. He thought maybe something was wrong at home, but now wasn't the time to address personal issues.

"Why don't you borrow one from Mrs. Bailey?"

Cramer nodded, standing immobile as Larkin looked over the scene.

The victim looked so small, lying crumpled in a fetal position. Larkin stooped to look without touching her. "Trudy Madison," he read her nametag.

Cramer shifted from one foot to the other. "Did you know her?" he asked.

"Not exactly…I know she's the one who took the pictures."

"Excuse me?"

Larkin couldn't fault Cramer for not remembering or taking the story seriously. Neither did Larkin at the time, but Casey's tale didn't seem so far-fetched anymore. He had never met Trudy personally, but he knew she was the one snooping around Lakeview, and it had gotten her killed. As he stared into the cold, blue, lifeless eyes he made her the silent vow that he made to every victim. He wouldn't stop until she received justice.

"Go wait for David, will you? You can show him where we are," he said to Cramer. "I'll stay with her."

"You don't think it happened like they said, do you?" Cramer asked Larkin who was still stooped beside the body.

Larkin looked up at him. "We'll know more after the forensic crew gets here."

Cramer knew that look. Larkin wasn't satisfied that a crazy patient murdered a nurse.

Larkin quickly interviewed a nervous Sam, then told him he could go back to the break room. Larkin never used a pen and paper when he talked to someone. He had a photographic memory.

David Blake strode into the room like a man with a purpose. He was one of the best forensic people Larkin knew. Larkin was never happier than when David decided to join their team. "Who found the body?" David asked.

"Sam Talbot. He's an orderly, one of the few people allowed on this floor. This wing is for the criminally insane."

"What did he say happened?"

"His theory is that Trudy was snooping around trying to prove they were mistreating the patients. He said that he and the other guys had to get rough with them sometimes to make them behave, and she didn't understand. He thinks she must have taken the keys after he left and decided to check on a patient. He believes she went to the wrong room, and the man inside killed her."

"She got the wrong room, all right," Cramer shivered. He had followed David Blake, their forensic man, back to the murder scene.

"Sam said that Carl broke the girl's neck. I never mentioned her neck being broken," Larkin told David, raising his eyebrows.

David put on his gloves and stooped to begin his preliminary. "That may not mean much at this point. You and I could tell at a glance because we've been trained. It's possible the killer has had some training also."

"Hell...The way her head is dangling, even I could tell her neck was broken," Cramer insisted.

"It's possible that I'm reading too much into it," Larkin admitted.

Blake was good at his job and Larkin knew because at the 17th Precinct they had gone through a bunch of candidates before David was hired. The man had begged, borrowed, and stolen to construct the crime lab their city owned. David had also insisted on handpicking his crew. When they swooped onto a murder scene, everyone knew their jobs; they bagged, tagged, photographed, and drew sketches of the body and the evidence surrounding it. His people weren't allowed mistakes. David Blake had zero tolerance for incompetence.

"What did you get from the position of the body?" Blake asked.

"It looks to me as though she was thrown inside and the body crumpled to the floor."

"The evidence shows she was grabbed from behind," David said. "See the bruising on the front of her neck?"

"I saw it," Larkin agreed.

"If she had just unlocked the door and stepped inside—how did the patient get behind her? The answer is—he didn't," David said.

"What do you think really happened?"

"I don't know yet, but it's not the way Talbot thinks. To make it work, she would have had to take the key, open the door, and turn her back on an insane man. Unless she was a complete idiot, she didn't do that. See the marks on her neck? They don't go all the way around. They're just across the front."

Larkin nodded. "That is my thoughts exactly."

"Let's take a walk down the hall," David said.

Larkin looked at him incredulously. "You didn't get your exercise this morning?"

"Just follow me," he said, as they moved along the hall. "Do you see the scuff marks on the floor?"

It was the first time Larkin noticed the smudges at intervals between the murder scene and the file room. "What do you make of that?" he asked.

"I believe someone carried her body from down the hall and every so often let her feet drag across the floor. She's a pretty tall woman, and she was dead weight. Her shoe soles are made of rubber. They left marks on the floor."

"Surely, she wouldn't have gone to a dangerous patient's room alone," Larkin surmised.

"What do you know about this case that you're not telling me?" David studied him in the dim light.

"We'll talk more at the station." Larkin sent a silent signal that he didn't care to discuss it here.

"Let's get back to the body," David said.

"How did you notice the scuff marks on the floor?" Larkin asked.

"I have low self-esteem; I always look down."

"And the moon is made of green cheese," Larkin chuckled, shaking his head.

The photographer was finishing up with the supposed crime scene when they returned.

"I took her right handprints, sir, but when I started to do the left, I noticed something in her hand." It was James Taylor, a new member of their crew, who spoke up. "I waited for you to get back, so you could take a look."

"You did the right thing, son," Blake encouraged him. He was fresh out of school, but he was excellent at his job. David had no doubt he would continue being an asset to their group.

She clutched a scrap of paper so tightly, that David had to break her fingers to retrieve it. "It's a business card," he said.

"Whose?"

"Dr. Casey West..."Do you know her?" David asked when he saw Larkin nodding his head.

Larkin put his fingers to his lips, again giving the signal, and reminding David that he didn't want to discuss it here.

"The card has something scribbled across the back," Larkin said, as David was processing the front for fingerprints."

David turned it over. "It looks like, Casey, Franklin owner. It's hard to tell. The writing, it's all run together"

"What do you make of that?"

"I think she left us a clue." David smiled and placed the card in a plastic bag, then slipped it in Larkin's shirt pocket. "Figuring it out is your job."

Cramer kept looking around and fidgeting. "You have to pee?" Larkin asked.

"I hate this place," he said. "It smells like urine and Lysol. It brings back too many memories."

Larkin knew Ted was thinking about the home where his grandfather spent his last days.

"What's our next move?" Larkin asked Blake.

"Well, we have fingerprinted each key on the ring. We printed the door to Johnston's room. I think the next place we go is the room at the far end of the hall."

"Weren't you going to go to the break room and take statements from the people who work this wing?" Larkin reminded Cramer.

"Oh yeah." Cramer looked mortified that he had forgotten.

Larkin decided they were going to have a long talk when they arrived back at the station.

"Don't forget to stop by Mrs. Bailey's office and ask for a writing pad," Larkin reminded.

"Sure," Cramer replied.

"What's up with him?" Blake wondered. "He seems a little distracted."

"He has a lot on his mind lately," Larkin said.

David shrugged. "It's just not like him. He usually keeps us laughing."

Suddenly, Mrs. Bailey showed up with a white-haired gentleman in tow. She walked up to them chattering as if she had drunk too much coffee.

"What are you people doing back here?" she challenged.

"We have reason to believe Miss Madison might have come here first," Larkin explained.

"That's crazy," the woman hissed. "She was always worried about the patients and our treatment of them. Why would she come back here where we keep our paper work? I allowed you to interview Sam Talbot before I sent him home, but you people are going too far."

Larkin flashed David a look when he heard Bailey had sent Sam home.

Blake had used the key marked "File Room" and his men were starting to process the scene.

"I'm Jerry Connors." The man with Mrs. Bailey held out his hand. Larkin shook hands with him, and Jerry continued, "I run this place. We're interested in giving you our full cooperation, but back here is off limits. The patients in this wing are dangerous individuals, and their records are confidential. If we let the police go poking around in them, we're leaving ourselves liable for a law-suit. Surely, you can understand that," he said, spreading his hands.

"We can get a judge to issue a warrant."

"I must insist you stop until you make that call."

Larkin put up his hand to the men. "Can we call from here?" Neither administrator looked happy, but Jerry nodded for him to follow and led him to his office to make the call.

After speaking to Judge Becket, Larkin learned they weren't going to get their court order. Larkin looked directly at Jerry Connors, suspecting that Judge Becket had already gotten a call.

In essence, the judge told Larkin he didn't have the proof he needed. Just because there were a few scuff marks on the floor it meant nothing. So what if her finger-prints were found on the doorknob. It just proved the girl was nosy and snooping around an area she wasn't authorized to be in. After all, that is what had gotten her killed.

Larkin hadn't mentioned the evidence to the judge, so he knew that either Bailey or Connors had already talked to him. The judge also told him to stick to processing the area where they found the girl's body and get back to the station.

How did the judge know what evidence they had? Larkin was angry when he hung up, but, as always, he had control of his emotions. They might have won this skirmish, but the war was far from over.

When Larkin returned to the file room, David and his crew stood in the same position as when he had left. Bailey was still there and Connors followed behind him.

Larkin told them. "We didn't get the order."

Everyone on the team knew what that meant. They gathered their gear and filed out. David was the last one to leave and as he neared the door, stooped and picked up a pencil and a flashlight off the floor. He slipped them in different plastic bags, and then left the room.

"I'm sorry, Mr. Larkin," Connors offered, "but we have to protect ourselves."

Larkin had no doubt about that, but from what was the question. "Is there anyone else we need to talk to?"

"Casey West, a new doctor here. I think she and the girl were pretty close. Since this is her day off, you'll have to talk to her tomorrow."

"I'll do that," Larkin made his way back to where the forensic team was finishing up with the body. Connors and Bailey made themselves scarce, probably because they knew this wasn't where the evidence was to be found. They were probably anxious to secure the file room. What they didn't bank on was David Blake and how well he could read a murder scene, or, in this case, a non-murder scene.

"Where did they go?" David asked as Larkin approached.

"I saw them both go into Bailey's office," Cramer said, as he joined them. "What happened with the warrant?"

"Someone talked to the judge before I did," Larkin said. "He knew all the evidence before I said anything. He told me a few scuff marks in the hallway weren't enough evidence for a warrant."

"What about her fingerprints on the doorknob? And the key?" David asked.

"It just proved the girl was nosy," Larkin repeated what the judge had said. "From what the judge understood, Trudy had been trouble from the start, and her disobeying the rules had gotten her killed."

"I have a theory," David said.

"So do I, but let's not discuss it here."

"We'll talk back at the office," Blake said.

Chapter 5

"Got time for a cup of coffee?" Larkin asked David Blake as they entered his office. Larkin strode behind his desk and sat down, offering his friend a seat as well.

"I can get it," Cramer offered. "I know how the boss likes his, how about you?"

"I drink it straight from the pot," David said. "Do you need some help?"

"I usually don't drink the stuff," Cramer replied. "I'm a bottle baby myself."

"He's a milk drinker," Larkin translated.

"They say it's better for you," David said. "I just don't know who they are."

Larkin wasn't convinced about the benefits; Ted was beginning to get a little chunky; however, it could as likely have been the rolls he ate with the milk.

"What do you think happened at the hospital?" Larkin asked abruptly.

"How do you read the evidence?" David countered.

"The first thing I noticed was that the position of the body was wrong."

"I agree," David said. "It looks to me as if someone half-carried, half-dragged her down the hall, opened the door, and threw her inside the room. I don't believe the patient messed with the body. The killer hoped that Johnston would abuse the corpse, but it looks as though he was frightened and steered away."

"Lucky for us he did," Larkin said. "Do you think the murder happened in the file room?"

"It's not what I think, it's what evidence is telling us. I could be wrong; I could be biased, but the evidence doesn't lie. I think the girl went to the file room where I believe she was going through the filing cabinet. I picked up a flashlight from the floor before I left the office. The drawer to the file cabinet had her finger prints on it, and so did the flashlight. She probably heard a noise. In any event, something alerted her to the fact that she wasn't alone. She stopped to write on the card you found in her hand. She was trying to leave someone a clue," David said.

"I think she found out something important that she knew was about to get her killed," Larkin said.

"Someone strong grabbed her from behind, put an arm around her neck. That's when she dropped her pencil and the flashlight. Both have her thumb-print on them," David said.

"Well, the pencil and light proves she was there."

"She was probably distracted by her attacker while she was writing, and she made a run for it. The breaking of her neck happened so quickly, she didn't have time to fight back," Larkin agreed.

"There was no skin under her nails," David said. "I also believe the perpetrator wore gloves."

"What better place to get surgical gloves than in a hospital."

"He made quick work of snapping her neck. Without letting her fall, he grabbed her just under her breast and carried her to where we found her. Whoever it was, he had to be strong. She was a tall girl and dead weight. That explains the scuff marks on the floor. I believe that every so often he let her feet drag." Blake pulled the bag that held the pencil out of his pocket and handed it to Larkin.

"Can we prove that it was this pencil that she used to write the message?"

"It's just a plain old No. 2 pencil," David said. "It doesn't point the finger at her killer, but it does give us a picture to what your girl was up to."

"Too bad we couldn't process that room." Larkin's jaw tightened.

David smiled again. "While you were making the phone call to the judge, the boys and I fingerprinted the file cabinet and the door knob."

"You fox, you!" Larkin exclaimed. "Too bad they won't allow us to use the evidence in court."

"That's true, but it gives us a better picture of what really happened. There was also a smudged handprint overlapping the girl's."

"This was on the doorknob?" Larkin was excited.

"I could just barely see a tiny bit of her little finger. It's weak. I don't think we could use it in court, even if Connors would allow it."

"Probably not," Larkin agreed.

Cramer returned with the coffee, and Larkin filled him in on the evidence as David saw it. When Ted Cramer heard the part about the judge already being aware of the evidence, he exclaimed, "Wait until you hear this! I was going to mention it before, but you and David were talking, and I forgot. When I went to ask Mrs. Bailey for the pad to take statements, I heard you and David talking as plain as day."

"What do you mean, you heard us talking?" Larkin exclaimed.

"There's a bug set up in the murder scene. There's a powerful microphone that can pick up every sound in a room. The receiver is and FM radio. I heard Bailey turn it off when I knocked, and she allowed me in her office. You can use a set-up like this in the car, office, or anywhere."

"Where would she get something like that?" Blake wondered.

"A lot of places really. You can order one from eBay."

"No shit?" Blake stared at the younger man incredulously.

"Cramer worked for a private eye before he came to us," Larkin explained with a smile.

"A sleazy one, I might add," Cramer muttered.

"Are you saying the director, what's her name…She had the murder scene bugged before we got there?" David gasped.

Cramer nodded. "That's how they knew what to tell the judge about the evidence."

Larkin couldn't believe that Cramer had waited this long to tell him something so important. He definitely needed to have a talk with him. It just wasn't like Ted to be so distracted.

"Who do you think killed her?" Cramer asked.

Karl and David looked at each other.

"You first," David said.

"I believe it was Sam Talbot who actually broke her neck. I just don't know why," Larkin said.

"Is he the guy who was supposed to have found her?" David asked.

"He's the one."

"I didn't see him around," David said.

"Mrs. Bailey sent all personnel to the break room, but after I interviewed Sam, she sent him home. She said it was because he was so shaken up from finding the body. I did insist on talking to him briefly before he left the area," Larkin said. "I noticed how nervous he acted. He kept stumbling over his words and looking at Mrs. Bailey. I think he'd been coached on what to say and he was afraid he would screw up," Larkin said.

"Do you think Sam Talbot is big enough?" David asked.

"He's definitely a big boy," Cramer said. "He's taller than me, and I'm well over six feet."

"He also has a few more muscles than you," Larkin said affectionately, patting Cramer's arm.

"Let's put it this way," Ted Cramer said. "He makes me look like a 90-pound weakling."

"Wow! You're a pretty good-sized boy yourself," Blake exclaimed. "It sounds like he could be the one."

"Oh, I believe he's the one who snapped the girl's neck," Larkin said. "I just haven't figured out why."

"Can we prove it?" Cramer wondered.

"I doubt it at this point," Larkin said.

"We could bring him in and lean on him," Cramer said. "He might crack and give us what we want."

"My gut tells me there's more to this than just Talbot deciding at the last minute to murder the girl."

"You think there are others involved," David said, nodding.

"Most definitely, but I don't want any of them getting suspicious. I want to make sure we have the evidence before we do anything. Connors is in charge, and he has friends in high places. We've found that out already," Larkin said.

"We found a smudged print over the girls on the doorknob. We also have her thumbprint on the key to the file room and the pencil found on the floor. We have Talbot's handprint on the front of the drawer," David said. "That should prove something."

"All Bailey has to say is, 'I sent Sam to look for a file. She's already told us she doesn't go to that wing without an escort," Larkin said.

"It looks like they have all their bases covered, " David said.

"So far..." Larkin agreed.

"I don't envy you on this one, ole buddy," Davis said, slapping Larkin on the shoulder.

"I believe after he killed her, he went back to the file room to see if he left anything incriminating. He had gotten rid of the gloves by then. He saw the drawer was left open, so without thinking, he put his hand against it and pushed it closed."

Larkin shook his head. "Did we get prints from everyone who works South Wing?"

"Yes, and a DNA sample as well." Cramer spoke up.

Taking fingerprints and DNA samples had always been Cramer's job, but Larkin was afraid that, as distracted as he was lately, he may have forgotten.

"We need to go over the evidence again, but a blind man can see there are several points that match the girl's prints, even though they are smudged by someone wearing gloves," David said.

"You've read the prints?"

"Yes, then I turned them over to Craig Harris."

Craig Harris was a fingerprint expert from the old school." A good deal of stuff was done by computer these days, but he did things the old-fashioned way—by studying prints with the naked eye.

Larkin insisted Mrs. Bailey give them a set of prints for everyone working there as of yesterday, and she complied. Larkin knew that it was a procedure the hospital insisted on for their employees. This information was something a friend of Larkin's, who used to work there, had told him years ago. That is where his photographic memory came in handy. When someone told him something, he saw it in pictures. It was the way his mind worked.

Larkin told Kathryn Bailey if she didn't supply the information, the police would have to take up more of their time fingerprinting all the employees. He also wanted a copy from hers and Jerry Connors. It was sure to take time from their busy schedule.

Since Cramer had already taken a set of prints from everyone who worked the area. This was good. Now they could compare them in case Mrs. Bailey had given them wrong information.

They probably felt pretty safe because whoever killed Trudy Madison was wearing gloves.

"Harry has her now. We'll know more after the autopsy."

Harry Merts was a personal friend of David Blake's. He was also a good coroner. David had high-jacked him from another police department out of state. He had chosen Harry for two reasons: he was excellent at his job and he liked the man.

"Why can't we arrest, old Sam?" Cramer asked. "He left his hand print on the drawer, even though the prints on the doorknob were of no use."

"He works the South Wing. Can't you see what a good lawyer would do with that? He has every right to be there. Trudy didn't. As for his print on the drawer, all Bailey would have to say is that she sent him after a file. She has already said that she is reluctant to go there. It would be only natural for her to send someone who works the floor."

"So what are we going to do? Let him get away with murder?"

"Not if I can help," Larkin said.

"What about the scuff marks in the hall?" David asked

"Let me get this one," Ted piped up. "The patients are all nuts. When they walk, they drag their feet."

Karl and David both laughed. That was the Cramer they both knew and loved.

Larkin sat for a time lost in thought. His gut told him who was behind the killing, but the why kept eluding him. One thing he did know was that he needed to talk to Casey West. What she disclosed didn't seem so far-fetched anymore. He also wanted to caution her to be careful. He had a strong premonition that she was in danger as well.

Larkin sat going over and over what Trudy had written on that card. He felt that it wasn't a coincidence that she had written it on Casey's business card. He wondered if the clue was strictly for Dr. West. It was time he paid her a visit at home. After all, he had her address on the card in his pocket.

Chapter 6

Larkin stopped by to see Harry Merts before going to Casey West's place.

Harry was short and stocky with a morbid sense of humor that would offend most civilians. He was dressed in scrubs; a mask covered most of his face. He stopped long enough to wave Larkin over when he saw him hovering by the door. Larkin wasn't fond of watching him cut up a corpse.

"What have you got so far, Harry?" Larkin asked.

"The cause of death is pretty obvious. She died of a broken neck. Whoever did it had to be one strong son-of-a-bi…" Harry let his voice trail away. Larkin wasn't fond of swearing, although he never said anything to the other men for doing it. Harry had heard through the grapevine how strict Larkin's parents were when he was growing up.

"What else?"

"Her neck is bruised. Take a look," he said as Larkin came close to the table. "By the size of the bruises, the guy must have arms like Virginia hams. There is also bruising under her breast."

"Could that have been caused by way the perp carried her?"

Harry thought for a second before answering. "That's very likely the way it happened. She has some cracked ribs on her right side. I believe he had a good hold on her. How far do you think he carried her?"

"About sixty feet," Larkin figured.

"Wow!" he exclaimed. "That's quite a feat. She weighed 180 pounds, and she was about five-nine. Just look for the biggest damn man working there, and you'll have your killer."

"The trouble is; I think we have two or three other big men who were hired for the same floor."

Larkin thought about Carl Johnston, the man who was suspected of killing Trudy. He was broad, but not that tall. Larkin would guess him to be about five-ten. "Would you do me a favor, Harry?"

"Sure, if I can."

"Would you measure the length of the girl's legs? They look awfully long to me."

"I already have that figure for you." He searched his papers, and then told him. "David asked me for the same measurements."

Larkin smiled. "Great minds do think alike," he said, slapping Harry on the arm.

"Like I said, it would take a strong son-of-a-gun to carry a girl weighing that much as far as you said," Harry informed him.

"What if he stopped a few times and let her feet rest on the floor?"

"He could have, I guess. She was dead weight, so I'd say he was one heck of a man if he didn't let them drag at some point."

"Anything else I need to know?"

"If it's any consolation, he killed her quick. She never had a chance to react before he broke her neck."

"David thinks she was distracted by something she was writing."

"What was she thinking? I'm being stalked by a killer; I think I'll stop and write a letter?"

"I think it's a clue as to who killed her. What she scribbled on that card, I mean."

"I hope you get him, Larkin," Harry looked intense. "He's extremely dangerous. You might want to look for someone who's been in the Special Forces. I believe he's a trained killer."

"Thanks, Harry. You've been a big help," he said, slapping the other man on the shoulder.

On the way back from the morgue, Larkin ran into Cramer and gave him a special assignment. "How about dropping in on our friends at Lakeview?"

"What am I looking for?"

"Anything that looks suspicious." The one thing that set Cramer apart from the crowd was his powers of observation. There was not much he missed, especially when it came to a crime scene.

"What I want you to do is make them nervous," Larkin said. "If they get scared, they're going to make mistakes."

"I can do that." Cramer smiled.

Chapter 7

Casey West was shocked when she answered the door—Detective Larkin! What are you doing here?" she asked. Her eyes were still beautiful even though they were red from crying. No woman had the right to look this good without make-up, Larkin thought. "May I come in?"

"Sure...Come on in," she said stepping aside for him to enter. "Have a seat and I'll make you some coffee."

"Thanks, but no," Larkin said as he surveyed her apartment. Her living space was a little bare, but looked modern, clean, and neat like its owner.

"Nice place you have here."

"Thanks…It's small, but I'm not here that often."

"I suppose you've been notified about your friend, Trudy…"

"I've been so upset since I heard the news," her voice choked.

"How did you find out?"

"Uncle Jerry called me."

"Uncle Jerry?" Larkin asked.

"I told you about the family friend who helped me get the job. When I was a little girl, he asked me to call him Uncle Jerry, and it just kind of stuck," she explained.

"What did he tell you happened?"

"He said that Trudy took the keys to the South Wing and, for some unknown reason, went to a violent patient's room. He said the man inside killed her."

When Larkin didn't respond, she said, "Isn't that what happened? Did I get the story wrong?"

"That's what the management is saying, but the evidence tells a different story."

Casey looked troubled. "Then what did happen?"

"We believe she was murdered in the file room."

"Oh my God!" she gasped. She turned an ash white and slumped into a chair. "It's all my fault." She began to cry again.

"How do you figure that, Dr. West?"

She reached for a tissue. "You know I told you that I thought the woman in room 12 was Arron's mother and possibly my sister?"

"Yes…" he affirmed, nodding.

"I—I told Trudy that the evidence was probably in the file room. Mrs. Bailey is always protective of the keys to that place," she explained.

"Did you tell Trudy you believed the woman she photographed was your sister?"

"Yes…Trudy and I became fast friends. In fact, we started taking our lunch breaks together. We were scheduled to have the same day off next week, and we decided we were going to spend it together." Her voice caught on a sob.

"And may I assume you spent your lunches discussing what was going on at Lakeview?"

"I'm so sorry, Detective Larkin," she said shaking her head.

"Did she tell you she was planning to go there?"

"We talked about it, but I never thought she would actually do it."

"Don't blame yourself," he said, patting her arm. "You didn't know, she'd be harmed."

"Looks like you have your murder, Mr. Larkin," she said. "Now what are you going to do about it?" she challenged.

"You're right, Dr. West. I'm sorry I didn't pay more attention when you first came to me. If anyone is to blame, I'm the guy," Larkin said.

"We both may feel guilty, but there's only one person who killed her. I want that person, or persons, to pay for their crime." Her voice was fierce.

"You may not believe me, but I feel the same way," Larkin said.

"I never expected you to come here today," Casey said. "Uncle Jerry said you would probably talk to me tomorrow at work. How did you get my address anyway?"

"I have reasons for wanting to talk to you in private. I told no one I was coming here today. I don't want to put you in danger and I don't want the killer to become suspicious of you. As for your address, I got it from a business card that Trudy had clutched in her left hand. Do you have any idea how she got your card?"

"Yes. I gave it to her the other day when we had lunch. I invited her to my house, but she didn't know my address. She was supposed to come to see me this weekend. I keep the cards with me to pass out to parents with troubled kids. I do after-hours counseling for people who can't afford to pay," she explained.

On hearing this news, Larkin's opinion of Casey went up a notch. "Trudy wrote three words on the back of your card. David Blake, our forensic guy, thinks she left us a clue."

"What did she write?"

"It looks like, Casey, Franklin, and owner. The letters all run together. You have to remember: she was writing in the dark while being stalked by a killer. I thought maybe, since it was on the back of your card, she might have been trying to send you a message. Does it mean anything to you? Would you be the owner of Lakeview by any chance?"

"Actually, Franklin was my last name at birth. But there is no way I own the hospital."

"That was your biological father's last name? Could he have owned the institution?"

Casey laughed. "No, I don't think so. Even if he had owned it, I don't think he would have passed it on to me. After all, he didn't think enough of my sister and I to keep us."

"Did Trudy know your name was Franklin?"

"Yes, I told her the day we had lunch. I had just paid a private detective big money to find out that information, and I was upset when I learned the truth. Trudy was easy to talk to."

"The clue was to you then," Larkin concluded.

"It could have been; I guess…"

"I think she knew using your real last name would get your attention."

"I still have no idea what she was trying to say to me." Tears streamed down her face. "How can I ever figure it out?"

"It may not mean anything. Try not to let it upset you." He patted her shoulder to comfort her. "I doubt we will ever know what she intended to say," Larkin admitted.

"Do you have any idea what it means?"

"It might make sense as time goes on," he replied. "At this point, I'd only be guessing."

"Trudy was an only child. Her mother's an alcoholic. Life hasn't been easy for her, and now it's over. From what she told me, she has always been a parent to her mother, not the other way around."

"In my line of work, I've seen a lot of kids in that same position."

"I'll bet you have, Detective Larkin, but so have I, and I haven't been practicing that long."

Larkin smiled. She had just let him know in a roundabout way, that she considered him old.

"Life is so unfair, isn't it?" She clasped her arms as if she were cold. She walked over to her only window and looked out at the city traffic.

"I was just thinking about my own life before you came. My real parents gave both my sister and me away, but a rich couple adopted me. I can't remember ever wanting for anything materially. They sent me to the best schools; I had designer clothes, plenty to eat. Even though they were killed, they left enough insurance to take care of me for the rest of my life."

"My dad's friend helped me get a job at Lakeview. What I'm getting at, Mr. Larkin, is some people seem to get all the breaks while others struggle all their lives, like Trudy and my sister."

"I know what you're saying. I, too, have enjoyed a comfortable background. Not on the same scale as you, but my folks did okay by me."

"I plan to see that Trudy has a decent burial," Casey vowed. "I've talked to her mother. I knew I had to do it early, or she would be drunk. We're supposed to make funeral arrangements tomorrow. I told her mother I would pay for everything and I would come by and pick her up in the morning. I'll beep for her. If she doesn't come straight out, I'll go without her." Her jaw tightened.

"I wish you would realize this wasn't your fault."

"Then why do I feel so guilty?" she asked.

"You don't owe the girl anything…"

"I do owe her," she said. "It was because of my situation that she was murdered."

"A funeral is costly," Larkin reminded her.

"I can afford it."

Larkin knew when to give up. "We need to discuss something else."

"What is it?"

"I think you're in danger there."

"At Lakeview?"

"Yes."

She stared at him. "Why so?"

"I believe there are things going on that certain people don't want known. They have already killed once to keep their secret safe."

"Do you think it has something to do with me believing the woman in room 12 is my sister?"

"I honestly don't know," Larkin said. "It could just be a coincidence, and Trudy stumbled onto something unrelated they wanted to keep hidden."

"You keep saying, they, as in a conspiracy. Whom do you suspect?"

"I hate to name names at this point, but I need you to promise me that you will be careful. Trust nobody."

"How can I do that if I don't know the people to watch out for?"

"My partner, Ted Cramer, dropped by Mrs. Bailey's office, while we were investigating the crime scene. As he approached the door, he could hear my men's voices coming from inside. When Mrs. Bailey heard Cramer, she turned off the radio she was using to receive the information."

"What are you saying?"

"She had the crime scene bugged before we got there. She wanted to know what we found out. That tells me that our Mrs. Bailey has something to hide."

"I knew there was something about that woman I didn't trust." Casey slipped off the couch and paced the room. "Oh my," she gasped. "I wonder if she has a bug planted in my office. There must be. When I first talked to Arron, do you remember me telling you how he responded?" Larkin nodded and she continued. "He said he had pretended to take his pills. He was coherent and we had a nice conversation about his mother. Since then, every time I see him, he's like a zombie. What if she heard him tell me about throwing his pills away? Now she is making sure that he takes the drugs."

"Tomorrow, I'll drop by your office, like I told Jerry Connors I would. I don't want anyone from Lakeview knowing I came to your apartment today. I don't want them considering you a threat."

"You're afraid I'll end up like Trudy, aren't you?"

He didn't answer.

"I'll be talking to you tomorrow, but I won't say anything I care about them overhearing. I want you to be careful what you say as well. Do you understand?"

"Yes. You're going to pretend it's the first time you're interviewing me, but it's just to keep anyone from getting suspicious."

"All the time, Cramer will be looking for the bug. If one is there, he'll find it."

"Why do I feel there's something you're not telling me?" she asked.

"How well do you know Jerry Connors?" Larkin was blunt.

"I've known him most of my life." She paused. "Surely you don't believe Uncle Jerry had anything to do with this?"

"Either Mrs. Bailey or Connors called the judge before I could. The judge already knew what evidence we had before I told him. After that, he refused to allow us to process the file room."

"Did Uncle Jerry give you a reason for not wanting the room searched?" She paced harder, a troubled frown on her face.

"Yes, Connors said that the patients' records are confidential, and we investigating them would leave Lakeview open for a law-suit."

"Well, there's your answer then." She turned to face him. "Jerry's been a friend of my dad's since I was a little girl. He and his wife socialized with my adopted family for years. He has been a pillar of strength to me since their deaths. I just can't believe him capable of something like this. I won't believe it, Mr. Larkin"

"Just be careful. My advice to you, at this point, would be to trust no one."

"You honestly believe he's involved, don't you?"

"I believe it's possible, but it doesn't matter what I believe. I just want you to be careful of what you say and to whom you say it to."

"Since Trudy's gone, I have no one I can confide in," she said.

"If you feel the need to talk to someone, call me."

She looked him up and down. Larkin was tall, clean cut, and handsome. He wore a pullover shirt and slacks. He gave the same impression of casual elegance as any man wearing a tailored suit, but she didn't see him as making a very good girlfriend.

"Thanks, Detective Larkin, and I'm sorry."

"For what?"

"I had you figured for someone who took the easy way out. It would have been easier for you if you had just accepted their version of Trudy's death. If you had, the case would have been closed by now."

"I go with what the evidence tells me." He shrugged his shoulders.

"Could I ask you a question? Why did you take such an interest in a girl that the world considered a nobody?" She searched his face.

"Maybe when I heard about Trudy, I recognized a fellow crusader for lost causes." He smiled.

Her voice caught on a sob. She half laughed, half-cried as she told him, "That was Trudy all right—a crusader for lost causes."

"I only know when I stood looking down at her crumpled body, I promised her justice. And that's what I plan on giving her."

As Casey was walking Larkin to the door, she stopped him by catching him by the arm.

"Let me help you, Mr. Larkin. Please…"

"It's too dangerous." He shook his head.

"You need eyes and ears inside of Lakeview. Let me do this."

"Why would you want to put yourself in danger like this?" he asked, staring at her.

She smiled through her tears. "Maybe I'm a crusader of lost causes as well."

Larkin smiled. "On one condition," he said.

"What is that?"

"We never discuss the case at that facility."

"Okay, but where are we going to meet?"

"Unless there is something that needs to be discussed right away, we will meet once a week at different restaurants."

"How will I get in touch with you?"

He took out his card and handed it to her. "It's numbers, for my cell, home, and office. Call if you need me, night or day."

"You're serious?" She studied him intently.

"As a heart attack," he said. "Your friend was murdered, and I don't think it was as simple as the management would have us believe. Oh, and I'd look for Jerry Connors to try to gain your confidence. Don't be tempted to tell him anything about what you suspect."

She paused, thinking the situation over.

"I mean it. Don't trust anyone," Larkin warned.

"Okay. I won't."

"Promise me."

"I promise you that I won't trust anyone."

"Now, repeat our plans for tomorrow?"

"You're going to ask me questions that we don't care are overheard."

"Right, and what is Cramer going to do while we talk?"

"Looking for the transmitting device…"

He smiled. "You might make a detective yet."

Chapter 8

On Monday, Karl Larkin and Ted Cramer showed up as promised for the fake interview with Casey West.

Cramer had been a thorn in Jerry Connor and Kathryn Bailey's sides all weekend. He showed up at all different hours, poked around the nooks and crannies. He stopped different employees and asked them questions.

By Monday, the two administrators had taken up residence in Bailey's office with the pretense of giving the detective privacy.

"Dr. West," Larkin greeted her. "I'm Karl Larkin, and this is Ted Cramer. I understand you and the deceased girl were good friends."

"Won't you sit down," Casey played along. "Yes, we were. I had just lost my parents, and she had a troubled home life—we both needed someone to talk to."

Larkin made plenty of noise when he pulled out a chair. He nodded at Casey while Ted proceeded to scope out the office. Cramer was like a bloodhound when it came to finding a bug. There was an artificial plant on the window ledge and underneath a leaf was the tiny microphone. Cramer lifted the leaf showing it to Casey and Karl.

Casey nodded at Cramer. She couldn't believe they were spying on her. They had overheard Arron telling her about throwing his medicine away. She suspected it all along, but now she knew for sure. Uncle Jerry would never be capable of such an act unless he was under Kathryn's influence, she told herself.

As Casey and Karl watched, Ted parked himself on the corner of Casey's desk and took out a bag of potato chips from under his shirt. "I hope you don't mind," he said winking at them. "It's near lunchtime and I get hyperglycemic when I don't eat."

"No…Go ahead." Casey stifled a snicker.

Larkin almost laughed as Ted bent forward near the plant and crunched down on the chips.

On and on the conversation went, and Cramer rattled the bag and crunched his chips. While Cramer made all the noise he could, Casey wrote on paper a time and place for Larkin to meet her. They chose a fast-food place nearby.

Fifteen minutes later, Casey and the two detectives moved to the hallway to say their good-byes. Bailey and Connors conveniently showed up just outside of Kathryn's door. Cramer flashed them a toothy grin and held the bag of chips out as an offering. If looks could have killed, he would have dropped dead on the spot.

"How is the case coming, Detective Larkin?" Jerry asked as he joined them.

"It's proceeding slowly," Larkin admitted.

"So sad," he breathed. "I doubt that mother of hers has the money to bury her. I hear they're dirt-poor, and the mother's a lush."

Cramer watched Larkin bristle.

"Her funeral was pretty elaborate," Casey's statement cut Jerry short. "As a matter-of-fact, I paid for it myself."

Connors looked shocked, but Larkin was developing a growing respect for Casey. Her statement made Cramer smile. He realized she was rapidly becoming a girl after Larkin's own heart.

"I didn't realize the two of you were that close," Jerry admitted.

"She confided in me about her home life, and I talked to her about my parents' accident."

"I'm so sorry about your friend's death, honey." Jerry's attitude changed abruptly. Larkin hoped that Casey could see through the phony sweetness. "But Mrs. Bailey and the entire staff tried to warn her, the South Wing was a dangerous place. We lock people up for a reason. Sometimes they escape and hurt either themselves or someone else. That's why we hire special people to work on that floor."

"Mr. Connors," Larkin interrupted. "I would like to interview you when you have the time."

"Why? I wasn't even here when Carl murdered the girl."

"I would like to go over the history of the patients who live on the South Wing."

Jerry Connors studied him intently. "Are you interested in our patients' mental health, Detective Larkin?"

"I'm interested in the ones who commit murder, Mr. Connors." The two men sized each other up.

"I'll get you a profile on Carl Johnston, the man who killed Trudy Madison. I'm afraid the other patients will remain a mystery to you. Their files are privileged information." Then ignoring the two detectives, he turned to Casey. "We have a monthly meeting scheduled for tomorrow at 9:00. It will be an opportunity for you to officially meet your co-workers."

"Should I prepare in some way?"

"No. It's just a chance to get to know people and familiarize you with the running of the place. I have to leave now—I have to meet with a patient's family. I'll see you tomorrow." He turned and walked down the hall.

"Friendly guy," Cramer said after he was gone.

"He has a difficult job with the running of this place," Casey defended.

Larkin just hoped that Casey didn't trust him enough to share what she believed about her sister.

Chapter 9

With a pleasant smile, Casey joined the others in the conference room. It was two days since Trudy's death and she had suffered through a couple of sleepless night. She tried to hide the dark circles under her eyes with make-up, but felt she hadn't had much luck. She had worked at Lakeview for two weeks and had run into most of her co-workers, but she had only spoken to them in passing.

She smiled nervously as Jerry escorted her to a seat at the left of a long table. While Casey looked around at everyone drifting in and the ones already seated, her eyes discovered a man she had never seen before. His hair was light brown. His hazel eyes changed color as he turned his head toward her and they caught the light. Seeing Casey caused him to do a double take.

A boisterous group of men dressed in white were laughing as they joined the female nurses at the far end of the table. Their chairs scraped the floor as they sat down.

A silent glare from Jerry sent the message to quiet down. They did, just as Mrs. Bailey entered carrying a folder in the crook of her arm. She took a seat next to Connors at the head of the table.

Jerry stood and addressed them, "Ladies and gentleman, welcome to Lakeview's monthly meeting. This is the place for you to discuss any problems you have concerning the running of this establishment. Any dilemma you have is a glitch that concerns us all, and we won't be satisfied until we take care of the situation. I know all of you are aware of the tragedy that happened last week, where one of our nurses visited an area that is off limits to certain staff. These rules are here for a reason. The South Wing is a dangerous place. That is why we have the big guys at the end of the table."

Sam Talbot held up a beefy arm and the other people in the group cheered. Connors signaled for them to be quiet, but he smiled. "I would like for you to meet a member of the staff who's been with us for a couple of weeks. This young woman is Casey West." Jerry stood behind her chair with his hands on her shoulders. "She has just finished her undergraduate work, and she will be doing her residency here with us. Some of you might have noticed her in the halls. Let's face it, folks, anyone this pretty is hard to miss."

There was applause around the table, which made Casey uncomfortable.

"Now, I won't you to meet our newest member, Dr. Marcus Kelly. Stand and take a bow Marcus." The man with the beautiful eyes stood and gave a mock bow. More applause erupted from everyone except Casey. She wondered who this man was, and by the feeling in her gut, she wasn't sure she was going to like the answer. "Marcus is another psychiatrist and my new assistant." More applause echoed through the room.

Jerry had hinted that Casey was to assume that position sometime in the future. She had envisioned herself studying under Jerry Connor, whom she considered the best. Now, some guy waltzes in and squishes her dream flat.

Jerry Connors went on and on, expounding on Dr. Kelly's illustrious credentials. Casey tuned in long enough to hear that in addition to his medical degree he had a Ph.D., the same as she did. So, the guy can dispense medicine and give therapy, and he has more practical experience. That was a big deal.

As Jerry continued his overly long introduction, Dr. Kelly turned to face her. The sour look on Casey's face made him shiver and turn toward the woman on his left who appeared duly impressed with a male with so much potential. She was old enough to be his mother, or at least an older sister, Casey thought unkindly. Not that she cared at all. Connors introduced this woman as a social worker named Peggy Adams. She held an M.F.C.C. degree and was licensed for marriage, family, and child counseling. Peggy was also new and was going to be in charge of scheduling all the out-patients with a doctor, if she was unable to take them.

Casey tuned out the rest of the introductions.

Lakeview was an impressive facility, large, but not huge. It didn't appear to be understaffed like other hospitals, but two full-time psychiatrists and a psychologist on staff seemed excessive. Casey needed to have a talk with Uncle Jerry after the meeting.

The last person Jerry introduced was the hospital coordinator, Kathryn Bailey, to the recent arrivals.

"Does anyone have any questions?"

Casey had plenty of them, but she thought it appropriate to wait until later to voice them.

"Am I to understand that Dr. West will be working under me?" A few people snickered at the new doctor's words.

"Yes, you will have as much authority here as I do when it comes to the people on staff and the patients. If I don't agree with you, of course I will have the final say.

"Is there any other questions?"

"What about the girl who was murdered? Are we safe to do our jobs?" a nurse at the end of the table asked. The crowd began twittering; obviously they were worried about the same thing.

Casey wondered when someone was going to address what had happened here. She looked toward Marcus and his face looked grave. She wondered if this was the first time he had heard about the murder.

"I told you before that you're safe as long as you stay out of the South Wing. The people back there are dangerous. We have the big guys here at the t able to handle them. As long as you go about your regular job and mind your own business, you're perfectly safe," Jerry said.

"Does anyone on staff have any other concerns?" Jerry asked.

When no one answered, he dismissed them telling them to go back to their duties.

Chairs scraped noisily across the floor. People broke into groups and chatted as they returned to work. Casey gathered up the books on schizophrenia that she had taken out of the library. Reviewing how to deal with one's own mentally disturbed family was probably a wasted effort, now that Pretty Boy was in charge. Casey had picked up the books because she feared inheriting the sickness that plagued her loved ones. She tried to push it from her mind, but she had a deep-down fear of it happening to her.

Once outside, Cassie confronted Jerry.

"I thought I would be working as your assistant," Casey said.

"That was the original plan, but I'm finding that I'm entirely too busy with running this place. It was much easier when patients were confined right here where we could keep up with them, but with all the out-patient programs these days, it's hard to do. I'm sure Dr. Kelly will make an excellent teacher."

Casey's blood boiled.

"He'll be taking over the care of Arron Thompson, as well."

"But you said the boy was going to be my patient," she protested.

"I'm sure there will be no objection to you helping with the boy," Marcus spoke up as he walked up to them.

She flashed him a scathing look and then turned back to Jerry. "So does this mean, I'll have no patients of my own?"

"You're inexperienced, Dr. West." Mrs. Bailey's voice cut through the hallway like a guillotine. "You're lucky we hired you in the first place. Dr. Kelly has the experience we need. He's your boss and if you're going to work here, you need to come to terms with that fact, right now."

Connors seemed uncomfortable with Kathryn's stern statement and began to fidget. "Honey, what Mrs. Bailey is trying to say is that you aren't familiar with our methods yet. I'm sure Marcus will give you more to do as time goes on."

She hated Jerry's patronizing voice; it brought back memories of her adoptive father when he didn't approve of her friends.

How generous of Marcus, she thought. The other workers who were close by seemed anxious about the confrontation and tried not to pay attention as they went about their duties.

"I have to leave in a few minutes, so if there is nothing else…" Connors said, looking at his watch. "I'm meeting with a couple about their disturbed child."

There was no talking to Jerry for he was half-way out the door. Casey was not satisfied with how things were turning out. She thought once of going after Jerry, trying to catch him before he could reach his car, but Mrs. Bailey stopped her by taking hold of her arm.

"Dr. Connors is busy and he's gone already." Kathryn's voice dashed all hopes of changing Jerry's mind. Sure enough, she saw through the entrance doors that his car was pulling out of the parking lot.

Mrs. Bailey then turned to Marcus. "We assigned you the big office next to hers. She pointed to Casey as if she were part of the woodwork.

"Call me on the intercom if you need anything, or just knock on my office door. It's the first door to the right as you face the time clock."

Casey turned to leave, but Marcus caught hold of her arm. "You seem upset: is something wrong? If I'm taking the office you wanted, I can use the smaller one."

She turned to stare up at him. He was over six feet tall and she could get lost in his beautiful eyes, nice brows, and strong chin. With him standing this close, his smell was intoxicating. She choked up. She couldn't begin to tell him what his taking over Arron's case would do to her. That meeting had dashed her hopes of helping her nephew.

"It's not about the damn room." She yanked her arm, but Marcus held tight and made her face him. Tears stung her eyes as she fought to keep them in check. A display of anger or a temper tantrum might get her fired. Then where would her sister and nephew be? "I have work to do," she said, this time pulling away from him. "I'll be in my office. You know which one it is. It's the tiny one next to yours," she said sarcastically, before pulling free from him and walking away.

"Look," he said to her retreating back. "We could have dinner tonight and discuss it. Get things ironed out…"

She turned back to face him. "I think there's a rule around here about employees dating their bosses. If not—then I'm making one." She about-faced and marched down the hall.

Just before she reached her office, he came up to her.

"Why don't you step into my office then, so I can give you your assignment for the day?" His smile was the most engaging one he could muster. In his bid to win her over, he was pulling out all the stops. She didn't doubt that showing his pearly whites had worked magic for him before, and it might even have worked on her, if the situation weren't so serious.

"Maybe we could discuss the boy you seem so concerned about?"

She stopped dead in her tracks and faced him once more.

"His name is Arron Thompson. He's eighteen years old. I've seen him a couple of times, and I seemed to be making progress with him. That's all."

"Okay, that's a start. See? It's not really so hard to talk to your new boss."

It was the wrong thing to say. The new boss crack grated on her nerves, but she let it pass. Casey had never been one to use her sex appeal to her advantage, but maybe this was a good time to start. She schooled her face into sadness, which wasn't a problem at this point, and followed him meekly into his office.

One whole wall was covered with windows that overlooked the manicured grounds and mature trees. There was enough sunshine flooding the place to brighten even her mood. It made her wonder why they stuck her in the little rat hole next door. Did Jerry plan to hire Marcus all along? Did he think of her as simply a charity case?

Marcus indicated for her to take the soft chair next to his desk. "Won't you make yourself at home," he said.

Casey took a seat and crossed her long legs. Marcus shuffled through a stack of folders and papers on his desk, placing a few loose papers into the file on top.

"Patient's files," he told her. "I was trying to familiarize myself with our cases." He laid everything aside and stared at her long enough to make her uncomfortable under his scrutiny. "The boy," he asked, "why does his case mean so much to you?"

"I—I…" she stopped for there was no way she could tell this stranger the truth.

"It's not that his case is more important than any other," she lied. "It's just that it was originally assigned to me.…"

"And now it has been given to someone else?"

"No, it's been given to you," she clarified, staring directly into his eyes.

"Your uncle is concerned that you're getting personally involved with the boy, Dr. West. You must know it isn't good to do that."

"What…?" Casey shook herself out of her stupor. Darn, he was good looking! But now was not the time for her to become distracted.

"I know you were taught not to get personally involved with a patient…That's Psychology 101." His eyes burned into hers until she turned away.

"Don't tell me my job, Dr. Kelly. I'm a good doctor and I've helped hundreds of patients. I'm not involved, as you call it. It was just that I felt I was making progress with the boy, and now, I find out that you'll be taking over." She looked away to keep him from seeing the frustrated tears that were forming in her eyes. Her eyes were expressive and she couldn't let this man know how much Arron's case meant to her.

"I'll make a deal with you, Dr. West. You can continue treating the boy as long as everything goes smoothly. I will check on his progress and sometimes sit in on your counseling sessions. Is that satisfactory?"

"I suppose I'll have to settle for that."

What did he expect her to do—jump up and down because he tossed her a crumb?

"You still don't seem happy," he replied.

"I'm ecstatic, can't you tell?"

"You're a hard woman to please." The way he was looking at her made her wonder if he meant something more than job wise.

"I know I can't prescribe medications, but I was hoping to persuade Dr. Connors to lower the boy's dosage. I think they're over medicating him. He's like a zombie. I mean, the first time I saw him; he spoke normally after I was told he didn't speak at all. He confessed that he had been throwing his medication away. Ever since then, he has been acting like a robot." She stopped, realizing how pathetic she sounded.

"May I call you Casey?" His patronizing voice brought back memories of the lectures her adoptive father gave her when she was a teenager. Marcus might have been the most attractive man she'd ever seen, but she couldn't let him get to her.

"Like I said before, we could have some lunch and discuss it more."

"I think we should remain professional," Dr. Kelly. As you pointed out, you are my new boss."

Marcus sighed and shook his head before he continued. "Casey, the boy has been diagnosed as a schizophrenic. You know what that means. There are times when he will appear normal. It's classic textbook. He'll never like taking his meds, but you know what happens when he doesn't. He will begin to hallucinate, and all the other symptoms will follow. I have been going over his file. It says that he thinks different patients here at the institution are his mother, isn't that true?"

She wanted to protest, but there was no way she could tell him what she suspected.

He patted her arm. "I know it's hard when you want them to be normal, and they're not."

Casey shut down. There was no use trying to make him see. He believed what the management was telling him and that was that. "I'll be glad to continue doing his therapy, if you will allow it." She rose, but he waved her back down.

"It might interest you to know that I checked this place out thoroughly before coming here. No matter what you think of me personally, I'm a good doctor. I had options about where I would take a position, but, after researching the different institutions, I decided to come here."

"I'm sure you were the pick of the litter, and Lakeview is blessed to have you." "You're impossible!" He hissed through his teeth.

Try as she might, she couldn't think of a reason why she felt so hostile toward this man. Like it or not, he was her new boss and she'd better get used to the fact.

"Would you like to know why I decided to come here?"

She had gotten out of her chair and now she stood by the door. "I'm sure you're about to enlighten me." She didn't want to appear curious, but she would like to know why, in all the places he could have gone, he chose Lakeview to apply for a job, and ruin her life. It was nothing personal, she told herself. He was just another obstacle in the way of progress with her nephew.

"I came here because this facility doesn't believe in what I call "crazy therapies." She looked puzzled.

"I don't believe in the rebirthing, re-parenting, regression junk that some weirdoes are throwing out there these days. I believe in science. We have medications today that help the mentally ill, and I believe in medication and therapy just as your uncle does."

"He isn't really my uncle you know," was all she could think of to say.

"What…?"

"Jerry Connors is not really my uncle. He's an old family friend."

He didn't have to say anything; his face said it all.

"I'm grateful for the job, Dr. Kelly; don't ever think that I'm not. Jerry Connors has always been a good friend to my family."

"Your parents, you mean."

Casey stared at him, wondering how much Jerry had told him about her.

"Yes, my parents…"

"By the way, I'm sorry for your loss."

Damn. Had Jerry given him her life history?

"Thank you, but life does go on," she said.

There was no need to tell him she had never really bonded with the West's and had never really known why until they were gone. She guessed it was true that blood was thicker than water.

"I'll try to be more professional in my approach to patients," she added.

"That's all I ask, Dr. West. I'll see that the boy is brought to your office immediately for a session."

She stopped short, remembering the bugging device planted in her office. She couldn't really remove it without them becoming suspicious. "It's so pretty today. Do you think I could have the session in the vestibule? It's not as depressing."

He paused for only a second. "Sure, why not. As long as there is no disturbance, I have no problem with it."

She managed a half-hearted smile of thanks before walking away.

Marcus stared at the closed door with a frown on his face. He just might have a problem with that one. The powers that be had warned him, but no one had told him how attractive the woman was and how she would affect his libido.

Chapter 10

Casey was anxious to talk to Detective Larkin after her eventful week at Lakeview. They met at the fast food restaurant and decided to eat in the play area. Casey felt it was easier to be inconspicuous if people were interested in watching their children as well as eating their food.

She wore a pair of shorts that made her long tan legs go on forever. She carried their food while he held her arm. Larkin smiled at the envy he saw on the faces of several young men.

"Let's sit here." Larkin pulled a table away from where the children were playing.

"How has it been going?" he asked as they placed their food on the table and sat down.

"So…so…" she replied, breathless.

"Do you need to be back at a certain time?" Larkin asked.

"I'm a doctor," she smiled. "I take as long as I like."

"Well, I'm a cop and I can always say I'm working."

She laughed and looked up from her food straight into the eyes of Marcus Kelly. He stood in a long line, right in front of the playroom door. She almost choked on a French fry.

"Oh my God," she whispered.

Larkin turned around to see what she was staring at.

"Turn back and put your face closer to mine. Pretend you like me."

Larkin did as she asked.

"Smile," she gritted through her teeth.

"What the heck!" Larkin found himself in a generous lip lock. He broke away in time to see the other man turn his back. He caught his breath and tried to focus his thoughts.

"Old boyfriend?" he asked.

She stretched her neck to see whom Marcus had brought to lunch, hoping it wasn't anyone she knew. No… The girl was young enough to be his daughter. When Marcus looked her way again, she waved. Reluctantly, he gave her a wave in return.

"Okay, what's going on? If he isn't an old boyfriend, who is he?"

"He is my new boss."

Larkin's drink went down the wrong pipe. He managed to swallow the liquid instead of spewing it on Casey. He was left coughing and spluttering.

"Are you all right?" Casey rose to her feet and began pounding him on the back.

"I'm fine—sit back down," he ordered, fighting to get himself under control. except for looking like an ass, of course. "You were saying he's your new boss. When did that happen?" Larkin wiped away the diet Coke that dribbled down his chin.

"I got the news the first thing this morning. I was under the impression that I was going to be Uncle Jerry's assistant. It turns out Marcus Kelly is going to wear the title instead."

"Bummer."

"Tell me about it."

"Why the sudden change?" Larkin took a drink and tried not to choke this time.

"You can relax now. They left while you were spitting and sputtering," she chuckled.

"You're the damnedest woman."

"How so?"

"You can sound bitter as hell one minute and laugh the next."

"Maybe I'm insane. I do worry about it, you know."

Larkin stared. The bitterness in her voice stung him. She shrugged her shoulders. "Insanity does run in families. My mother was schizophrenic; so is my sister and maybe my nephew. I might be crazy, too."

Larkin reached across the small table and caught hold of her hands. "There is nothing wrong with you."

"Maybe I'm just imagining a conspiracy going on at Lakeview. I mean, what possible motive could anyone have for keeping my sister and nephew from getting better? Maybe, I let Trudy draw me into this paranoid theory because I am freaking nuts."

"You're not crazy."

"You must be the only one who doesn't think so."

"Your friend was murdered. There is no denying that."

"What if it was just like they say? She wandered into a violent patient's room."

"That could have been what happened, but the evidence says otherwise. We think she was killed in the file room and dumped where we found the body."

"Who are we?"

"I'm talking about my forensic team and myself." Larkin said.

"You're sure of that?"

"Yes…" My forensic team is the best, and we're all sure of it."

"I take it the head of CSU is a personal friend of yours," Casey said.

"Davis Blake, is a friend, but he finds things that other people over look."

"And he's positive she was killed in the file room?"

Larkin nodded. "I sent Cramer, my partner, back over to Lakeview after they stopped us from collecting any evidence. Cramer caught Sam moving files from the murder scene to Mrs. Bailey's office. I think they were afraid we might still get a court order and come back to search. I believe the room held something incriminating to someone at Lakeview."

"Oh my God," she breathed. "I was going to tell you about that. That same day, I stopped by my office for a patient's file. It was my day off. They weren't expecting me to be there. I heard Mrs. Bailey talking to someone. She must have left the inter com on by accident. I could hear through the speaker in the corner of my office. Her voice was plain, but the male with her was speaking so low I could hardly hear him. I don't think the man was close to the microphone. They were discussing who should take the files to their home. The man must have wanted her to keep them in her safe because she was questioning as to why he didn't keep them himself. I could tell she was angry about being the one asked to take them home. She told whomever she was talking to that they needed to rewrite them just in case the police got a warrant to search their homes. He told her there was no need to rewrite these files; he would make damn sure the police never had a chance to see them. He wanted her to keep the evidence so she couldn't deny she wasn't involved. By what she said, he also wanted them kept for a reference, to make sure they did everything right."

"Finally, she must have agreed because I heard her door open and someone leave. I opened my door a crack, and saw Kathryn come by my office carrying a folder bulging with papers. I shut my door quickly because I thought the man might follow her, and I didn't want either of them to know I was there."

"Are you sure it was the same day you found out about Trudy?"

"I'm positive. I was so upset, and I knew I wouldn't sleep that night. To have something to keep my mind occupied, I decided to go over a new patient's folder."

"Did you recognize the male voice?"

"No, I didn't."

"Do you think it was Connors?"

"He was speaking so low, and he was too far away from the mike. I couldn't really tell."

"How long has your new friend been there?"

"You mean Marcus?"

Larkin nodded.

"Monday was his first day on the job, but he could have been hanging around the place before and I never noticed."

"You don't seem fond of him," Larkin observed.

"He's the cat's meow, according to Uncle Jerry and Mrs. Bailey."

"Jealous?... Forget that crack," he said waving away the French fry she offered him.

"Yuck. Plain fish without tartar sauce," she wrinkled her nose. "How does a grown man live on that?"

"I usually bring my lunch from home. Didn't they teach you in medical school about fat and cholesterol?" He shook his head. "Do you realize how many grams of fat are in a double cheeseburger?"

"I bet you don't eat doughnuts either." She giggled. "You're very unique for a cop, aren't you?"

"Is that a nice way of saying I'm a geek?"

"You're a very good looking and sensitive man, Detective," she said. "Are you blushing?"

"We were talking about your boss, and how you don't like him."

"Frankly, the man is a patronizing ass."

"Tell me more about him."

"He's a psychiatrist. He has a Ph.D. in psychology, the same as me. He's doing the job I thought was going to be mine. What's not to like?"

"Do you think he knows anything about the murder of Trudy Madison?"

"Only the story all of us have been told," she said, finishing off the last of her sandwich.

"You have a gigantic appetite for a little woman," he remarked.

She chuckled. "No puny salads for this gal," she said. "I don't think Kelly is in on any conspiracy, if there is one," she said.

"Are you beginning to doubt?"

"It just doesn't make any sense. Why would someone harm an innocent boy? What reason would they have?"

"You're naive about the ways of the world, aren't you?" Larkin said.

"What do you mean?"

"Some people would kill for fifty cents. I see it every day in my line of work."

"But my sister and Arron have nothing in the way of assets. Jerry told me the state is paying their bills. If that's true, the money hardly covers their meds."

"Your friend found something in those files that got her killed. I keep going over and over what she wrote. Franklin and owner... What does that mean?" Larkin asked.

"I wish I knew," she replied.

"Is it possible that you're the owner of Lakeview?" Larkin asked.

Casey laughed. "You must be as crazy as they think I am."

"I've said it backward and forward. It has to mean something." He was shaking his head and frowning.

"Maybe she didn't get to finish what she started to write. Maybe it was her way of getting my attention."

"If your biological father owned this place and Trudy found that out. Maybe he willed it to you before he passed away."

"If I were the owner," she said fiercely, I would fire old' Kelly's ass tomorrow and the next to go would be that Bailey creature."

Larkin chuckled. She was kidding, but it had given him an idea. It might be worth looking into who did own Lakeview. Casey had mentioned to him once that her adoptive parents had been rich. Maybe Mr. West or her biological father had an interest in the hospital.

"I'm going to have to be getting back," Casey said after a time. "I'm supposed to meet with Arron this afternoon. I've been meeting with him in the vestibule. The room is much more cheerful, and hopefully, it isn't bugged like my office."

"How is it going with him? Have you seen or heard anything suspicious?"

She hesitated. "Not really except they removed the files."

Casey inhaled deeply. "I did ask Jerry to see the list of meds the boy is taking, and he said he would get it for me. I know he's busy, but he's never given it to me. He keeps putting me off."

"You said you weren't allowed to prescribe medicine?"

"Besides Jerry, only our resident psychiatrist can do that."

"Would that be Marcus Kelly?"

She nodded.

"You're concerned about the medication?"

"The boy is so vacant, and his expression never changes. The first time I saw him, his big brown eyes were so expressive. Now they're sad and full of pain."

"It has to be hell seeing these people go through this misery every day," Larkin sympathized.

"It is worse when you know you're related to them," she admitted. "I feel so helpless."

"There might be a way of finding out what you want to know."

"And how is that?"

"You have to know how attractive you are, Dr. West. Maybe you could use some of your womanly wiles on the new guy."

"I'd rather charm a snake," she said.

Larkin laughed. "He might be one and the same."

"Very true… I'm really not the type, Mr. Larkin."

He believed her, or she would have tried to play him the first time they met.

"It's up to you of course. I guess it amounts to how much you want something."

She stared at him for a few seconds. "How about you, Mr. Larkin, have you ever used your manly wiles to get what you wanted?"

Larkin looked embarrassed. "I can't really say that I have, but then again, I don't have the assets that you have."

"You're an attractive man, Mr. Larkin, and I'm sure you wouldn't have trouble, if you turned on the charm," she said. When he didn't answer, she continued, "I don't think you're capable of what you're suggesting I do."

"I suppose you're right. So, where does that leave us—doing it ethically?"

"I guess so." She smiled. "I'm beginning to like you more and more."

"Same here… It's nice to meet someone with character for a change," he said, raising his eyes to meet hers.

"I think our next meeting should be at my house," Casey suggested. "We can't take a chance on running into anyone else we know. Come over Saturday. You can park your car in my garage."

"I don't think so. The neighbors aren't blind and I would hate to ruin your reputation."

"Let me worry about that, Mr. Larkin."

"I'll park my car on the street," he said. "That way the neighbors won't think we're up to something."

"If that's the way you want it."

Larkin smiled. "What if Kelly spills the beans about us being together?"

"He has no idea who you are."

"I think he'll ask," Larkin was sure of it, the way the man looked at him.

"It's really not any of his business. If he asks, that's what I'll tell him. Besides, he probably won't even ask."

"Oh, he'll ask all right. I saw the man's face, and he didn't like us being together one bit." Larkin was quite sure of that.

"Why would he give a hoot?"

"Maybe he has the tiniest bit of interest."

"Interest?" she scoffed.

"In you…"

"I don't think so. All he wants is to be the big duck in the puddle at Lakeview. I'll let him know in a hurry that he has no control over my personal life."

Larkin smiled. He understood Casey's jealousy. He had been the same way when his first partner made detective before him. The man was one hell of a cop, but he died in the line of duty shortly after getting the position. Larkin often wondered what would have happened if he had gotten the job instead. Would he have been the one to die? Life was mysterious and unpredictable.

"Let's make our next meeting Saturday then. What time?"

"How about noon? I'll make us lunch."

Larkin smiled at her quick decision. She certainly wasn't wishy-washy. "That sounds great."

"What would you like to eat?"

"Surprise me," Larkin said, and then saw visions of junk food dancing in his head.

"Okay, but don't be shocked if I serve you left over pizza." she threatened as he started to leave. His exaggerated cringe made Casey smile.

His expression changed abruptly. "Casey, be careful. I have a gut feeling about this one. Someone is playing for keeps. I still don't like you snooping around Lakeview."

"Don't worry. I won't make it as obvious as Trudy did. I'll be fine," she assured him."

But Larkin did worry about her. He was determined to have Clinton Cummings, their computer expert, look into Connors and Bailey's background, and while he was at it, he just might have him look into Sam Talbot's as well.

Clinton Cumming was the newest member of the team hired by David Blake. Larkin smiled as he thought about how much Cummings strayed from the computer geek-type you usually saw in the movies. He was tall and buff and more of a health nut than Larkin. He lifted weights to stay in shape, but computers were his babies. Larkin figured he took them to bed with him at night. He had a set-up at work that intimidated Larkin just to walk by it. It was fortunate that the powers that be allowed David's team a generous budget for the CSU.

Chapter 11

A few days later, Casey had another depressing session with Arron. The child was unresponsive and lethargic. Marcus and she had spoken very little since their McDonalds run-in. She bit her lip and knocked briskly on his door. Arron was too important to let her feeling toward Marcus get in the way of the boy's care.

"I'm sorry to bother you, but there is something I need to discuss," she spoke as soon as he opened his door.

"Then please come in." He stepped back to allow her to enter. "I was going over some case files that needed updating," he said. "What is it you would like to talk about?"

"It's about Arron Thompson..." She plunged right in.

"How did I know that was coming?"

"The boy is listless. He stares straight ahead like a zombie when I talk to him. I think he is on too much medication." There, it was out.

"Dr. West, I have gone over his records, and from what I've read, his condition is serious. We have to give him a pretty high dosage of a psychosis drug, plus a tranquilizer. I know that you found him responsive that one time..."

"But that first day that I talked to him, he seemed normal," she interrupted, shaking her head. "He said he had been throwing his meds away."

"Yes, and it was recorded that he had a screaming fit that same night. He was hallucinating about seeing things."

"Why wasn't I notified about this? He was supposed to be my patient. Why didn't Dr. Connors tell me this?"

"In all due respect, Casey, Dr. Connors is the one who prescribed his medication. Could it be he knew you were so involved with the child that you couldn't see reason?"

"Did he tell you that?"

"Not in so many words, but he implied it. He explained that losing your parents had been a traumatic experience, and he believed that you might have transferred the affection you felt for them to the boy"

"So, now Jerry thinks I'm crazy. Is that why he put you in charge of the boy instead of me?"

"Anyway, Dr. Connors says the child is a danger to himself, and now you want me to lower the boy's dosage. With your vast experience, I suppose you just want me to ignore his history and discontinue his meds altogether?"

Her jaw clenched. The man was an ass. "I'm sorry to have bothered you, Dr. Kelly. I'll be going back to work now." She got out of her chair and walked slowly to the door.

"I know it's none of my business, but don't you think you ought to be getting your life back on track. It's been what, a year since your parents died?"

She turned slowly back to face him. "What are you babbling about?"

"I mean dating a guy old enough to be your father, for one thing."

For a second, she was at a loss. Then she realized he was talking about Detective Larkin. "It's my business what I do after I leave this place. Or do you want to control that as well?"

"You must not be proud of it, or you wouldn't be trying to hide."

"Maybe I knew how people like you would react."

"There's only one reason I know for hiding a relationship, and that is because one or the other of the couple is married. Oh my God… The guy's not only too old for you; he's married, isn't he?"

"I haven't tried to hide anything. And you don't have to worry about my private life, Dr. Kelly, and how about you. You were with a girl young enough to be your daughter."

"That was my kid sister. She's home from school and she met me for lunch."

For some reason, she hated him believing something so awful about her, but she couldn't share Larkin's identity with him. She had to let him believe the worst.

"The way I see it; Jerry Connors has given you every chance in the book. If it were up to me, I probably would have fired you the second day you were here. Why would you question someone with credentials like his about the medication he is prescribing for one of his patients?"

"I need to go back to work."

She reached for the door, but he caught her arm.

"Just remember that you're working for me now, and if you can't come to terms with the way I do things, I won't hesitate to remove you from the boy's case. Is that clear?"

Tears burned Casey's eyes and she turned her back to him. She refused to let him see her cry.

"Do you understand?"

"I understand completely," she said without looking at him.

"Look, I think you have the makings of a good psychologist. I've watched you with other patients. You're great with them. There are areas you need to work on, but I have faith that you will get it together."

"In what areas," she moved her fingers in quotes, "do I need work?"

"You tend to get personally involved. When you do that, you get too close to the problem, and you don't help yourself or your patient."

"What you're saying is, it's wrong to sympathize with people…"

"I'm saying you have to put your feelings on the back burner when you're dealing with the kind of people we do."

"You mean crazy people?"

His eyes narrowed. She had pushed the right button. "I mean disturbed people. To be able to help them, you can't allow yourself to become emotionally involved. I'm sure you learned that in Psychology 101."

"Not all of us can completely switch off our feelings," she snapped, implying that's what he did.

"Not all of us wear them on our sleeves either."

"It's probably easy for someone without feelings," she baited him.

"Watch it, Dr. West," he warned. "You need to get it together before you do permanent damage to yourself or a patient."

"Are you talking about my personal life?"

"Like you said, that's your business. The patients here at this hospital happen to be mine."

She would get no help in this office: she could see that now. Without looking at him, she turned and walked out the door.

Chapter 12

The next day in her own office, Casey moved the plant with the listening device onto a hallway table. After searching for additional bugs, she sat for a long time wondering how she could help her nephew. She poked her head out of her office and glanced down the hall looking for the nurse that dispensed medicine. Nancy Harper was the one passing pills and Casey quickly pulled her aside.

"Did you need something, Ma'am?" The girl had been chatting with a maid working the area and seemed to resent the intrusion.

"Yes, I need Arron Thompson's medication records."

"Ma'am, I've been told that you weren't allowed to alter the dosage for any of our patients." Nancy looked uncomfortable.

"Who told you that?"

"Dr. Kelly, did, Ma'am. He said I was the one responsible for getting the right meds to everyone. It would fall on my shoulders if anything was changed."

"I just wanted to see what dosage he's taking, not change anything." Casey gave her a sweet smile.

Nancy hesitated. "I guess it'll be alright for you to look at his chart. I'll bring you his file after I'm through here."

"Good... That way I can get a more accurate view of his case."

About fifteen minutes passed before Nancy brought the chart to Casey's office.

"Thanks, Nancy. I'll check it out and have them back before lunch."

The girl nodded and turned to leave.

Casey's blood boiled to find out Marcus suspected she might try to lower the boy's dosage on her own.

She winced as she reviewed Arron's file. He was small for his age, and his dosage would take down a large man. She didn't know how, but she was going to find a way to lower it.

The next morning, while Nancy was wheeling out her medication cart, Casey made her way down the hall. A cleaning woman stopped Nancy, and they moved farther down the hall to gossip. It was something the nurse did every morning and Casey had observed her actions. If she wasn't talking with one of the maids, it was another co-worker. One of the staff would find her and they would move away from everyone else.

Casey simply walked by her cart where the little medication cups sat on a paper with the patient's name in bold black letters. Her eyes skimmed quickly until she found A. Thompson and quickly replaced the original pill with one of a lower dosage that she had in her pocket. It took only a second to change one pill for the other and then walk away. She hurried by Nancy and the maid as though she was passing to go to another part of the hospital.

There was a difference in the color of the pill. Casey held her breath and prayed that Nancy wouldn't notice. She stood in the doorway of her office and watched until Nancy returned. The girl looked at her watch and hurried away with the cart. Casey breathed a sigh of relief when she saw the nurse leave her nephew's room and move on to her next patient.

Casey took a deep breath to still her rioting nerves. She hoped she wasn't making a mistake, but she had to know if the boy really needed such strong medication.

For the next two days, Casey waited for someone to distract Nancy when she brought the medicine around. It was never a long wait until another worker would seek out the nurse for a gossip session. While Nancy chatted, Casey substituted the psychosis drug with a look-alike placebo. The meds nurse spent so much time gossiping in the morning, she really didn't have time to check if someone had altered the patient's dosage. Casey counted on that. The pill she exchanged was the same color. The placebo was a tiny bit bigger than the other drug, but Nancy never noticed.

Casey observed Arron over the next three days. He seemed the same, only staring straight ahead and acting as though he was unaware of his surroundings. Every day, she took him to the vestibule for a session, hoping no one placed a bug there as well.

A week passed. Casey walked Arron to the vestibule and started a conversation, as usual. "Arron, how are you today?"

Arron turned his head toward her.

Casey's mouth dropped open.

He didn't speak, but his eyes followed her every move.

"Are you feeling better?"

He didn't say a word. For one whole hour Casey had a one-way conversation with someone who refused to talk back. Yet Arron would look at her when she asked a question. She knew she had to be patient and wait on him to feel comfortable before he would speak to her again.

Casey was reluctant to end the session, not that she had a choice. The hour was almost over and a nurse would come in a few minutes to take Arron back to his room. She had other patients she was scheduled to see. Casey looked up to see Mrs. Bailey coming toward them instead of Nancy, her stomach tied in knots.

"Arron, if you can understand what I'm saying, you need to pretend that you don't see or hear us. If you want to get better, we have to do this together."

"How is the boy doing?" The older woman queried, glancing around as she came up to them.

"About the same, I'm afraid," Casey sighed. Her heart choked her; she prayed that Arron wouldn't turn his expressive eyes toward the woman when she spoke.

When he fixed his gaze straight ahead, his eyes blank, Casey smiled. He was off the psychosis drug and had been for over a week. She breathed a sigh of relief. He understood what she wanted him to do.

"I told Nancy that I would take Arron back to his room. She's doing something for Dr. Kelly."

"I can do it," Casey volunteered. She looked at her watch. "I have 15 minutes before my out-patient arrives." Actually, she only had about 12, but she didn't want Mrs. Bailey to spend any more time with Arron than was necessary.

Mrs. Bailey glanced at her own watch. "I do need to catch Dr. Connors before he leaves. He's going to see the mayor today about putting a stop to that dreadful detective who's always hanging around asking questions."

Casey knew she meant Ted Cramer. Larkin kept his distance; he was afraid that Marcus Kelly would recognize him as the man from the restaurant.

"I'll be glad to take the boy back to his room," she assured Mrs. Bailey again.

"Thanks… I'll be leaving early today, so I'll see you tomorrow," Kathryn said, after a moment of hesitation.

After Kathryn was gone, Casey put her arm around Arron's shoulders and watched as the boy smiled. "You did great!" she said, hugging him.

Chapter 13

It was never good when, District Attorney Deets called them to his office. Larkin rarely saw eye-to-eye with the man and neither did Cramer. The DA presented himself as being tough on crime, but in reality, he was willing to look the other way if he thought something would hurt him politically. Everyone who worked with him knew he was maneuvering himself into becoming governor in the next election.

"Why don't you both have a seat," Deets said as they entered his office.

Larkin noticed the two chairs placed in front of his desk. Usually, there was one. The two detectives did as they were told and waited for him to tell them why they were here.

"It's come to the attention of our mayor that we're poking around in a case that should be closed." He stared at Larkin.

Larkin bristled. He hated it when Deets used we as if he had contributed to the case. "What case would that be?" Larkin snapped.

"I'm talking about the nurse over at Lakeview who was killed while snooping around an insane patient's room."

"That's not what the evidence shows—" Larkin stopped abruptly as Deets held up his hand.

"I don't want to hear your suspicions. Unless you can give me hard evidence, this case is closed."

"We have to investigate to get evidence," Larkin snapped.

"You can't hang around Jerry Connor's establishment and harass people. He has friends in high places, the mayor being one of them."

"He and that old hag who runs the place had a bugging device set up at the crime scene," Cramer growled.

"It's a mental institution, for heaven's sakes. They have cameras and listening devices set up all over the place. Do you think they do that just to spy on the police? They have to watch these people or they'll try to escape. Jerry Connors is a respectable man. I play golf with him and the mayor," he boasted. "I can't see him conspiring to cover up a murder."

"The girl was murdered in the file room, and there is evidence, she was carried and thrown into the patient's room." The chair screeched across the floor as Larkin stood.

"Even if that's the case, the girl was snooping in a place where she had no business."

"Damn it, Deets. Why don't you for once stand up and do the right thing?" Larkin glared at him.

Deets got up from his chair. "You don't get it, do you, Larkin? There are people who matter and there are people like this girl…"

"Who doesn't?" Larkin gritted his teeth.

"You know what I mean…"

"I know exactly what you mean," Larkin said.

Cramer rose also. He was afraid Larkin was going to get a handful of Deets's shirt.

"Let's face it. The girl was a trouble maker…"

"So it's okay if someone murders her?" Larkin ask. He inched his face closer to Deets.

"That's not what I meant… The girl's mother is an alcoholic, and she isn't going to make any waves. Jerry Connors is a friend of the mayor and of half the judges in this town."

"I don't care if he's president of the United States… if he's doing something illegal, I'll hang his ass," Larkin said.

Cramer caught hold of his boss. If Larkin was angry enough to say ass, he just might take a swing at Deets.

"Watch it, Larkin. I could have you fired," Deets threatened.

"Go ahead. But don't think someone else is going to work his butt off to make you look good."

Cramer tried pulling Larkin away.

"Calm down, Larkin," the district attorney said. "You know I would never do that. You're a damn good cop."

"I've made you look good for years," Larkin snapped.

"And I am eternally grateful for that. You only have one fault that I can see…"

"What's that?… I believe in justice for everyone?"

"You don't know when you're out gunned," Deets said.

"What do you mean by that crack?"

"You don't know when to let go."

"If you mean allowing someone to get away with murder because they're a big-wig in the community, no, I don't."

Deets sighed and shook his head. "My hands are tied on this thing, Larkin. I'm in the same boat you are. My ass is in a sling."

Larkin stared at him for a time. "I guess you're right. I'll stop Cramer from hanging around Lakeview."

"Just when I was beginning to enjoy making them nervous," Cramer smiled.

Deets glared at the younger man. "Keep him away from there," he ordered.

"This thing isn't over by a long shot. Something is going on at that facility and someone committed murder to keep it quiet. I need to find out more about Jerry Connors and Kathryn Bailey."

Deets squirmed. "I'm warning you to leave this thing alone."

"And I'm warning you," Larkin said, pointing his finger under Deets's nose, "I'm about two steps away from handing in my resignation. Do you know who is next in line for my job?"

Deets swallowed and answered, "Probably Clay Howard?"

"Yeah—It is Wrong Way Howard. We'll soon see how good you look if that joker takes over. He has that nickname for a reason," Larkin said.

"He's been promoted in a timely manner."

"He was promoted because he's close to retirement age. People feel sorry for him, because he can't do anything right. If I'm gone from this department…"

"I'm going, too," Cramer said.

"Don't threaten me, Larkin."

"You know damn well that your career has taken off because we hand you the evidence on a silver platter. Cramer and I make you look good."

"What are you trying to say?"

"I'm saying, without Cramer and me, your career will be in the crapper."

"I know how you feel, Larkin, but I can't let you do it," he whined.

"What's the matter, Deets? Doesn't your ass-kissing extend to the mayor?" Larkin asked.

"We'd better go, Larkin," Ted remarked trying to pull his boss away. He had never seen him so angry. "We're making it worse by staying here."

Larkin paused at the door. "You know, there's a very wealthy young lady who works at Lakeview. If something should happen to her, I will take it personally, and I will hunt the guilty party down if it takes me to my dying day. I have a few friends in high places also."

Larkin turned to leave, but Deets called him back. "Look, if you can do some investigating on the outside… Just promise me you will stay away from Lakeview."

"What about the woman I told you about? Who will be there for her if I'm off the case?"

"Larkin, I sympathize with you…"

"Yeah. Your sympathy does her a hell of a lot of good,"" he said before stalking out of the office. Cramer followed, slamming the door.

"Cramer!" Deets followed the younger man out into the hall while Larkin continued on.

"Yeah?" Cramer turned to face him.

"Stay away from Lakeview, and that's an order."

Cramer stopped, but he didn't turn around or say a word. Then he followed Larkin back to their office.

"That takes care of that," Larkin said as Cramer took his usual seat on the desk's corner.

"My hanging around made them nervous, like we thought? Cramer said."

"Tomorrow I'll get in touch with Casey. We're supposed to have lunch at her house— and don't give me that crazy grin. I'm old enough to be her dad."

"Some women like older men."

"I don't go for younger women."

Cramer had his doubts that Larkin would ever get over Cassie Thompson. For two years, Cramer caught Larkin deep in thought or staring into space. He denied it, but Cramer knew he was thinking about her.

"What about you, Ted? What has been going on with you lately? You seem awfully absent-minded. Is there a personal problem I ought to know about?"

Cramer slid off the desk and walked to the windows. "Kim and I are fighting a lot lately," he said, without turning around.

"What about?" Larkin said to his back.

"She wants to have a kid, and I don't want one right now. It's no big deal."

"I know women well enough to know that it can be huge," Larkin said.

"I'm just not ready to have one right now."

"Why not? You two are pretty well set up financially since your grandfather passed away, aren't you?"

Larkin was sorry the minute he opened his mouth, but it was too late to take it back.

"I just wanted my kid to have grandparents like I had when I was growing up. My mother and I aren't on the best of terms. Kim's parents are always traveling to other countries. They wouldn't make good grandparents at all."

"I know it's none of my business, and I'm a fine one to talk, but I've never been sorry I patched things up with my folks before they passed away."

"It's an entirely different situation," Cramer countered.

"Same result." Larkin said.

Cramer came back to his perch on the corner of Larkin's desk.

"What do you mean?"

"It's a cold world out there without family is all I'm saying."

"Sometimes it's just as cold with one," Cramer said.

"Is this about your mother not taking your grandfather in?"

"She knew how badly he hated living in a rest home," Ted accused

"In all fairness, Ted, the woman had a job. Taking care of an Alzheimer's patient is a full-time task in its-self."

"I offered to pay a nurse to watch him during the day." Ted jumped to his feet and paced the floor.

"I'm going to have to get you a desk of your own," Larkin said, changing the subject.

Cramer laughed. "I've perched on the corner of yours so long I doubt I could be comfortable if I had one."

"We have plenty of space for one," Larkin said.

"I guess it's because we don't spend enough time in the office to become uncomfortable," Ted said.

"You're probably right." Larkin agreed. "People won't stop killing each other."

"Anyway, my grandfather left my mother well off. She didn't fail to take the money."

"Let's get back to the point, Ted. It's a big responsibility to keep track of someone who wanders away. He did that several times as I recall."

"She just didn't want to be bothered with him."

Larkin dropped the subject. Cramer wasn't ready to forgive.

"I think you need to settle this issue. It seems to be affecting your work as well as your personal life."

"I know, and I am sorry about that. I'll try harder."

Larkin knew firsthand how painful it was to be estranged from one's own family.

He knew Ted's father had walked out when Ted was just a baby, and now that his grandfather had passed on, Ted's only close relatives left were his wife and mother.

But right now they had bigger problems. Larkin would have to explain to Casey why he was taken off her friend's case. It made him angry because District Attorney Deets thought Trudy didn't matter. In reality, Larkin knew Deets could get him fired and he had invested too much in his career to have that happen. He had to face it. They were banned from Lakeview, and officially removed from this case.

Chapter 14

Saturday, Larkin arrived early at Casey West's apartment. Casey showed him into her living space. She had only a few homey touches that made the place her own. The lack of pictures and knick-knacks reminded him of his own house.

Her living room contained a leather easy chair, an upholstered love seat, and a table. Larkin wondered if she ever spent time relaxing. He doubted it. A desk with an office chair sat against the wall opposite the love seat. Books and papers were stacked next to her PC and printer. Next to a stack of books, an empty glass rested on a lone coaster. It didn't take a detective to figure out that this was where she spent her time.

"I made tuna salad sandwiches," Casey said. She had come out of her tiny kitchen with a platter of food and two glasses of diet Coke on ice. "If you'd rather come to the table, we can do that instead."

"No, no…Take the chair," Larkin insisted.

"I don't mind the love seat," she smiled, placing a nice china plate and a glass of the soda on the table beside him. She offered him the platter of sandwiches, from which he took three diagonally cut portions.

"Potato chips?" she offered.

"No, thank you," he said, as he sat and placed a coaster under his drink. "I have to stay away from salt; it raises my blood pressure. It's a heredity thing that makes me susceptible to hypertension."

"I have no idea what health risks I have except the obvious one," she said sadly.

"You mean your mother's illness?"

"Yes." She nodded, then took her own plate with two whole sandwiches, stacked with potato chips, and sat down across from him.

"How have things been at Lakeview since the murder?" Larkin asked. Casey's face grew troubled. "Not well I'm afraid."

"How so?"

"I tricked a nurse into letting me see Arron's chart. I wanted to know how much medicine he was taking."

"What did you learn?"

"He's taking an adult dose of Thorazine. I mean a dose that would knock a huge man to his knees. Then a dose of Valium at night."

"And you think they're deliberately over medicating him?"

"Yes, I do. Psychologists can't prescribe medicine, but we do have to study it in school. The dosage goes by body weight, and he's small for his age. I knew I had to do something about it."

"Is it possible that it takes that amount to relieve his symptoms?"

She stared at him for a time without really seeing him.

"Maybe," she said at last, "but I don't think so."

She wondered if she should confide in him about withholding Arron's medication. Instead, she changed the subject. "How is the investigation coming along?"

"Not well, I'm afraid." Larkin always hated telling a friend or family member that the investigation had stalled. "My superiors have taken Cramer and me off the case."

"I was afraid of that." Casey shifted in her seat and stared at him. "I talked to Mrs. Bailey and she told me Jerry was going to put pressure on the higher-ups to stop Cramer from hanging around Lakeview."

"Well he did, and they did," he said, taking a sip of his soda.

"This sucks," she said.

"It proves one thing to me. The management has something to hide."

"I think it's Mrs. Bailey's influence on Jerry." Casey sighed.

"Are they involved?" Larkin asked.

"I've heard rumors." She shifted in her chair.

"Have you seen any indication of an affair?"

"They spend a lot of time in her office together, but it might just be business." She shifted her eyes, and then set her drink on the table.

"So you believe there is something between them?"

"Everyone needs companionship, Mr. Larkin. And there is no accounting for taste."

"How about you, Dr. West, has your boss made a play for you yet?"

"Heavens no. I would kill him. Anyway, our relationship is nothing like that," she said. "I don't have any time or inclination to look for love right now. I have too much to sort out."

"I've discovered that when you have too many complications in your life already, love usually finds you," Larkin said.

She looked at him as though he'd lost his mind.

"No, trust me. Marcus Kelly has no desire to become involved with me."

"What about Jerry Connors?"

"No. Of course not."

Larkin shrugged. He knew what a body like hers did to a man. It wasn't too farfetched to think Connors had an ulterior motive for hiring her.

"Jerry's a good man, but he seems lost after his wife passed away. Lakeview, and maybe his relationship with Kathryn Bailey, is all that he has now," Casey defended him.

"I'm not saying there's anything wrong with him having a girlfriend. I'm just trying to look at all the facts."

Casey was still defensive when it came to her family friend. She trusted him too much, but Larkin couldn't fault her for that. When it came to having friends that is the way it should be.

"You've said before that you think he is reacting this way only because of Kathryn Bailey's influence?"

"Absolutely," she said, nodding her head. "Don't you?" She took a bite of her sandwich.

"I wish I was that sure," Larkin admitted. "All I know is that he was the one to put a halt to the investigation."

"Does this mean the case is closed?" she asked after she had chewed and swallowed.

"I won't close a case that fast," he told her, taking a bite of his own food. "I hate someone telling me my case is over before I'm able to set it right."

Casey smiled. She and the detective were a lot alike after all.

"I think Cramer and I will work quietly behind the scenes. I want to find out who the owner of Lakeview really is."

"Do you think finding the owner is relevant to this case?"

"It may not be," Larkin admitted. "I keep going back to the clue Trudy left us. Your real family name and owner…Maybe if we can find out the actual name of the owner, he might override Connor's decision and let us continue our investigation. Do you think your real father might have been the proprietor?"

"I told you no. My real father is dead and he didn't care enough for my sister and me to take care of us when he was alive."

Larkin nodded, but he still looked thoughtful.

"What if it means nothing? What if it just means the killer stopped her before she could give us the rest of the clue?" Casey asked.

"I've got a gut feeling about this. It was important enough that she sent you a message while being stalked by a killer. What about you?

Have you witnessed anything suspicious? Is there anything happening at Lakeview I ought to know about?"

Casey shook her head. She paused, deep in thought. "I keep thinking of how much courage it took for Trudy to go to that file room," Casey said at last.

"Yes, it did," Larkin, agreed.

"Because she suspected things weren't right, and she knew it had something to do with my family. I feel so guilty. I talked too much to her about the situation."

"Look," he said reaching out to touch her shoulder. "Trudy was the kind of person who spotted things that were wrong and tried to correct them. People like her will always try to remedy the situation. I know because I'm the same way. It had nothing to do with you."

"I wish I could believe that."

"How is the boy doing since you took over his treatment?" Larkin tried to steer the subject in a more positive direction.

Casey avoided his eyes. "About the same, I guess."

"Why do I suspect there is something you're not telling me?"

She hesitated. "For some time now, I've been substituting a placebo for his anti-psychotic medication."

"Wow!" Larkin stared at her and swallowed. "Do you think that's wise?"

"I weaned him off of it gradually, giving him a lower dosage, and then going to the placebo."

"It was easy for me to get what I needed. The medicine is kept in a storage room, but any of the staff can walk in and get what they need. There is a pharmacist who gives out the meds every day. She gives them to Nancy and Nancy puts them on her cart, and passes them out. I go while the pharmacist is on lunch break and get what I need. I take several pills at one time, so there is less danger of me being caught."

"That seems awfully negligent." Larkin said, "just to walk away from a room full of medicine, and leave it unattended."

"Not really. Drug addicts want to get high, not take downers." Casey smiled.

"I thought you agreed not to change his medication."

"I did what I felt I had to do." She shifted and avoided his eyes. "The boy was a walking zombie. The psychiatric nurse who gives out the medicine likes to talk. I made sure someone was around to distract her, and then I made the switch."

When Larkin didn't say anything, she looked at him. "I suppose you're going to tell me that I'm breaking the law, and you want me to stop?" she said, taking a drink of her diet soda.

He hunched his shoulders. "My hands are tied, I've been taken off of this case, remember?"

"Thanks..." She breathed a sigh of relief.

"But what happens if something goes wrong. At the least, you could lose your job, or be prosecuted if your boss presses charges."

"I'm willing to take that chance."

He continued to stare at her.

"You think I'm doing wrong?"

Moments passed before he answered. "There are times I take liberties with a case if I feel it's necessary. I trust my gut feeling. I'm hoping it's the same with you."

She swallowed hard. "I feel that I'm doing the right thing, if that's what you mean. Yesterday, when I spoke to him, he actually looked at me."

"Do you think he recognized you?"

"I know he did. He didn't speak during the session, but he looked at me several times as if he understood what I was saying. I had taken him to the vestibule, and when I saw Mrs. Bailey coming toward us, I told him if he understood what I was saying, not to look at her when she spoke to us. He kept his eyes fixed straight ahead, so I knew he understood what I wanted him to do. I think there's an intelligent boy in there, Detective Larkin, and I plan to bring him out, no matter what I have to do to make that happen."

Larkin thought of telling her that she was too close to the situation to see it for what it really was, but thought better of it. The determined set to her jaw indicated it would be useless for him to protest.

They both jumped when the doorbell rang.

"Are you expecting someone?" Larkin asked.

"It must be that crazy parcel post man. He's on a new kick refusing to deliver my packages unless I'm home to sign for them."

She hurried to the door expecting a delivery-person, and she was shocked to see Marcus Kelly instead.

"What are you doing here?" She tried closing the door before Marcus spied Larkin.

"I brought your next week's work schedule. Mrs. Bailey said you left without getting yours on Friday. Since you had Monday off, she needed to get this to you today. I told her I passed right by your place on my home, and I would drop it off."

That he lived anywhere near her was news to Casey, but she didn't say so.

"Thanks, but I'm a little busy right now."

"I can see that." He glanced at Larkin's car parked in front of his.

"Just give me the damn schedule, will you, and be on your way."

"This is Saturday. Shouldn't he be with his other family?"

"What makes you think my affairs are any of your business?"

The phrase was hardly out of her mouth before she regretted her bad choice of words.

"You're right. Your affairs are hardly my concern." He handed her the paper and headed toward his car.

She regretted that Marcus thought she was having a fling with a married man, but the important thing was to help Larkin find Trudy's killer. That and see that her nephew could live a normal life.

Marcus stopped at his car parked on the curb right in front of her house, and looked back at her. "I thought you would be glad of the extra time to spend with your lover. Why look so gloomy?"

"Just get out of here before he sees you," she gritted.

Casey was surprised when he shrugged his shoulders, slipped inside his car, and peeled away from the curb.

"It seems we aren't safe meeting anywhere, are we?" Larkin asked as she stepped back inside. Casey realized he had watched everything from the window. "I think he has the green-eyed-monster."

"I think the jerk just gets off on spying on me." She took a deep breath.

"Maybe he has orders to spy on you." Larkin stood with his dishes, ready to carry them to the kitchen.

"Do you think he's involved with whatever is going on at Lakeview?" Casey asked.

"He may be," Larkin admitted, "or it may be that he's interested in you."

Casey shook her head. "To tell the truth, he doesn't like me very much. I know he doesn't have any confidence in my work."

"Never sell yourself short." Larkin patted her shoulder. "You know people, and that's a big plus. You were convinced that something was wrong at Lakeview before anything happened. Maybe it was woman's intuition, I don't know, but you have something going for you. You're a beautiful, intelligent woman and that is definitely working for you."

"Look, it's about a thirty-minute drive to Lakeview, and I need to get over there to exchange Arron's pill."

Larkin was silent.

She added, "You don't approve of me doing that, I know."

Larkin struggled to keep the troubled frown off his face. "How are you going to explain being at Lakeview when it's your day off?"

"I'll just say I forgot something else."

"Don't do anything to make them suspicious. I don't want to investigate your murder."

"I have to do this for my family and for Trudy. Otherwise she died in vain."

He nodded and readied himself to leave. "Remember—if you need me, call day or night," he said, before walking to his car.

Chapter 15

Arron who hadn't had his meds in over a week, met with Casey in the vestibule. Nancy brought the boy in and settled him at their usual table. As soon as Nancy left, he turned toward Casey. His big brown eyes looked bright and clear. A tiny smile played around his lips.

"You look happy today," Casey said, her heart racing faster with anticipation.

"I saw Mrs. Bailey leaving the building as the nurse was bringing me here," he said.

"You spoke!"

"I'm old enough to talk, don't you think?" Arron said.

"It's just that it's been such a long time since I heard your voice."

"I must be getting used to the pills they're giving me," he said.

"I've been slipping you a placebo; do you know what that is?"

"Not really…"

Casey had to remember that he was only nine when he was brought here. He probably hadn't been taught anything since.

"Don't you like Mrs. Bailey?"

"She's what my dad would have called an old- battle- ax." The mischievous smile spoke volumes.

"Where is your dad?"

Arron hung his head and squirmed. "I don't know. He deserted my mom and me the last time she was sick."

"When is the last time you saw him, Arron?"

"It was the day that they brought us here." Casey swallowed. "He brought you and your mother to this place?"

Arron shook his head. Shadows darkened his eyes. "A man came to the house. He was the one who took us away."

"Was your dad there at the time?"

"That day, I got up late. Before I went to the kitchen, I heard my dad yelling at my mom. He said she was crazy."

As Casey watched, his big brown eyes filled with tears.

"He said he was going to send her away. I yelled 'no' and ran to her. I threw myself in her arms, and she held me. He tried to pull me away, but I held onto her. He gave a hard jerk, and I fell down. I was screaming and he slapped me hard. He said that I was crazy as she was, and he was going to send both of us away. There was a knock at the door, and when my father answered it, there was a two strange man wearing white. One man said he had come to take my mom away. When he tried to take her, I kicked his shins and tried to bite him. My dad became angry and hit me again, knocking me across the floor. He told the men that we were both crazy, and he needed to take us both. Then the big man made a call. When he got off his phone, he agreed to take us both, but he said he couldn't give my dad any more money."

Casey cringed, imagining the hell this child had been through.

"Your dad sold his wife and child?" Casey was appalled. "Are you sure money was exchanged?'

"Yes."

"And it was your father who received the money, and not your dad who paid the other man for your stay here?"

"They gave my dad money, and then they brought us here." His eyes held a faraway look and Casey knew he was reliving that horrible day.

"What happened then, Arron?" Casey whispered through the lump that threatened to choke her.

"We've been here ever since."

"What did your dad do after they gave him the money?"

"He counted it, and then he left the room."

"Wow!" Casey was stunned. "How much did he give your father?" The amount didn't really matter. She was just curious to know the going price for one's family.

"I really don't know. It was several dollar bills."

"I can't believe this."

"He didn't even say goodbye to us," Arron said, reliving the pain.

Casey squeezed his hands. She couldn't hold him like she wanted because she was afraid of arousing suspicions.

"I'm so sorry you had to go through that, but I want you to know I'm here to help you. I just need you to trust me," she spoke softly. She reached forward squeezing the boy's shoulder. "What they did to you is horrible and I promise you that they're going to pay. Do you understand?"

Arron nodded.

"Have you seen the man who came to get you working here at Lakeview?"

He nodded again.

"Do you know who he is?"

He shook his head. "I've only seen him a few times."

"What does he look like, Arron?"

"I don't know. He's big, and he dresses in white, and he's mean."

Sam Talbot—it had to be. She was just as sure that Talbot was acting for someone else. However, who would give Arron's dad money for two mental patients? It made no sense. They should have charged his father for their care, not given him money.

She hoped that the trauma hadn't clouded Arron's memory. No matter who paid whom, the boy had been through a traumatic experience, and she needed to steer away from the event.

"Tell me what you like to do for fun, Arron?" It was difficult, but she plastered a smile on her face.

"I like video games." he said halfheartedly. His dad had gotten him a game-boy in happier times.

"What else? Do you like any other kind of games?" Playing a video would call attention to the fact that Arron was off his medication. One thing about this whole episode, it had verified that the boy was normal and very intelligent besides. She didn't know why someone was trying to prove otherwise, but she was determined to find out.

"I like card games."

"Playing cards?"

"Rummy…My dad taught me rummy."

"I'll get us a deck before the next session."

"I'm pretty good," he boasted.

"I'll clobber you tomorrow at rummy," she said, smiling.

"I don't think so."

"Arron, we have to be careful," she warned. "You'll have to sit with your back toward the door. If I see someone coming toward us, I'll kick your shoe underneath the table. You stare straight ahead as usual. Do you understand?"

He nodded. She kicked his shoe underneath the table, and he went into his act.

"Good," she breathed. "I think we're ready."

"Why are you helping me?"

Casey stared into his expressive eyes.

"Because I don't think you're disturbed at all," she said.

"Why does everyone else think so?" His eyes drilled into hers.

"I honestly don't know, Arron. Maybe they don't know you like I do."

"Promise me that you won't let them hurt me like they do my mom."

Casey's eyes welled with tears. It was getting harder and harder to switch his medications. Since Larkin had been taken off the case, she wondered how she would be able to prove what was going on.

"Promise me!" His eyes looked like a hunted animal. "Don't desert me like everyone else."

Tension crept into her neck and shoulders. She clasped hold of his arm. "They'll be coming for you soon," she said at last. "We have to play the game."

"Promise me!"

Nancy's footsteps echoed down the hall. Arron fixed his stare on Casey one more time. She nodded and put her finger to her lips.

"I'll do my best, Arron," she whispered, "I promise. This hour she spent with him went so fast."

"She knew she shouldn't have made that vow. She couldn't keep changing his medication forever. How was she to assist him further? She didn't have a clue. She was allowing the gut feeling Larkin talked about lead her.

The boy needed hope and so did she. She felt Larkin was her friend and he wouldn't give up on finding out what was going on at Lakeview. She also knew it was going to be more difficult for all of them since he had formally been taken off the case.

Chapter 16

The next morning, Casey almost collided with Sam Talbot, who was just leaving Mrs. Bailey's office. Kathryn had added a new patient to her schedule, and she stopped by to talk to her about it. She felt she had her hands full watching out for Arron.

She heard Kathryn say, "Thanks Sam," as she neared the door. Standing in front of the doorway, she noticed a mysterious look passed between the two of them.

"Come in, Dr. West." Mrs. Bailey sniffed, and then she pulled a tissue out of her pocket. A glass vial slipped out and rolled across her desk. The older woman snatched it up, but not before Casey saw the six microdots inside. When Mrs. Bailey realized Casey was staring, she quickly spoke. "I picked up some beads for my niece to make a bracelet. She's retarded, and my sister likes to keep her busy making things. It gives her a break and keeps the girl from whining."

Casey nodded.

"I just wanted to discuss the new patient that someone put on my schedule."

Kathryn looked through the papers on her desk. Casey hoped she believed she'd fooled her. Thanks to her self-destructive friend, Jimmy Dillon, she knew acid when she saw it. The two of them had gone to college together. The way he abused drugs, Casey had gotten an education about all things drug-related.

Casey wondered if Mrs. Bailey and Sam had just finished snorting something. That would explain her sudden case of the sniffles. Could drugs have something to do with what was going on here? But if it was about drugs, how did it involve her sister and her nephew?

Casey couldn't make sense of it. She gave herself a mental shake and went about her business with an uneasy feeling which lasted the rest of the day. Should she say something to Uncle Jerry about what was going on? In the end she decided against it. She believed the rumors about Kathryn and him being involved. She had even caught them in compromising situations. She supposed there was nothing wrong with that. She also had heard about Bailey being involved with Sam Talbot and figured that this was one love triangle she wanted to steer clear of. Besides, Arron's progress without medications put a whistle on her lips and a song in her heart that obliterated any thought of baser things.

Casey and Arron surveyed the vestibule. Their usual table was occupied, so they were forced to sit side by side on a small couch to enjoy a game of rummy.

She and Arron giggled and talked their way through the different hands. It was when Casey's spine began to tingle that she looked up and froze.

Kathryn Bailey stood at the entrance to the vestibule glaring at them. Casey kicked the side of Arron's foot, causing him to go into his vegetable act.

"Arron!" Despite the sharpness of Kathryn's voice, Arron remained frozen in place. "It's time to go back." Casey quickly gathered up the playing cards while Mrs. Bailey came up to them. When Arron stood to his feet, Kathryn placed her arm around his shoulders and started to lead him away.

"Is this a new procedure?" Kathryn asked, as Casey pocketed the cards into her smock.

"I thought the cards might stimulate him." The feeble explanation was the best Casey could think of on the spur of the moment.

"And how did the cards work?"

"He seemed to like them."

Casey lowered her eyes.

"You're five minutes late for your new out-patient's appointment," she accused.

"I'm sorry. I didn't realize. It won't happen again. Do you want me to drop Arron by his room on the way back?"

"I'll take care of Arron. You just make sure you get to your other patient," Mrs. Bailey said, practically tugging the boy away.

Casey watched them go. Dread filled her heart. She knew Bailey had seen too much. She felt helpless as she stood there watching them go. All she could do is pray that her nephew would be all right. The new patient that Kathryn had added to her schedule was an effort to take away precious time she could spend with her nephew. Casey knew that, but management had the power and there was nothing she could do about it.

Chapter 17

Casey stayed at Lakeview later than usual that evening. Her nerves were on edge. How much had Bailey observed between herself and Arron? She didn't know, but she wished she did.

That evening, screams shattered the silence. The halls filled with motion. Arron. Casey raced into the hall. Marcus, Mrs. Bailey, and several nurses crowded around him.

Arron was shouting, "Get the snakes off of me! Can't you see them? They're red and green and they're crawling all over me! Help me! Please!"

The boy had super strength. Marcus gave him an injection to knock him out. Then Sam picked him up and carried him to his room. Casey followed, watching with horror as two nurses snapped restraints on his legs and arms, chaining him to the bed.

Marcus waved everyone else out of the room as he examined the boy. Casey moved to the doorway and watched. A few moments later, Marcus stepped to the door and ordered a nurse to give him another sedative if he was violent when he came around.

How could she have done this to him? Casey thought. She had ignored the dangers everyone had warned her about. The boy really did have problems, and she was so sure he was normal. She had to let someone know it was all her fault. She knew it was grounds for her being fired, but she had to tell someone anyway. The boy's well-being depended on it.

Marcus waited until he was sure his patient was asleep before stepping into the hall and putting his arm around Casey. He led the dazed Casey away from the room. "He'll be all right now," he whispered close to her ear.

Mrs. Bailey barked, "I need to talk to you, Dr. Kelly."

"What is it, Kathryn?" he replied.

"I believe you should have a talk with the nurse in charge of dispensing the medicine. I noticed earlier this afternoon that the boy didn't seem to be medicated." Her stare threw daggers at Casey. "You see what happens when these patients aren't kept on their meds."

"Are you implying that he hasn't been receiving his medication as was ordered?" Marcus snapped.

"I'm saying that perhaps Nancy was told not to give him his meds." She still glared at Casey.

"I'm responsible for prescribing his medication, and I have not changed anything. I'll look into the situation, Mrs. Bailey. If I find the nurse was remiss, she will be fired."

"Let me know what you find out," Kathryn said. She flashed Casey a hateful look, and then she turned and walked down the hall.

Marcus called Nancy into his office while Casey waited outside. Nancy emerged, her eyes red from crying. Casey swallowed her pride and knocked loudly on his door.

"Can I talk to you?" she asked, when he answered.

Marcus checked his watch. "Why not? I have a million things left to do, and I'm already fifteen minutes late for a meeting," he said.

"It's important..."

"Come on in," he said, standing aside.

"I'll get right to the point," Casey said as she entered. "This thing with Arron is entirely my fault."

"How so?" He asked his eyes narrowing.

"Nancy had nothing to do with it. I don't want you to fire her."

"Are you saying you ordered her not to give the boy his medication?"

"No—not exactly…"

"What exactly did you do?" He glared at her.

"Nancy likes to talk. I always made sure there's someone handy for her to talk to. When she brought out the medicine cart, I would substitute his meds with a placebo."

"You what…?" His voice was like a physical blow. He clasped her arms so hard it cut off her circulation. "Are you crazy?" he hissed. "Don't you know the danger you put that boy in? How long has this been going on?"

"About three weeks," she admitted.

"What's with you and that boy? What made you believe he didn't need his medication?"

"He acted so normal," she defended.

"Remember your training for God's sake. Schizophrenics can seem completely normal at times until they go off the deep end. I know you were taught that in school."

"I don't believe the boy is schizophrenic."

"And he just went into hallucinations for no good reason?" he snapped. "I mean, you're such an expert, being out of school, what? Six months and all?"

"Red and green snakes. Red and green snakes," she repeated. That's the answer," "What the hell are you babbling about?" Marcus snapped.

"I have this friend who was into drugs when we were in school." He took LSD and he said his trips were always in Christmas colors. That old bitch saw how well Arron was doing and she drugged him."

"What?"

"Bailey, she drugged him."

"What are you talking about? The boy wasn't drugged, that's the problem."

"No— I was in Kathryn's office today and when she pulled out a handkerchief, a vile with LSD microdots slipped out."

"I can't believe you would stoop so low as blaming someone else for your incompetence."

"I'm telling you the truth. Kathryn drugged him."

"You're accusing the woman who runs this place of using unauthorized drugs on a helpless boy?"

"Yes. I am," Casey declared.

"She said they were purple beads for her niece's bracelet, but they weren't."

"Have you used illicit drugs before, Dr. West?"

"No, I have never taken drugs. I told you that my friend did. I've nursed him through countless bad trips. The more I think about it, the more I'm convinced that Kathryn drugged Arron."

"I thought you were here to do the right thing. Take the blame for your actions. Instead you decided to take the childish way out and blame your actions on someone else."

"The boy is not schizophrenic. You believe what you want to believe," she snapped.

"I choose to believe what makes sense."

"Do you? Have you ever known a schizophrenic to have an attention span long enough to play a game? To be organized in his thoughts as to be competitive. Have you known one who could concentrate for any length of time?"

He stared at her.

"Well, have you?"

"No—but…"

"No buts. They can't do it, and you know they can't. Arron is able to do all of those things."

Marcus shook his head. "You're too close to this boy to see the truth."

"He can laugh and share without becoming agitated."

"It usually doesn't happen that way, but I have seen times in patient's lives when they appeared to be normal."

"Arron Thompson was a happy normal boy for three weeks, until Kathryn caught us having fun yesterday."

"What do you mean, she caught you?"

Casey's eyes filled with frustrated tears. "We always sat at the same table where I could keep a watch for anyone coming or going. When I saw someone coming, I would kick Arron's toe to warn him, and he would go into his act."

"His act…?"

"He would immediately stare straight ahead, pretending to be in the same stupor they always brought him to me in. We called it the game."

"And he understood, 'the game?' He made quotation marks with his fingers.

"Yes, he did," she vowed. "Yesterday that monster caught us before I could warn him."

"What on earth would be her motivation to sabotage the boy's efforts to get well?"

"I know it sounds crazy, but it's true." Her eyes begged him to believe her.

"You say the boy hadn't had any of his meds for two weeks?"

"More like three," she admitted sheepishly.

He seemed to think the situation over for a few minutes before he spoke. "I'm going to have to tell Jerry about this."

"You're a doctor. I know you have probably seen patients before who have been on LSD."

He held up his hand to stop her. "This is just too incredible to believe," he said, shaking his head.

"I told you about my friend who gave me an education in drugs. And before you accuse me of being on them, I've never taken, nor will I ever take any illegal drug. I've been with my friend through good trips and bad ones. I've seen the effects of LSD."

Marcus shook his head.

"Jimmy told me about everything being outlined in red and green. I remember his eyes being all pupils. You looked at Arron's eyes. Were they dilated?"

"I have to go," Marcus said.

"Sometimes Jimmy saw horrible things, sometimes they were funny. I remember one time he laughed because the cars looked like frogs hopping down the highway." She caught hold of his arm when he tried to leave.

"You said Kathryn told you they were beads in the vile."

"Yes... She gave me a lame excuse about them being for her niece."

"There you go. You were mistaken about what you saw."

"I know what I saw." She stared directly into his eyes. "I know you don't want to believe me, but deep down, I think you know I'm right."

"I can't believe in some wild conspiracy involving a kid that these people want to harm. No one else in their right mind would…"

"That's where you're wrong, she said inhaling sharply. "Trudy believed it. That's why she's dead."

"You mean that nurse who was killed by a patient?"

"She wasn't killed by a patient. I don't believe it for a minute, and neither do the police." Casey said.

"If this girl's death was a homicide, why aren't the police still investigating?" "I know you've heard the rumors about Trudy's death." She tried to steer him away from the fact that Larkin was still investigating.

"I talked to Jerry about it and he told me the investigation was closed. That the girl was a trouble maker who snooped around a violent patient's room and he killed her."

"That is not what happened. A patient didn't kill her."

"How many others have you convinced of this great conspiracy plot?"

"Detective Larkin believes it." She had to tell him something; otherwise he would surely fire her. "He's the older man you saw me with."

"You're dating a cop?"

"I'm not dating him. I'm his eyes inside of Lakeview."

"Are you saying the incident isn't closed?" he asked.

"I know you must be thinking I'm paranoid."

"No, I think you're crazy."

"I've said too much," she replied. "What I'll do is give you one of Detective Larkin's cards. If you don't believe me, you can get in touch with him." It was too late. She had blurted out things to Marcus she shouldn't have said. Larkin was already off the case and what would happen to her family if she lost her job? What If she was no longer here?

"What do you plan to do about what I told you?"

"I don't know yet. But something will have to be done."

"Are you going to recommend to Jerry that I be fired?"

He paused in thought. "I have to think some things through," he said at last. "I believe there are details you're not telling me about the situation. If that is true, it would be a good time to start spilling your guts."

"I'm sure there are things you're keeping from me as well," she said.

"Look…You have to give me something here if you think your job is worth saving. Or do you believe I'm part of this big conspiracy?"

"Maybe you are."

"Oh my God… You're suspicious of everyone, aren't you?"

"I'm beginning to be."

"You said the police believe there is something going on. Why?"

She turned to leave. "There's not much I can say, if you think I'm crazy, is there?"

"I think your parents' deaths may have caused you to feel insecure. Seek out an older man. Maybe cause you to distrust people who're trying to help you."

He still believed she had a relationship with Larkin.

"There is no older man, I told you."

"I've seen the guy. Remember?"

"Okay. I'm going to level with you. The guy you've seen me with is investigating Trudy's case."

"You said the guy I saw you with is a cop?"

"Yes."

"I see."

"What do you see?" She made quotes with her fingers.

"Let's face it. A woman like you could get a man to do anything. Believe anything you asked him to. He wants in your panties."

"We're friends, that's all," she said.

"I saw him kiss you, remember? I caught him at your house. Why? isn't he coming here if he's really investigating a murder?"

"Jerry put pressure on the district attorney to drop the matter. Larkin is now working behind the scenes."

"Don't kid me. I say, he's working to get in your underpants," Marcus said, "if he hasn't already."

Her hand shot out before she could stop it, slapping his left cheek hard. He pulled her to him for a punishing kiss. The kiss softened. Her body pressed into his. When he finally pushed her away, they both gasped for breath.

"I know what you do to a man." His voice was husky with passion.

"Why do men always think everything is about sex?" she snapped.

"Because it usually is," he said.

"The police believe that Trudy was killed in the file room and that her body was dumped in that patient's room. That's what the evidence shows, Dr. Know-It-All. If you don't believe me, call this number." She handed him Larkin's business card. She had called him so many times she knew his cell phone by heart.

"I still say that the man is probably going along with your theory just to…"

"Get in my pants," she answered for him.

"I was going to say humor you, but that, too." He smiled.

"You're impossible," she hissed.

"The police really believe it was someone other than a patient who killed her?"

"Yes. It's not only Larkin, but it's his whole forensic team."

"Why are they involving you?"

"I was Trudy's friend. I asked Detective Larkin to let me help them."

"Discover this great conspiracy, right?"

"I've been honest with you. If you fire me, the police will have no way of knowing what is going on here. They've been pressured into giving up the investigation. Why would the management do that, if they don't have anything to hide?"

Lakeview has a reputation to uphold. I can certainly see why Jerry doesn't want a bunch of cops hanging around. I, for one, don't think there is anything going on. But I do have the feeling that you're still not telling me everything."

She wanted—no, she needed to confide in someone—but she couldn't trust him with the secret information about her nephew and sister.

"Please don't take me off the boy's case. Just this one time, give me the benefit of the doubt. It's important." Her eyes begged him to understand.

He considered the information for a moment as he walked to the window and looked out, and then he turned back to her. "I'll take care of the situation with Mrs. Bailey and Jerry, but I will be handling the boy's case as of this instant. Is that understood?"

She started to say something, but he cut her off with a wave of his hand. "This is the deal, take it or leave it."

"Are you going to put Arron back on his original medication?" She held her breath.

"I'll evaluate him myself and draw my own conclusions. There will be no interference by you in anyway. This ought to satisfy Mrs. Bailey and your uncle."

"What will you tell them about what happened?"

"I will tell them that I'm not sure what happened, but that I have taken over the boy's case to see that things are done right."

"Please don't put him back on that medication," she begged.

"I'll do what I think is right for the boy. You have no bargaining chips, Dr. West. As of now, you're on probation, and I will be watching you very carefully. If I see you hanging around that boy, I will fire you myself. Do you understand?"

"Yes, I understand." Her voice was chipped ice.

Casey turned toward the door. Tears threatened to spill over. Damn her carelessness, damn her arrogance, Damn her big mouth.

Damn it all, but she didn't want the stinking man to think badly of her, and of this minute he thought she was freaking nuts.

"Casey, you need to trust me," Marcus's words surprised her.

She looked up at him abruptly.

"I'm serious. I think you have a lot of issues when it comes to trust."

Her hand rested on the knob. She couldn't argue with the truth. She had never really trusted her adoptive parents. She tried to think of all the people she had trusted in her life and came up empty. No, there were two people she trusted, and the revelation shook her to the very core. She had trusted Trudy, and she trusted Karl Larkin.

"Casey, one last thing, he said. "This is your last chance. Don't blow it."

His statement caused her to pause before opening the door. He didn't need to explain what he meant. It wasn't a threat; it was a promise. If she screwed up one more time her job would be a thing of the past. She would have such a bad reputation she would never be able to work again. She might even lose her license.

Without answering, she slipped out into the hall and headed toward her office. She had brought this all on herself. She was so anxious to help her family that she'd thrown caution to the wind.

Chapter 18

Casey had no idea how Marcus explained to Jerry and Mrs. Bailey why he removed her from Arron's case. No one mentioned it, and soon, things were back to the normal routine. Nancy didn't lose her job, but Casey noticed that she never strayed from her medicine cart anymore to engage someone in conversation.

Casey wondered what Arron must be thinking. Did he feel she had abandoned him like everyone else in his life had?

She tried to find out what treatment Marcus was using for him, but the nurses were evasive, and she knew it would be a mistake to ask Marcus himself. He might be working with the management. It was certain he wasn't prepared to listen to anything against his idol, Jerry Connors. She tried to watch the boy from a distance, hoping somehow to keep him safe. She was bone tired from staying after hours. She pretended she was working on the cases Marcus assigned, but she suspected everyone knew why she was staying late.

Larkin fumed when Casey told him about the drugs Sam Talbot brought into Lakeview. It made him want to rip Talbot's and Bailey's heads off. He did put a tail on Talbot. Within a week, the police arrested him for possession.

When Talbot never showed up for work the next day, he called Bailey and she sent a lawyer who represented Lakeview to bail him out of jail.

In the meantime, Sam admitted buying drugs for Kathryn Bailey. He insisted he didn't know how she planned to use them. The Lakeview lawyer showed up and put a quick end to the interrogation, just as Larkin began questioning him about Trudy's murder.

Larkin warned Casey by cell phone what had happened with Talbot.

When she arrived at work the next day, Mrs. Bailey's door was closed. Casey sat in her own office pondering a way of using the information about Talbot. She thought about going to Marcus and telling him about Talbot admitting he had gotten the LSD for Kathryn. She still couldn't prove Kathryn had given it to Arron. She decided to keep the information to herself. Larkin had cautioned her not to trust anyone at Lakeview.

Some savior she was. She couldn't think of anything she could use to her advantage. She wished she knew which room her sister was in. She wanted to go there so badly, but she promised Larkin she wouldn't do anything dangerous. She kept remembering how her friend Trudy was murdered and she knew if Sam Talbot caught her in her sister's room, he would kill her as well. The management would put the blame on her poor sister. If only the police would hold Sam because of the drugs, she could explore the South Wing without fear of getting caught. Everyone used to take turns staying the night at Lakeview, but since Sam Talbot was there anyway, his coworkers all were allowed to go home. He had lost his apartment for to not paying his rent. Kathryn talked Jerry into letting him crash at the hospital until he was back on his feet.

Casey felt the only reason Jerry and Kathryn allowed him to stay was because it did them a favor as well. They breathed easier knowing Sam Talbot would take care of any problem. Casey believed he'd d been ordered to dispose of anyone he found snooping around his area. She knew Sam was watching her and she was anxious when everyone else left the building.

She felt so helpless. No matter how many late nights she spent at Lakeview, fear kept her away from Arron and her sister. She not only feared losing her own life, but she was afraid if she made waves they might retaliate against Arron or her sister.

Chapter 19

"We have problems," Sam told Kathryn as soon as she let him into her office. He walked straight to the chair beside her desk and flopped down without so much as a how- do-you-do.

"What kind of problems?" Kathryn moved to stand in front of him. She found him less intimidating that way.

"The police caught me with a little weed. They booked me and they want me to rat out my supplier."

"I know that. I was the one who sent the lawyer—again—or did you think it was the good fairy?" she asked, through gritted teeth.

His eyes narrowed. He didn't care for the old crow's attitude. "My court date is in two weeks. They won't do much. They never caught me selling, and I only had enough for my own personal use. They also questioned me about the drugs I got for you."

"What did you tell them?"

"I denied getting you drugs."

"Did they believe you?" she snapped.

"They knew about the drugs you used on the boy. Don't ask me how, because I didn't tell them anything."

"So where's the problem?" She asked walking closer to him.

"They grilled me about Trudy Madison's murder. They say they have my fingerprints on the doorknob and my palm print on the file cabinet."

"They have nothing. I sent you for a file, and you retrieved the one in question, and then pushed the drawer closed."

"They also say they have evidence that I carried her body, letting her feet drag across the floor."

"They're only guessing. How could they know?"

"It's uncanny. How did they figure out what really happened?"

She reached over to put her hand on his shoulder. "Look. You tell them nothing, do you hear? They're guessing, and they don't have diddly-squat."

"I just wanted you to know if I go down, I won't be going alone..."

"Don't threaten me, Sam. You aren't equipped to deal with someone like me. If it comes down to it, we will provide you with the best lawyer's money can buy. Just keep your mouth shut about us." She moved in front of him and gave him a warning look. "Just remember...I'll always be one step ahead of you."

"Oh yeah?"

"That's an amazing comeback, Sam."

He stood up, towering over her. "I might not be as smart as you, but I'm strong enough to snap your neck, just like I did the Madison girl's."

"Shut up. Don't you know I have this place bugged?"

"You just remember what I told you," he said moving toward the door.

"Get back to work and forget about all of this. Jerry made sure those two idiot detectives can't hang around here anymore. They're just trying to scare you into confessing. I'll talk to Jerry and have him put pressure on them again." She walked to the door and opened it, inviting him to leave.

"I thought maybe we could have a little session," he moved in close to her. "I could use a stress reliever after that bout with the detective and his buddy," he said, hunching against her.

"Are you crazy? I have to deal with the situation you've gotten us into. Just remember I pick the time and the place for the action."

"You'd better make sure Jerry gets rid of the cops fast. They make me nervous asking me questions."

"I'll talk to him right now. Just get back to work and leave everything to me."

"What about the fine?"

"I've paid it already. Just don't bring up my name or that you supplied me with anything. Do you understand?"

Sam stared at her for a moment before turning to go back to work. He wasn't about to tell her that her name had already come up, not before he confirmed she had paid his fine anyway.

Kathryn closed the door behind Sam. She hurried to her desk and paged Jerry. Within five minutes, Jerry stormed into her office.

"I was in the middle of a business meeting, Kathryn. What the hell is so important?"

"The police picked Sam Talbot up for drugs again yesterday evening."

"So? What so different about that…The man has been sleeping on the vestibule couch for two months because he can't keep a roof over his head. I'd rather guessed he had a problem in that area. Didn't you?"

"Do you remember me telling you that I had a suspicion about the boy not being on his meds?"

"Yes, I remember," he huffed.

"Well, I caught Casey West and him laughing and even sharing a hug. It was plain to see he wasn't on the drugs you prescribed for him. So I took matters into my own hands."

"What do you mean you took matters into your own hands?" His eyes widened.

"I had Sam get me some microdots…"

"You gave the kid LSD? Are you crazy?"

"I had to do something. You're so damned busy you don't have time to stay focused on what's going on. I had to make it look as though the kid was hallucinating so Marcus would put him back on his medication. I also had to convince that idiot you hired, that he needed his meds."

"You're the idiot, Kathryn. You could have killed the kid. If he had been taking what I prescribed for him along with the LSD, he would have died."

"All the kid represents is another problem I have to deal with," she said.

"All we need is another death around here to explain, Kathryn."

"I know that, Jerry, but I couldn't think of any other way to handle it."

"Do you think Casey talked Marcus into taking him off the meds I prescribed for the boy?"

"Yes, I do."

"I'll have a talk with him and find out what's going on."

"I'm just so tired of keeping up with all the lies," Kathryn said. "The pressure is getting to me, Jerry."

"Just remember what you're doing this for, Kathryn."

"I don't know if the money and the early retirement are worth it anymore," she said as she stared at him. Or if you're worth it, she thought.

He took her into his arms. She stiffened. "I promise; I'll be more aware of what's going on."

"I hope so." Kathryn seemed to breathe a sigh of relief.

"You know that Sam Talbot is loose cannon," he said, after holding her for some time.

"I know..." She could feel the tension mounting once again. "He said that Larkin and his partner questioned him about the Madison girl's murder while they had him in custody."

"I was afraid of that," he said pushing her away. "It's your entire fault. You're just like that drug addict boyfriend of yours. You can't do without the coke."

"It's just to take the edge off," she said, trying to hug him once more.

"At least we got rid of those nosy detectives. Thanks to you, they aren't allowed to come here anymore," Kathryn said.

"That doesn't mean they can't go to your house and pick you up like they did Sam. If they obtain a warrant they can pick us both up," he said, running his fingers through his hair.

"Can't you call your friend the mayor again? Can't he get them off our case?"

"What do you suggest I tell him, Kathryn? I have a couple of junkies working me, and will he please have the cops ignore them while they work with mental patients?"

"What about talking to one of your judge friends you play golf with?"

"You just don't get it do you?" He gave her a hard glare that made her cringe. "I have a spotless reputation in this town. I've gone out of my way to be a pillar of the community. Didn't I tell you that we need to keep a low profile if this thing was going to work?"

"I—I'm sorry, Jerry. It would have been fine if that dimwit we hired to do our dirty work hadn't gotten picked up for buying drugs."

"What do you mean we hired? I told you it was a bad idea from the start. He's just smart enough to blow my whole damn plan, Kathryn. If the cops lean on him, he'll spill his guts and take us down with him."

"Do you want me to fire him?"

Jerry shook his head. "You're not any smarter than he is, are you?"

"What do you mean?"

"He would definitely talk to the cops then. I was thinking about something a little more permanent."

"I don't know," she gasped. "We already have one murder to explain."

"He's into drugs. Everyone knows that. It won't be a far stretch for him to be killed because a drug deal goes bad."

"Don't we need him to work the South Wing?"

"We lock the patients in. They're not nearly as dangerous as we've led people to believe."

"We could hire a hit man."

"That's another bad idea," Jerry said.

"Why?"

"Because the more people who know about a murder, the greater the chances of getting caught."

"What do you have in mind?"

"I should make you shoot the bastard, since you screwed up so badly."

"I—I can't do that."

"Don't panic. If I want something done right, I do it yourself. But you're going to help me."

Bailey swallowed hard. How did she know she wasn't going to get out of this so easily?

"Do you know where the old quarry is?"

"Are you talking about the one just outside of town? It hasn't been used in years," she said.

"Do you think you could lure him out there?"

"I may be able to...why?"

"Because, when he's dead, we could dump him, car and all, into the quarry. It would probably be years, if ever, before they find him."

"How will we explain his disappearance?"

"He doesn't have any family, but a grandmother, and she's in a nursing home in Virginia. If the cops or any of the staff asks questions, I'll tell them because of the drugs I had to fire him, and I figure he took off to avoid the charges against him."

"That's brilliant, Jerry," she exclaimed. "It's so simple, it just might work. That's all we have to tell everyone. It ought to take us out of the hot seat."

"Just remember, Kathryn, "people on drugs screw up. If you don't stop snorting cocaine, you might be next."

She swallowed. She didn't like to be threatened, but she knew the man was playing for keeps. She realized he wouldn't hesitate to eliminate her as well. She was in a dangerous position, simply because she knew too much.

"I'll be more careful," she vowed.

"No, you will kick the habit. All we need is the cops believing something drug related is going on at Lakeview. It'll call attention to us, and that I don't need. Do you understand?"

"I do, but we have a bigger problem."

"And what is that?" His eyes narrowed.

"Our fake Ruth Thompson, showed up in my office the other day. She was all upset because Casey West came to her house, looking for her sister. You told me that Casey had no idea she'd been adopted?"

"I didn't think she did." Jerry looked worried.

"I think she's looking for her family, and I suspect she thinks the kid is her nephew. That's the reason she has such an interest in the boy."

"He is her nephew, Kathryn. Just shut up and let me think."

"We need to get rid of her as well," Kathryn said.

"We just can't go around killing everyone who gets in our way. That detective Larkin would be all over us if something happened to Casey. Even if she suspects Ruth Thompson is her sister, she doesn't know for sure, or I think she would have already confronted me. We have to keep her from finding out anything else before we can get our phony Ruth to sign the papers. After they're signed, no one can stop us. In the meantime, we need to keep a close eye on her."

"What if that detective talks to the fake Ruth? You know how unstable the woman is."

"Don't worry, Kathryn. I've already dealt with the problem. I'm always two steps ahead of you."

"What do you mean?"

"I have this little cabin on a piece of land beside the lake. It's very remote and no one will find her there. The neighbors will see her packing to leave and she is going to tell them she is going on a vacation."

"You never told me about this place."

"It was on a need to know bases and you didn't need to know."

"It's your call..." You always think you know what's best."

"I do know what's best, Kathryn." His expression was the smirk she despised.

"It scares me that our phony Ruth is getting cold feet."

"I reminded her of the money she's to get, when it's over?"

"Of course you did." Kathryn's sarcastic remark caused him to flinch. "It might come as a shock to you, Jerry, but money isn't the motivating force for everyone in this world."

"And who would that be, Kathryn? Not you, I wager."

Kathryn moved away from her desk to a closet where she had set up a mini bar. Taking the lid off a bottle of bourbon, she poured herself a shot. "Want one?" she asked.

"You didn't ask me to set up the booze supply in here?"

She threw the shot down the back of her throat and grimaced. Jerry studied her disapprovingly.

"If you can think of something besides booze and drugs, you might be able to help me with the plan," he snapped.

"I think Casey is the most dangerous of all. "We need to get rid of her, too." Kathryn moved closer to him.

"Leave Casey alone and concentrate on Sam." How do you think we ought to do it?"

"I don't know. You seemed to be the expert in that department," she snapped.

"That may be true, but at least I don't call attention by drugging kids," he retorted.

"If it hadn't been for me giving the kid acid, Marcus wouldn't have taken over the boy's care. You should be thanking me, Jerry, instead of criticizing."

"That remains to be seen."

"What do you talking about?"

"We'll see if it comes back to bite us."

Kathryn shook her head.

"Let's get back to Sam," Jerry said.

"What's the plan for luring him out to the quarry?"

"I'm leaving that to you." His eyes narrowed. "From what I hear, you're pretty good at handling the old boy."

"What do you mean by that crack?" she queried.

"I think you know exactly what I mean."

"No, I don't," she snapped.

"I've heard the rumors, Kathryn."

"What rumors?"

"That you service the old boy every once in a while."

"Where did you hear that?"

"Don't act so outraged, Kathryn. Everyone knows about it. I personally don't give a damn. It's not like you're my one true love."

His words cut to the quick. She did love him, and no matter how mean he was to her, she always came back for more.

"I don't care who else you screw as long as things go according to plan. What I don't like is something calling attention to Lakeview, like drugs for instance."

"I told you I would be more careful," she snapped.

"And I told you that you were going to kick the habit cold turkey. You can take as many drugs as you want to after this thing is settled. Up until that time, you'll be discreet in all your dealings, is that understood?"

Kathryn's nerves grated at the way he snapped orders. More and more, she found herself turning against him. At first, she went along with his plan out of love. Then she was lured by the promise of money. Now, she continued on because she feared him.

"When this first started you kept me in the loop. I knew exactly what the plan was."

"You still know the plan, Kathryn."

"I don't like this thing with Casey. You said she didn't know she was adopted, or that she had a sister and nephew. I think she knows everything. Why else would she react the way she does with Arron. She may even know the woman we released if not her sister."

A troubled expression crossed his face. "Give it up, Kathryn. I'm not getting rid of Casey."

"I still say having her at Lakeview is dangerous."

"And I say having her on the outside, snooping around, would be even more dangerous."

"It's your call," Kathryn said.

"You damn right it's my call, and don't you forget it. There is no evidence left at Lakeview she can find."

"Thanks to me incriminating myself with those files," Kathryn snapped.

"Stop being such a martyr. You'll get paid for your efforts."

"What if that detective is working the case on the outside?"

"I don't think he has given up like his superiors told him," Jerry admitted. His frown deepened as he considered it.

"Even if the phony Ruth goes away, there'll be questions."

"She has moved to the cabin already, Kathryn. I told her what to tell the neighbors. She doesn't socialize much. They'll soon forget all about her."

"What about Larkin? He'll never stop snooping."

"I'll have my friend put pressure on him again. I have influence in this town, and I plan to use it to the hilt. If that detective doesn't back off, I'll see to it he won't be able to get a job as dog catcher."

Kathryn stared at him. She had never seen a man more determined. He was a formidable enemy. She sure didn't want to cross him.

"When are we going to take care of Sam?"

"Tonight...Just have him at the quarry at 10:00. I'll do the rest."

Chapter 20

Sam Talbot left work at 9:00. Everyone had gone home early but Casey. She couldn't leave knowing that her nephew was in a nearby bedroom, possibly drugged while her poor sister was locked in a room worse than a prison cell.

She hated that isolated wing of the hospital. She agreed with Trudy: Lakeview treated the patients living there less than humanely.

Casey sighed. Since Marcus took over Arron's case, she had little to look forward to. Helping other patients seemed futile when she couldn't do anything for her own family. She should be more like Trudy. Maybe she should just take the keys and go to her sister's room. Check on her.

She poked her head into the dreaded hallway and looked around. She wondered if Trudy had felt the same way that fatal day she decided to go to the file room. She wondered if her heart pounded as hers was doing now, or if her blood pumped until she could hear it in her ears. She hurried back to the reception desk.

The forbidden wing drew her toward it with a devilish force.

There is no one here but you, a little voice enticed her. She had watched Sam leave early. That was odd for he never left at night since Trudy was killed.

The keys hung above the reception desk. She stretched up and touched the cold metal bulk, feeling each groove as she contemplated searching for her sister. Trudy said the woman was either in room 10 or

12. Knowing Bailey, she might have switched the patient's rooms, just to throw her off track.

Casey slipped the ring into her pocket, trying not to think about the danger as she caressed the keys. She swallowed hard. "Trudy, were you this petrified? she asked, feeling Trudy's spirit close by. But Trudy was dead and she might be warning her not to fall into the same trap as she had. She whipped the keys from her pocket and hung them back where they belonged. Arron's face appeared before her. A countenance filled with such joy from winning a hand of rummy. Then later, Arron walking around like a zombie. He and her sister had no one else they could depend on. She had to take a chance.

Everyone else had let them down. Ruth's father had given her away, and then her husband had sold her. For some reason, she couldn't grasp why the management wanted Ruth and her son at Lakeview. None of it made any sense.

Like Marcus, she had trouble believing that her Uncle Jerry, whom she'd known all of her life, had anything to do with what was going on. She was, however, becoming more and more suspicious of him as time went by. Unless he was hiding his head in the sand, he had to know what his supervisor was doing. What reason did they have for keeping her sister a prisoner and Arron drugged until he couldn't function? That answer evaded her.

Steeling her nerves, she snatched the keys from their hook again. The coldness of the keychain reminded her of the danger she was in. A shiver traveled her body. Did a goose just walk over her grave?

She couldn't over-think this or she would lose her nerve. If she didn't do something to help her family, was life really worth living anyway?

Trying not to think, she moved forward. All she had to do is put one foot in front of the other and move down the depressing hall-way. There were little windows in each door and she would have to look through the windows until she found the right room.

The staff left a night light on in the rooms in case of emergencies. She decided that she could at least look in the two rooms Trudy had told her about. She could locate her sister tonight and then devise a plan to actually go to her room sometime in the future. All the doors were locked; no patient could escape. The danger to her was low.

Casey hurried to the double swinging doors that bore the "Authorized Personnel Only" sign. She touched the raised letters on the sign, swallowed the lump of dread in her throat, and pushed the doors open.

The hallway was dimly lit and quiet as death. What a horrible place to live. She thought again of her poor sister.

The furnace rumbled to life. Casey jumped. The floor protested her weight by popping and cracking as she began her trek down the hall. It was just the floor settling, she told herself. It happened in old buildings, and this part of the establishment was not part of the remodeling the place had undergone in the last few years. She whirled around and searched for a person behind her. She felt as if she were being watched. Had Sam Talbot only pretended to leave and then sneaked back into the building? She paused to wait for her heartbeat to settle. Even if she was alone, she knew that this was still a dangerous place.

Trudy said her sister's room was located somewhere in the middle of the hallway. Casey slid along the wall to the room where she planned to start her search.

Nothing was causing a commotion tonight; it was the quietest that scared her. For the first time, she realized how still it was without the healthcare workers moving about and the patients sleeping.

Stopping at room 10, Casey stood on her tiptoes; putting her hands on both sides of her face, she peered through the glass. In the muted lighting, the room appeared to be empty. She moved to room 12. She could see Johnston's form in his bed covered from head to toe in a dirty blanket. Since Trudy's murder, the staff refused to go near room 13 which was the murder room, so Johnston was moved.

Room 14 was next, and she hoped it belonged to her sister. It took all the nerve she could muster to put her face up to the window. Suddenly, another face appeared in the window on the other side of the glass. Casey jumped back, cramming her fist in her mouth to squelch her scream.

The woman on the other side of the glass stared at her with the frightened eyes of an animal. Her long gray-black hair was matted around her face.

Casey clasped her chest and took a deep breath. Could this wild thing really be her sister? She did resemble the woman in the photo. Casey had to know for sure.

She steeled her nerves, and rose on tiptoes, to look through the glass once more.

The woman was still there, and even in her neglected condition, Casey could tell she was the same woman as in the picture Trudy had taken.

As Casey unlocked the door, her sister scampered back and sat on her bed, staring at Casey with frightened eyes. Her mouth was moving, but no sound came from her lips. Instant tears sprang to Casey's eyes. She realized that the woman was omitting a silent scream. What torture had this poor human endured? By using physical violence against her, they had trained her not to make a sound, but Ruth was screaming inside. As Casey watched her, she felt her own heart breaking.

Casey's stifled her own scream as her voice caught in a sob. Tears ran freely down her cheeks. She vowed not only to help her sister but to alleviate the suffering of the others living on this wing. She didn't know how, but some way she would do it. They were people, not animals, and somehow she would stop this abuse.

With determination, Casey took a step toward her.

Ruth cowered on her bed as she approached.

"Ruth," Casey soothed as she approached her. "You're all right."

"No." The woman mouthed the word and struck out at her.

"Ruth, it's okay. I won't hurt you," Casey promised.

Her sister wore a dirty gown that reeked of urine. Casey's blood boiled. Trudy was right in her estimation. They did treat their patients on this wing as though they weren't human.

Along one wall were built-in drawers that Casey opened to find one old hospital gown with the ties missing.

In the left corner of the room was a smelly toilet and dirty shower. Casey itched to give Ruth a bath, but knew she had to take this slow and easy.

Casey threw the gown back into the drawer and walked slowly to the bed. Ruth was agitated as it was. Somehow she would have to gain her trust before she could even clean her up.

"Ruth, will you let me sit with you awhile?" Casey said, soothingly.

Her sister never answered. She rocked back and forth on the bed moaning to herself. Casey caught hold of her hand. Ruth never jerked it away as she expected, but she didn't display any knowledge that Casey held it either.

Her hands were filthy, her fingernails long and claw-like. There was no excuse for this. If these patients were violent, they should be sedated if it was necessary for performing basic cleanliness.

For over a half an hour, Casey talked to Ruth. She put her arm around her sister's shoulders. They rocked gently back and forth in the rhythm that Ruth orchestrated. Casey's felt her sister's pain physically. She was determined to spend what time she could with Ruth because she might never get another chance.

Eventually, Ruth fell asleep. Casey was reluctant to let go of her, but she knew Ruth needed to rest. She had learned one thing tonight. Her sister had responded to basic human kindness. Ruth was disturbed, but there's no way Casey would consider her violent. She knew this was probably the first and last time she could spend with her until she and Detective Larkin could find out what was going on here. As long as Talbot worked this floor, she knew it would be too dangerous to visit with Ruth.

As she had held Ruth close to her tonight, she vowed that things would change. She was determined to find a way.

It was so cold in this room and her sister never had a blanket. There wasn't even a sheet on the thin mattress where she slept, only a dirty top sheet to cover her with.

She laid her sister gently down against the pillow. Ruth moved automatically into a fetal position. Cassie bent down and kissed the sleeping woman. She slipped out of the room, making sure she locked the door before heading back to her office. A Thumping noise echoed in the hall. Her heart caught in her throat. Had Sam Talbot returned to murder her?

She pushed the double doors open a crack so she could view the front doors and the vestibule in front of her. Someone was moving around, but she couldn't distinguish where the sound was coming from.

Her hand knocked against the bulge of keys in her pocket. Somehow she had to get them back before anyone knew she had taken them. Casey looked both ways, then hurried to the reception desk and returned the keys. She managed to place them on the hook despite her shaking hands.

The noises came from Mrs. Bailey's office. Casey looked at her watch. It was two in the morning. Why in the world would that woman be here at this time of night?

A loud bang reverberated. Casey jumped. Kathryn must have dropped something.

Moving quickly, she hurried to her own office and slipped inside. Once she thought about leaving the building, but she was afraid Kathryn would catch her before she could escape.

For thirty minutes, Casey listened for the rustling in the Bailey's office to cease.

Finally, she heard Bailey's door open and someone walk by her office. Footsteps sounded by her own door. Instinctively, she reached out and locked it. The footsteps suddenly stopped. Her hand was still on the knob when she felt it turn in her hand. She raised her hand to her mouth and tried not to scream.

After finding her door locked, the footsteps continued down the hallway.

Casey eased the door open slightly to make sure Mrs. Bailey was gone. She gasped when she saw Marcus Kelly's back as he left the building.

What was he searching for in Kathryn's office? It was another unanswered question.

Chapter 21

Kathryn Bailey pulled her car into the entrance of the quarry. The chain that once kept people out had been torn down by vandals. It was dark and eerily quiet behind the mountains of old rock. Kathryn breathed deeply and slowly as she drove over the chain that was now flattened to the road. It was spooky back here. She hoped Jerry and Sam showed up soon.

She watched her timepiece click away the minutes. Every second felt like an hour while she waited for her intended victim to show. Tick-tock. Her time-piece counted another five minutes. Sam was late and so was Jerry. Which one would get here first?

Tick-tock.

Five more minutes passed, and other thoughts crowded her mind. What if Sam and Jerry planned to team up and murder her instead? It could be a set-up. She started the motor, tempted to leave the stillness of the quarry, when she saw headlights at the entrance. She switched off her own lights but not before she recognized Sam's old rattletrap. He pulled up beside her and parked.

The plan was for him to bring her the cocaine and she would in turn give him money and sex. She hurried out of her car to meet him.

"Do you have the goods?" Kathryn looked around. The great mounds of dirt and gravel hid them from the road.

Sam handed her the drugs.

"Your car or mine," he asked, smiling.

"I don't care, but we need to hurry. Sometimes the cops check back here for teenagers making out."

"Let's do it in yours." Sam smiled. "I have junk in the back seat." He had been afraid that she would make some excuse about not giving him sex, but she seemed as anxious as he did. She was dog-ugly, but she was a good piece of ass, especially in the dark. He could pretend it was the new doctor. What's her name? It was Casey, now, there was a looker.

"Are you going to take off your clothes?" Sam asked.

"Just my underpants and hose and not all the way," she grunted as she slid them down her thighs. Jerry could be there any minute. Sam was a good lay and sex would definitely keep him occupied. The fact that she might get caught made her that much hotter. "Just pull your pants down and give it to me hard and fast, baby." The man was a stud, and she didn't have to wait around for his Viagra to work.

Sam quickly stripped his pants to his knees and joined Kathryn who was already lying on the back seat.

"Unbutton your blouse," he commanded. Pushing her bra up his mouth sucked in one of her sagging breasts. She grabbed his huge erection and guided him inside, moaning as he entered her. Kathryn urged him into the rhythm she wanted by placing her hand on his hipbones, setting the pace.

The blood soared to Kathryn's core. Pleasure mounted. She was ready to burst when Jerry's car pulled into the driveway, shining his lights on Sam's vehicle. She thrust her hips into Sam's, desperate for release. Her breath caught in her throat. The world exploded as she climaxed like never before. Sam collapsed against her letting her, know he had done the same. She drew a quick breath, before she shoved him off her.

"There's someone here," she told him, knowing full well who it was.

Sam struggled from the car, stumbling to pull up his pants while shielding his eyes from Jerry's bright headlights.

Kathryn stripped off her underpants the rest of the way and threw them on the floorboard. She straightened her own rumpled clothes. "You're late," she snapped as Jerry stepped into the light. The gun in his hand cast a long shadow.

"Would you have wanted me to be any earlier, Kathryn?" he asked as she finished buttoning her blouse.

"It's not like it looks. She was the one who came on to me," Sam exclaimed.

"I don't doubt that at all, Sam, but what I can't allow is for you to bring drugs into Lakeview. I've given you every chance, but you had to get in trouble with the law. I allowed you to live at the facility when you lost your apartment. I never even charged you rent. And this is how you repay me, by calling negative attention to Lakeview."

"I got the drugs for her." Sam pointed to Kathryn.

"You had better hurry. The cops check back here sometimes for kids making out," Kathryn said through gritted teeth.

"You bitch!" Sam stepped toward her. "You set me…"

A shot rang out. A hole appeared between Sam's eyes. He fell against Kathryn; his blood smeared her suit as he went down.

"God, Jerry! You could have warned me to get out of the way," she snapped as she pushed at Sam who lay on her foot. She stepped away from the body, withdrew her handkerchief from her pocket, and began dabbing at the blood on her legs.

"Forget cleaning up! You have to help me get him back to his car."

"Why didn't you force him back into his car before you shot him," she snapped, still wiping at the smeared blood.

"Why didn't I just ask him to get back into his car and shoot himself?" Jerry hissed.

Kathryn grumbled as she took hold of Sam's legs. Halfway to the car, she let them fall.

"Why did you park so close beside him?" Jerry complained. "You know what we planned to do with the body."

"I was the one who got here first. Remember?"

"We're going to have to put him in your car."

"Hell no!" she said "That's a brand new vehicle. I don't want blood all over the damn thing. Let's put him in your car."

"I'm not going to sink my vehicle in the quarry," Jerry told her.

"And what am I going to say happened to mine?"

"Say someone stole it."

"Think, Jerry...I can just move my car back."

"And what if the cops come by while we're playing musical vehicles?" Jerry spat. "We will just have to carry him around yours then."

"Well let's hurry up," she said.

"Get his keys," he ordered.

"Why don't you get them?" Kathryn stared at Sam's body, which was slumped almost face down and to one side, blood still pouring from his head wound.

"You're more familiar with his body," Jerry snapped.

Kathryn stepped forward, squeamish about reaching into her dead lover's pocket. "The keys are not here."

"Isn't he left-handed?" Jerry asked.

Kathryn tried jamming her hand into his other pocket, but Sam was lying more toward his left side and she was unable to get the keys.

"You're going to have to help me turn him over," she snapped as she pulled at Sam's body.

"Can't you do anything?" Jerry stepped forward, grabbed Sam's belt, pulling him onto his back.

Kathryn bent and grabbed his keys. When she came away with blood on her hands she wiped it on her skirt before handing them to Jerry.

"Don't give them to me. Put them in Sam's ignition. "We'll move his car as close to the edge as we can. I'll position my car behind his."

Jerry put Sam's car in neutral and they pushed it as close to the edge as they dared. Kathryn couldn't suppress a shiver. It was a long way down over the jagged rocks. She sure didn't envy Sam being the one who was about to make it his final resting place. She moved away from Sam's car fast. She knew Jerry was angry and she didn't want to tempt him to push her over as well.

Jerry pulled behind Sam's auto, got out, and motioned for Kathryn to come and help him.

Despite the clouds beginning to form, the moon shone brightly enough that they could see all too well the task that lay ahead of them.

"Are you ready to try again?" he asked.

A puddle of blood encircled Sam's head. "It's a good thing we killed him outside. This would have been a mess to clean up." Kathryn said. It was surprising what one thought of in a situation like this.

"I thought you were in a hurry?" Jerry snapped.

Kathryn lifted Sam's legs once more while Jerry caught him under the arms. Sam's legs felt nailed to the ground. Kathryn stumbled and almost let him drop again.

"Sometime tonight, Kathryn," Jerry remarked.

"The man's a moose," she snapped.

Another set of headlights drove slowly by the entrance to the quarry.

"Oh, my God—it's the cops," Kathryn breathed.

"Just hurry up," Jerry ordered. "Before we have to kill them, too."

"You can't be serious?" She stopped to look at him. The shadows hid his expression, but the hardness of his voice made her shiver.

"I've never been more serious in my life."

The cruiser drove slowly on past. Kathryn sighed in relief. She had planned only one murder tonight, and she drew the line at killing a cop.

"Come on," Jerry ordered.

"I can't do this. It's too hard," she whined, exhausted.

"We're almost there. Just keep going."

They were about three feet from Sam's car, but it might as well have been a mile. Headlights moved toward the entrance again. Jerry and Kathryn scurried behind a mound of gravel, which hid them from the road. A single streetlamp near the entrance illuminated the side insignia of the police vehicle.

"We can't kill a couple of cops," Kathryn's voice came out as a hiss.

A car door opened and Kathryn gasped.

"We aren't going to panic," Jerry said softly near her ear. "We won't do anything unless they head back here."

"Then what?..." Kathryn whispered back.

"I'll have to shoot them both and have them join old Sam."

A shiver ran up her spine. There was no mistaking the lack of feeling in the man. He was a psychopath, something she had suspected for a long time. She stared at him in the faint moonlight. For the first time, she realized just how dangerous he was.

"I didn't see anything." The cop's voice carried on the chilly night air. "I say let's get back to the station. It's past quitting time, and the ole lady is bitching about me working late all the time."

"I thought I saw some vehicles when we drove by."

"So we have a few teens making out. We both came here and did the same thing when we were kids. "Leave them alone. This is their parents worry."

Kathryn held her breath. The first man looked around for some kind of movement, and then slipped back into his car. The motor roared to life and then faded away as in the distance.

Kathryn exhaled. The poor bastards never knew how close they came to never going home again.

"Hurry up!" Jerry hissed. "The idiots may come back."

Kathryn sprang into action. She lifted Sam's legs and tried not to stare at his lifeless eyes as they half-carried and half-dragged him the last few feet to his car.

With her help they hoisted him into the driver's seat. Sam's stiffening corpse slid almost back out the door. Jerry released the seat and pushed it back, giving them more room to operate.

"I'm going to lift him into the seat again, and you need to hold him there until I can lift his legs. After he's inside, just let him slump over the steering wheel. Are you ready?"

She nodded and took hold of Sam's bloody head.

"Grab his shoulders and hold them, while I put his legs in." Jerry demanded. "He's dead, Kathryn. He's not going to bite you."

Kathryn hated the feel of the corpse. Sam's body was cold, clammy, and almost impossible to manipulate.

Jerry moved Sam into position against the back of the seat. "Now hold him there while I fasten his seat belt." The, body fell against Kathryn, who was bent over, smearing the side of her face with blood."

"Yuck!" Kathryn gagged, loosening her grip.

"Hold him, damn it!" Jerry ordered as he caught Sam's shirt to keep him from falling over. "Never mind…I'll hold him. You can fasten his belt."

Kathryn pushed Sam's head back against the seat with her shoulder while she struggled to fasten his belt.

Jerry popped the car into neutral and slipped into his own vehicle.

Kathryn stepped aside as Jerry placed his bumper against Sam's and gave the final push, sending the other car over the edge and into the water below.

She stood watching the automobile disappear in a swirl of bubbles. She turned and again dabbed at her filthy clothes with one of her lacy handkerchiefs.

Who knew that murder would be such hard work? She would never forget this night as long as she lived. It was finally over and all she could think of was a long, hot shower. She stared at Jerry in the bright moonlight. He looked sinister and dangerous. She shivered.

"I'm going to go home and take a bath," Kathryn said, as she moved toward her car.

"Wait a minute, Kathryn." The way Jerry said her name made her skin crawl and fear creep up her spine. She stopped and turned around slowly realizing Jerry was pointing the gun at her.

"What are you doing? We need to get out of here," she said.

"Get in your car," he ordered.

"That's what I'm trying to do," she snapped.

"Get in and put on your seat belt."

"What are you planning, Jerry?" she asked, staring at him.

"You've become a threat to me, Kathryn. And when someone becomes a liability to me, I have to eliminate them. You're about to join your lover in the quarry."

"Surely you must be kidding." She sputtered. "You need me, Jerry, to help you carry out this scheme of yours."

"You've gotten sloppy, Kathryn," he said and cocked his gun. "You started bringing drugs into Lakeview, and sleeping with scum."

"Things will be different now. I promise. I won't be getting drugs anymore, you'll see. Sam's gone. I don't have a supplier. It'll be just you and me, like when we started."

Jerry laughed. It was a very unpleasant sound. "Did you really think it was a permanent thing with us? I'm so far above you, Kathryn. I'm surprised that even you can't see that. I've thought this through, Kathryn. If the cops do find Sam and you at the bottom of the quarry, they'll find evidence that you shot your lover and then committed suicide, by driving your car over the cliff."

As she watched, he put on surgical gloves.

"They won't find my prints because I'm about to wipe mine clean. They'll find yours because I'll place the gun in your cold, dead hand."

"No one else will help you like I do. You need me, Jerry."

"Actually, I have already solicited someone to take your place. I offered this person the same amount of money as I did you. Now get in your car."

In the distance, the thunder began rumbling. A bolt of lightning streaked across the sky.

"Bring on the rain," he said to the darkening sky. "Even God wants me to succeed in this," he said. "He's going to wash away all of the blood."

"You're crazy!" Kathryn exclaimed. "The gun is registered to you, Jerry."

It gave him pause for thought. She was right. He would have a hard time explaining why she had his gun. Then he brightened. "I'll just tell them that we were lovers and you must have stolen it. I've already reported it missing. You see, everything is taken care of."

"I know you, Jerry. You don't like complications. If Sam and I both disappear, Larkin and his buddy will bug you every minute."

"I can't let you live. You might decide to go to the cops because you're afraid of me. I'll tell the detective you and Sam ran away together."

"I won't tell any of this, Jerry. I swear on my mother's grave."

"No, I have to kill you, Kathryn. I just can't trust you anymore."

It was then that her mind came up with a plan. She didn't want to take a chance of Jerry shooting her. "She knew Jerry was dead serious and she was grasping at straws, but it would give her a fighting chance The fall would probably kill her, if not, the icy water would do the rest. "I can't shoot myself, then drive my car over the cliff."

"What are you babbling about?" he snapped.

"If you don't shoot me, the cops will just think I shot Sam then committed suicide."

He seemed to think over what she said.

"Okay, but let's make it fast. Get in your car and do it now, before I shoot you where you stand."

"Okay, Jerry, I'm getting in," she said moving to open the door." She couldn't believe she was discussing her death with him as if they were talking about the running of Lakeview. It was all so surreal.

He waved the gun at her and for a second she contemplated tackling him. There was no way she could attempt it without him shooting her.

Slowly she slipped behind the wheel, still with the door open.

"Start the damn car and put it in neutral," he yelled.

Her hands shook so violently she could hardly comply. There was no way she could attempt a run for it. Why had she left her own car so close the edge? She saw no way around it. She was about to plunge over the drop off. It was early spring, but the water was freezing at this time of year. Hopefully, she had talked him out of putting a bullet in her head.

Still holding the gun in front of him, he said. "Start your vehicle and move it as close to the edge as possible."

"Jerry," she called, hitting the button and letting her window down.

"What do you want now?" he asked.

"I would like to know one more thing before you kill me. Is it Marcus who's helping you?"

He didn't answer. He motioned with the gun for her to sit up straight in the car.

"I knew it," Kathryn snapped. "How do you know you can trust him? He's sweet on Casey, you know."

Jerry made no response.

"I have those files in my apartment. If I disappear, the cops will search my place."

"Don't you worry, Kathryn, I have thought of that. I have a key to your place, remember? And I know the combination to your safe."

"Please Jerry. I'll do anything." Her hair straggled around her face in frizzy wisps. Dirt and dried blood encrusted her face.

The woman was a mess. How could he have ever had sex with someone so ugly? Reaching through the window, he grabbed her, causing her to hit her head hard against the door.

"Don't beg, Kathryn. It doesn't become you," he said. "Now sit up straight and take hold of the wheel."

Screaming and crying, she did what she was told.

He motioned for her to fasten her seatbelt, and she complied.

"I should have let you shoot me," she said.

"You're not worth wasting a bullet on, your stupid bitch." He was wearing gloves, but he clasps the gun in her hand then grabbed it back and threw it over the cliff. If the police happened to ever find it in the quarry, it will have your prints on it."

She frantically shook her head.

He reached across her, putting the car in neutral.

Kathryn pushed at the door.

Using his hip Jerry held it closed, and with Kathryn screaming in his ear, he used the window frame for leverage, and gave one last adrenalin inspired push. Kathryn joined Sam in the watery abyss.

At the edge of the quarry, Jerry watched until the car lights sank into the deep. He had some cleanup to do, but his two main problems along with their cars were gone. As soon as he retrieved the files from Kathryn's safe, all the evidence against him would disappear, just like the two people who dared to get in his way. The only people who knew enough about his plan to send him to jail for the rest of his life.

The rain began pelting him as if on cue. He walked to his car, removed a trash bag from a box in the trunk. He spread it over the seat of his Lexus. He had gotten Sam's blood all over his clothes, and there was no way he wanted to get it in his vehicle. Once home, he'd burn his bloody clothes in the fireplace and all traces of his crimes would vanish up in smoke.

As he worked the cleanup he whistled a merry little tune, knowing his problems were gone and he was one-step closer to the prize.

Chapter 22

Kathryn closed her eyes and held her breath as she plunged into the freezing waters. Somewhere, Sam was in the quarry with her, but Sam had a bullet in his head. She hadn't swum in years, but she knew she had no one to rely on but herself.

As soon as the car was submerged, she pulled herself through the opened window and kicked to the surface. Jerry hadn't thought of everything. She had wound the window down so she could plead for her life and to give herself a means of escape. He hadn't insisted she wind it up, probably thinking the car would fill up faster. She surfaced in the middle of the murky pool. She would have to swim about twenty feet to the jagged edge. She looked around for Jerry as she treaded water to stay afloat. To her left, there was a small tree that appeared to be growing out of the bank.

With long strokes, Kathryn pulled her almost numb body toward that bush. Her limbs were stiff and unresponsive by the time she reached the water's edge. She stretched her arm to reach the lowest branch of the tree and missed. She swung forward again. "Shit!" she exclaimed. She shivered. With a lunge, she grasped the limb and pulled herself up onto the narrow ledge of the quarry.

Her teeth chattered uncontrollably. She knew she had to get to someplace warm or die of hypothermia. Through sheer willpower, she began to scale the steep slope in front of her. She would be doing well and then she would slide almost all the way to the bottom. She began proceeding slowly, making sure her foothold held. She moved in a straight line up the slope. It was the steepest but also the shortest way to the top.

She was about halfway there when a rockslide began pelting her head with small stones. She held on to a spindly bush until it was over and she could move again. It would help tremendously if she could see where she was going, but clouds were quickly covering the precious sightings of the moon. When she felt she couldn't take another step, she thought of Jerry and how he'd used and betrayed her. The anger kept her moving upward. She vowed, if she didn't die from exposure, she would get even. Jerry Connors had crossed the wrong girl.

Suddenly, she was at the top, but what would she do now? She couldn't go back to her old life. Someone working for Jerry would put a bullet in her the next time. A pair of headlights swept over the quarry, causing her to duck her head into the shadows. She waited for the crunching of gravel to cease before pulling herself the rest of the way out. Jerry must have been waiting to see for sure that she was dead, and she had almost shown herself, thinking he was gone.

Lightning lit up the pitch-black night. Her whole body convulsed in shivers. She might have survived a watery grave only to die of exposure. It was early March, but it was way too early in the season to be outdoors and soaked to the skin. For the first time since she was a teenager, she was without transportation, cold, and feeling sleepy. While she was in the quarry, her only thought was getting out. Now she had a bigger problem. She couldn't walk home, it was too far, and she would freeze to death.

Feeling the lump in her pocket she remembered her cell phone. She took it out and quickly dialed 911. There was no response. She tried again, but to no avail. Her phone hadn't survived the water. Drawing back, she threw it over the bank to join her car, Sam, and their vehicles. Even though she was in a jam, Kathryn smiled. If she could stay alive, she knew where all the bodies were buried.

Suddenly, the storm loosed its full fury. Thunder crashed and lightning played around the quarry. Kathryn didn't know which way to go, but she knew she wasn't safe around water in the middle of an electrical storm. It was about five miles back to town and another fifteen minutes until she could get home. The way her body was shaking she knew she would never make it without help.

She scanned the area. Darkness surrounded her except for the circle of light from the streetlamp at the entrance. No houses. No people, just herself alone and, shaking from the cold.

She once again thought of Jerry's betrayal and told herself she hadn't survived the deadly plunge just to freeze to death.

When the lightning began exposing the area, she could see the sheer drop-off she had survived. She gritted her teeth with determination. She had almost had to climb straight up to get to the top. More than once, she came close to falling back into the quarry. Several times she slid halfway down the mountain. Her fingernails were torn and ragged; her body was bruised and bleeding from scaling the jagged rock wall.

She hurried to the entrance.

Standing around wasn't an option. She needed dry clothing and someplace warm. She might as well start hoofing it back toward her home, and pray that another vehicle would come by before she froze to death.

Chapter 23

James Claiborne and Molly Rucker drove home on the deserted back roads after a night on the town.

"That was an awesome movie, wasn't it?" Molly asked.

"Oh yeah, I loved that the good guy walloped the bad ones in the end," James chuckled.

"James! Look out!" Molly shouted and pointed.

James slammed on his brakes. A woman frantically waving her arms stepped into the middle of the road.

Her clothes were wet, torn, and dirty and they clung unflatteringly to her body. Her eyes and hair were wild and disheveled. Blood and rain soaked the front of her suit jacket. Her knees and hands were scraped and raw. She ran forward and placed her palms on the hood of his car.

James rolled down his window. "What's the matter?" he asked.

"I've been involved in an accident," she shrieked. "My car went into a ditch back there" she said pointing back behind her.

"Do you want us to drive you to the hospital?"

"No, I just need you to take me home."

Through chattering teeth, she gave the man her address. James looked at Molly, who simply shrugged and folded down the back of her seat allowing Kathryn entrance to the car.

"I'll need to take Molly home first," James said.

"That's fine. Kathryn would agree with anything. She could feel the warmth of the car heater and it felt wonderful.

"I have a blanket in the trunk for emergencies. I'll get it for you." His seats were leather and the wetness wouldn't hurt them. James hurried around the car and took the blanket out of the trunk.

"I appreciate this," Kathryn said. "You two probably saved my life."

Kathryn placed the blanket on the seat, sat on it, and covered herself with the other side. Her teeth chattered so much that she knew the couple could hear them. His old jalopy was a far cry from her BMW, but it had a good heater and it was heaven to her at this point.

"I hope I'm not putting you out too badly," she said, once she was warmer and able to talk.

Kathryn was too upset to notice the look that passed between the couple.

"If you drop me by my house, I will make it worth your while."

"I still have to get Molly home first," he said, glancing at his watch. Another look passed between the couple. "She lives in town, too and we have to drive right by her place to get to yours."

"That's fine." Kathryn said. She was beginning to warm up and knew she was going to make it. She was ready to agree to anything. She was going to live.

When they arrived, Molly gave James a quick kiss, said she would call him tomorrow, and jumped out of his car.

Finally, James pulled into Kathryn's driveway.

"The spare key is in a fake rock in the flower bed on your right," she chattered. "Would you…?" Her other one was in her purse, and it was in the quarry.

"Sure," James said. If he were lucky, he might get a few hours of sleep before going to work. He didn't relish leaving his GPS alone in a car with what he now considered was a strange, maybe even crazy, woman.

Since he'd signed on as the good guy, he might as well carry through. It would take away another few minutes of his sleep time, but she said she would make it worth his while.

As soon as she saw that he had found the key and was opening the door, Kathryn exited the car, the blanket still around her as she walked stiffly toward him.

"Are you sure you don't want me to drive you to the hospital?" James asked.

The woman looked dead on her feet, as he placed her key in her hand

"No, thank you," Kathryn said as she entered her house and motioned for him to follow.

"Wait here," she said, as she walked down the hall to a bedroom. Kathryn went to the painting on the wall, opened it, and worked the combination of the safe underneath. She removed a folder, a pistol, and an envelope of emergency cash. She took out a one-hundred-dollar bill and slipped her pistol into her pocket along with the rest of the cash. At this point, she was safety conscious and trusted no one. If the guy decided to rob her, he would get a big surprise. The way her day had gone so far, it just might happen.

"I really think you should see a doctor," James told her, when she came back into the room.

"I'll be fine," she told him. "I'll call the police and report the accident, and then I'll call my sister to come and run me to the hospital."

"On the way back to town, I didn't see your wrecked car." James frowned.

"It's concealed by the brush," she lied. "Here, this is for your trouble." Kathryn handed him the money and then the blanket.

James was shocked at the amount. "This is way too much."

"Just take it," she said abruptly. "You earned it, but I really need a hot shower and to put on dry clothes." She also needed to call a cab and have them take her to the airport. She knew she needed to get out of town fast. She doubted that Jerry would come looking for the files tonight, because he assumed she was dead. He would be there, or have someone else looking for the folder the first thing in the morning. He'd be shocked when he found her safe open and the papers he needed were gone. She wished she could see his face when he found out his precious files were missing.

"Thank you," the man said, heading for his car. It brought her back from her musing when he let the door slam behind him.

When James got back into his car he called Molly. "Can you talk?" he asked

"Yeah, he came in and went straight to bed."

"That was really weird," James said.

Molly knew what he meant. It was crazy the way they could read each other's minds.

"I think we should report it," Molly said.

"And have your husband find out where you were tonight?"

"Good point. Maybe we should just forget tonight ever happened."

"We should make a vow never to tell anyone," James said.

"As far as I'm concerned, tonight is lost from my memory," Molly said.

"I agree," James said, starting his car and pulling out of Kathryn's driveway onto the road for his drive home.

Chapter 24

The next day, Casey found the gossip around Lakeview interesting. Sam hadn't spent the night in the vestibule as he usually did, and neither he, nor, Mrs. Bailey had shown up for work this morning. That was odd, because everyone said Kathryn had never been late or absent since she came to work at Lakeview.

Jerry called a special meeting with Marcus and Peggy Adams, the social worker. Casey heard him page them this morning.

Casey felt like it was the perfect time to hurry to Arron's room to check if Marcus had reinstated his medications.

She was almost to his room when she saw Marcus coming back down the hallway.

She'd give anything to know where he was going in such a hurry.

"What's going on?" she asked as he hurried past her.

"We don't really know. Jerry says it's not like Kathryn to miss work."

"That's what I've been hearing from the staff," Casey agreed. She could certainly attest to that. Kathryn was a bitch, but she was a prompt bitch. The woman seemed to be everywhere always breathing down her neck.

"Sam isn't here either, and none on the staff has heard from him since before quitting time. One of Sam's friends said he had to go out for a while last night, and he covered for him. Sam indicated to him that he had a hot date."

"I thought he was living here?" Casey said.

"Your uncle is very tolerant, if you ask me. He is scrambling now to make up the slack." He stopped. "Is there something you needed?"

"I was just curious like everyone else why those two weren't here."

"No one seems to know what's going on, and if that's all, I really need to take care of something that Jerry wants me to do."

It was strange how he was so casual with Jerry's first name. Where did that put Marcus, if Larkin was right about Jerry being involved in something illegal?

"I was wondering how Arron is doing?"

"He's doing fine," he assured her. "If you're asking if I have continued his medication, it's none of your business."

Casey dropped her eyes to hide the hurt.

He softened his voice. "I told you—you need to trust me. Even, if it's only my ability as a doctor." With that he slipped inside his office and closed the door behind him. The man infuriated Casey.

If Kathryn was truly gone, then maybe, she could finally confide in Uncle Jerry? After all, he had been an old family friend as long as she could remember.

He was nice to the people you believed to be your parents, a little voice reminded.

Casey knew that she needed evidence and what she was after was in the files that Kathryn removed from the South Wing. The couple she had overheard talked about Kathryn taking them home and securing them in her safe. Even though Casey had followed her one day to find out her address, she knew she couldn't risk being arrested for breaking and entering.

The old bat was probably just at home sick. There was no sense in getting her hopes up that she was gone for good. On the other hand, if Kathryn did run off with Sam as the rumors circulating around the workplace indicated, then today would be the perfect time to search her home for evidence.

* * * *

Jimmy Dillon was only person she knew who could pull off breaking and entering, along with safe cracking among other things. His name was really James. It was ironic that his mother had given him the same name as the famous outlaw, or maybe it had been an omen of things to come. There didn't seem to be a lock that he couldn't pick, or a safe he couldn't get into, especially if it meant scoring his next hit. He had practiced mainly on his rich parents' storage places.

It had been a few months since Casey had talked with Jimmy. Much to her adoptive parents' dismay, she was one of the few friends who had kept in touch with him after he was kicked out of college. About ten o'clock that morning Casey asked Marcus if she could take some personal time. After checking the schedule, he agreed with a shrug, saying as long as she was back by two in the afternoon to do her outpatient session.

Casey hurried home, changed into jeans, and programmed Jimmy's address into her GPS. She made her way across town to the seedy neighborhood before she let herself decide it wasn't wise. She knew she should have called him first, but without a face-to-face meeting, it was too easy for him to say no.

She pulled up to the rundown building and wondered if she ought to go inside or turn around and head back home.

She knew it was difficult for Jimmy to find a place after he had been thrown out of so many apartments for not paying his rent.

She exited her car, walked up to the door, and pressed the doorbell. She didn't hear it ring, so she banged on his door. She was about to leave when she heard the rustle of footsteps coming toward the door. Casey gave one last loud knock and Jimmy opened the door.

He sported a scruffy beard and badly needed a haircut, but he was still as good-looking as she remembered. It took a few minutes before he recognized her. When he did, he grabbed her in a bear hug, lifting her off the ground, and declared, "Damn—it's Casey West!" As if she didn't know who she was.

He put her down slowly. A sour smell invaded her nostrils from the inside of his apartment.

"What brings you slumming, girl?" he asked as he made a path through the empty beer cans covering the floor by kicking them as he went. He swept papers and trash off a kitchen chair, objects and paper flying in different directions, as he moved it into the living room. He indicated for her to sit in the chair and he took an easy chair opposite her.

Four cases of beer were stacked at arm's length from his recliner.

Casey sighed. "You'll never change, will you, Jimmy?"

His eyes swept the stacked cases. "I have a goal in life…Cirrhosis of the liver," he quipped and popped the top on another beer.

"I can see that you're well on your way to achieving it," she scolded.

"You haven't changed either." He gave her his famous grin. "You're still the nagging, pushy dame you always were, but you're also the only one who gives a damn whether I live or die." He stared directly at her, a frown creasing his forehead.

"I just wish I could convince you to give a damn about yourself," she spoke softly and held his gaze. "Have you heard from your parents lately?"

"Humph…" he replied. "They're somewhere on a cruise, having a wonderful time. I heard the news from one of their snooty friends. They're determined to keep me informed. "He took another drink of beer, and glanced down, hoping to hide the longing in his eyes from Casey, but she read him too well.

"I'm sorry I brought them up." Casey reached forward to pat his arm.

"I know you didn't make the trip across town just to see my sorry ass," He took a sip of his beer. "I don't suppose you want a beer?"

"I'll come right to the point. I need your help, Jimmy."

Jimmy let out a sigh and slid back in his chair. "That's got to be a first. Usually, it's the other way around. Whatever you need, girl, you know you've got it."

"You haven't heard what it is," she warned.

"I might not have the talents you need."

"You're just the person for the job—if you'll do it."

"How could I say no to someone who is always pulling me out of a jam? Things like getting up in the middle of the night to bail me out of jail."

"I just don't want you to feel obligated, is all." Her gaze drifted to the overflowing ashtray beside her chair.

Jimmy jumped up and grabbed it, dumping it in the trash.

"You didn't have to do that," she said as he made his way back to his own seat and fell into it.

He smiled. "I forgot how sensitive your nose is."

"We're such opposites." She frowned, then gave him a sad smile. "I don't know how we ever became friends."

"You were taken with my painting, as I recall. "For once, I got lucky." He smiled at her. "You know I love you baby."

"As I do you," she said."

"I suppose you know the Wests died in a car crash?" They were getting too melancholy. She hoped he would change the subject.

"I heard about your parents, and I wanted to call. I just had no idea what to say," he said, hanging his head.

"It's okay," she assured. "I know how you are."

"I did feel for you. I know how hard it is to be alone."

"Going through their things, I found out that they weren't really my parents."

"Bummer," he said. "That had to be a shock, huh?"

"I found a file with a picture of my sister. My birth parents gave us both up for adoption. The reason, I assume, was because my mother had mental problems."

She waited for him to make some kind of crack but was surprised to see his concern. He listened intently as she proceeded to tell him everything that had happened in her life lately—up to the point where Marcus took her off Arron's case.

Jimmy was silent.

"Do you think I'm crazy? That I'm just imagining everything?" Casey asked.

He frowned as he processed the information. Finally, he said, "Maybe, if I didn't know you so well, West."

"So you don't think I'm crazy?"

"You're the most together person I've ever known." He set his beer on the table, pushing magazines aside to do so.

"Thanks."

"You said you needed my help. You want me to go over to Lakeview and slap some of these Delberts around for you?"

Casey laughed as she remembered his favorite name for people who did stupid things. "It's nothing like that," she assured him.

"I would, you know. Anyone messing with my girl is at the top of my shit list."

Casey laughed again and clasped his arm. "I need you to break into a house and open a safe for me."

"Whoa!" he exclaimed. "My skills are a little rusty at best." He stared at her. She stared back. He continued. "I might still have the knack."

"What?" she asked, as he continued to stare.

"This is just so out of character for you."

"Desperate times call for desperate measures."

"Can I ask whose home we're about to invade and for what reason?"

"Kathryn Bailey's…I suspect that is where those files I told you about are located. I overheard a conversation about where they moved them. It was after the nurse I told you about was murdered."

"She was your friend?"

"Yes… she's the one who tried to leave me a clue about something she found there. She wrote it on the back of one of my business cards. The people who run the place have friends in high places, and they stopped the police from investigating the file room where the authorities believed the murder happened. Later that same day, Mrs. Bailey took the files in question home."

"Let's go see what's in those files." He swallowed the last of his beer and stood.

"You mean now?"

"Why not?"

"It's broad daylight…"

"This is the best time. People are least suspicious than if you're slinking around after dark."

"Are you drunk?"

He laughed bitterly. "Honey, I'd have to drink a couple more of those," he said, pointing to the cases of beer by his side. "Are you getting cold feet?"

"Let's go," she said. She grabbed her jacket and headed to the door. "Anyway, I have a cop friend who'll put in a good word for us if we get caught."

Chapter 25

They decided not to drive Jimmy's beat-up rattletrap to Kathryn's place. Casey wanted something reliable if they had to make a fast getaway.

"Are you ready?" Jimmy asked as they sat in front of Kathryn's house.

"I'm ready," she said, swallowing.

"Then go ring the doorbell."

"What? What if she's home? What if she's just sick?"

"That's what we need to find out," Jimmy said.

"What do I say if she answers the door?"

"Just tell her since she didn't come to work this morning, you were concerned about her, and you decided to check and see if she was okay. This isn't brain surgery, West."

"I can't help it," she snapped. "I've never done this before."

"Stick with me, sweetie, and I'll give you an education."

"Thanks but no thanks. This is the last time I'll be doing anything like this," she assured him.

He chuckled and indicated for her to get out of the car.

Looking around, Casey realized it was a quiet neighborhood. The street was deserted. She rang the bell once, but no one answered. She waved to Jimmy to join her.

"I don't think she's here," she said as Jimmy bound up to her.

Jimmy took something out of his pocket that looked like a keychain. On it was Allen wrenches filed down to a fine point. "My set of keys," he said.

Casey surveyed the distance between Kathryn's door and her vehicle and wished she hadn't insisted Jimmy park so far way. The distance was good if she didn't want the neighbors connecting a break-in with her vehicle. It wasn't good if she and Jimmy had to get out of here in a hurry.

Jimmy, who had been studying the lock, slipped his keychain into his pocket. "We aren't going to need these," he said. "Give me a credit card."

"What?"

"I'm not going shopping. Just give me one."

Casey hurriedly extracted her beat-up Visa out of her wallet and handed it to him.

"You must have been opening a few doors with this yourself," he commented. "Would you hurry?" she asked, fidgeting.

"We're in," he said after sliding the card in the crack between the lock and the door. "These locks were around in the 70's." He pushed the door open a little to prove his point. "This must be a crime-free neighborhood," he said stepping inside. "That's good. The neighbors won't be expecting a break-in."

She followed him inside.

"Be sure to lock the door behind you. And keep your ears open."

"You need to hurry and unlock the safe." Casey closed the door and clicked the lock.

Jimmy smiled at her nervousness. "I have to find it first."

"Don't look at me; I don't know where it is."

"Calm down, West. You always get testy when you're nervous," he accused. "You're going to help me look for it. It's probably in a closet or behind a picture." When he saw the look on her face, he added, "Didn't you ever hunt for Easter eggs? Just start looking around."

From the entrance door, Casey could see a living room and beyond it a small kitchen. To the left was another open doorway where they could see a bed. To the right and down the hall were another bedroom and a bath.

"You going left or right?" he asked.

"I'll take the bedroom on the left." Casey swallowed. The room was kind of small and Casey doubted it belonged to Kathryn. She could see that the bed was made and no one was in it.

"What are you waiting for?" he asked when she didn't move.

"What if she's in there? In bed…Asleep, or dead? She may be incapacitated and she can't get up."

"Or… she's waiting on you with a gun." He laughed at her frightened look. "Don't worry. They say only the good die young and if this is true, from what you've told me, that old broad will live forever."

"Keep your voice down."

"I'll go with you." Jimmy chuckled. "And there's no need to whisper," he said in a normal voice, which seemed much louder, breaking the quietness.

"Shhhh," Casey cautioned putting her finger to her lips. "We don't want the neighbors to hear us."

Jimmy laughed again. "Wait a minute. I saw a little room on down the hall I need to visit. I have to recycle some beer."

Casey waved at him to go ahead, and then walked toward what probably was the master bedroom. She opened the door slowly and breathed a sigh of relief. There was no one there, but the room was steamy, as if someone had recently taken a shower in the adjoining bathroom.

Kathryn's bedroom held a king-sized bed with built in bookshelves on each side and a matching dresser and chest of drawers. The dresser drawers spewed women's underclothes. The bedspread was burgundy with drapes to match, and there was a walk-in closet full of expensive designer clothes. Mrs. Bailey did indeed live well.

Casey ran her fingers over the velvet bedspread. "She has very good taste and obviously likes luxury," she said, as Jimmy joined her. I just can't imagine someone who liked such nice things running off with Sam Talbot, who doesn't have the proverbial pot. Something is wrong with this whole situation."

"We need to hurry," Jimmy said. "Her clothes are still in the closet. That means she'll be back. "There is something in the other room you need to see," Jimmy said, taking hold of her arm, and pulling her toward another small bedroom at the back of the house.

"You found the safe!" she exclaimed, "and you already have it open."

"When I left the bathroom, I decided to check the room back here. I found the safe alright. As you can see, it is wide open."

"Tell me you have the files."

The room held an exercise bike, an assortment of fitness equipment, and a picture lying on the floor. But the safe was a gaping cavity built into the wall.

"This is how I found it," he said, putting his arm around her shoulders.

"Damn!" She must have taken the contents with her."

"It looks to me like she might have been sending a message to someone," Jimmy said.

"What do you mean?"

"She would have closed the safe unless she wanted someone to know she had the contents with her."

"Maybe she was just in a hurry."

"That too," Jimmy said. "Either way, our job here is done."

Casey frowned her disappointment.

They started out of the room, but Jimmy stopped her.

"What is it?" she whispered.

"Someone is unlocking the door."

"What are we going to do?" Casey hadn't heard a sound at first now she could hear the rattle of the lock.

"We're getting out of here," he said as he grabbed her and pulled her toward the bedroom window. Jimmy unlocked it, pushed it up. Casey looked down at the ground, four feet below.

"I'll go first, and then I'll help you down." With that, he pushed himself through the window and jumped to the ground. Wasting no time, Casey crawled through the window and when Jimmy clasped her around the thighs, she let go. Over-balanced, they both crashed to the ground, right on top of Mrs. Bailey's roses. Jimmy quickly scrambled to his feet, pulled Casey to hers, and headed in a run toward Casey's car. She hopped in and crouched down in the seat, telling him to get them out of there.

"Don't you want to know who our visitor is?" Jimmy asked.

"I already know who it is," she hissed. "I recognize his car."

Jimmy looked up at the man who stared out of the open window at them as Jimmy pulled his vehicle away from the curb.

"You can get up now," Jimmy said, as they sped along toward his apartment. "I think you forgot to tell me about him in your little story."

"His name is Marcus Kelly, and he's a thorn in my side," she said, straightening her clothes.

"Oh yeah. The guy looked at me as if he'd like to screw my head off and throw it at my dying ass. You know—sort of like how all your other boyfriends used to look at me."

"They thought you were after the same thing they were." She giggled.

"I would have been if I hadn't been so strung out on drugs."

"No, Jimmy. You always respected me whether you were drugged or sober." She stared at him as he drove. "I have always appreciated that."

They drove along in silence for a time. Jimmy glanced over at her. "Why is it when you find someone who gives a damn about you and who you respect above everyone else, you can't go all the way and fall in love?"

"I don't know, Jimmy," she sighed. She knew what he was getting at. She loved him like a brother, but she'd never thought of him as a lover. It was the same with him. It was one of life's ironies, she guessed.

"There must have been something incriminating to Kathryn in those files." Casey wasn't aware she had spoken aloud until Jimmy answered her.

"I have a feeling that was what your old buddy, Marcus, was after, don't you?"

"He must have been the one I overheard in the office that day."

"He went straight to the room the safe was in," Jimmy said, raising his eyebrows.

"You think he's involved in whatever is going on?"

"I don't know, but I'd be careful if I were you. If he did commit murder, he won't hesitate to do it again."

Casey shivered as she realized there was no way she could trust anyone at Lakeview. The only people she could trust were Jimmy and Detective Larkin.

"Marcus could have been drawn to that room because we were making so much noise trying to get away." She suddenly realized that she didn't want to think of Marcus as being involved.

"Why was he at the house in the first place?"

Casey hung her head because she didn't have an answer.

"He could have been just passing by and thought someone was robbing the place," she snapped.

Jimmy gave a deep belly laugh. "If you're going to be my partner in crime, you're going to have to grow a pair."

"What do you mean?"

"You sounded like a wild-cat, kicking and clawing the siding on the house, then falling out of the window."

She hit him on the shoulder, and they both laughed as they thought about how pathetic their escape had been.

Casey sobered. "We could still be caught," she said. "What if Marcus calls the police?"

"I'm sure if he had, they would have picked us up by now," he said. "I know your friend got a good look at your car and maybe even your license number."

"Then why didn't he call the police?"

"Maybe he was afraid of explaining what he was doing in a missing person's home," he replied. "Maybe there was hanky-panky going on between Bailey and this guy."

"He did have a key to Kathryn's place." Casey said, not liking the implication of that. It was bad enough thinking of Jerry being involved with that woman. An affair between Marcus and her was just too ridiculous to consider.

"Well, I don't care why he was there, but I'm just happy that he didn't call the cops." Jimmy parked the car and turned off the engine. "Maybe I need to park your car in the garage my landlord provides."

"There's really no need. It was stupid of me trying to hide from him. He knows my car," she said slapping her forehead.

"I'm sure glad I didn't take mine," Jimmy said.

"Are you in trouble again, Jimmy?" she asked.

He turned to face her. "Not at this particular time. I've given up drugs, you know."

"And replaced them with beer?"

"It's cheaper. At least I don't have to rob people to support my habit."

"It's still a means of escape."

He smiled sadly. "Are you psychoanalyzing me, West?"

"You know it's true, Jimmy."

He hung his head. She continued, "You know you're not really hurting your parents, don't you, Jimmy? It's like you said, they don't give a damn about what you do. They're so self-involved, they aren't aware you're even trying to kill yourself."

"Whoa—punch in the gut. You always did lay it on the line, didn't you?"

"It's because I do give a damn, Jimmy," she said. She touched his shoulder and made him turn to look at her.

"I know," he said at last. "One thing I always loved about you is that you gave it to me straight."

"Are you ever going to do something with your life, Jimmy?"

"I forgot what a pain in the ass you can be, though." He smiled.

"Well, are you?" Casey asked.

"You're talking about the guy who flunked out of college, remember." His hands clasped the steering wheel.

"It wasn't because you're dumb, Jimmy. It's because you didn't try."

"Anyway, it's all water under the bridge."

"You could take some adult college courses."

"It costs money, and I'm between jobs right now."

"How about I pay for it?"

"You know me, West. I'm not a sponger."

"You'd rather steal."

"Low blow, West. You know I only stole from my parents and their rich friends.

I was like a modern-day Robin Hood."

"I know you were doing these things to get your parents' attention, but the police are not that understanding."

"I was doing it to pay for my drugs. That's why I'm on probation."

"Why didn't you tell me, Jimmy? I could have gotten you in all kinds of trouble, for nothing."

"It doesn't matter, baby," he said. "It felt good doing something for you for a change."

"It will matter a great deal if Marcus calls the police."

"I don't think he called them or they would be after us by now. He's probably just another guy who's sweet on you. If he rats you out, he knows he won't have a chance with you,"

"The man can't stand me."

Jimmy gave her a doubtful look.

"Now about the money you need to go back to college?"

"I'd forgotten what a pain-in-the-ass, nag you are. We've been down this road before, and the answer is still no," Jimmy said.

"Why?"

"I won't be obligated."

"I told you that you'll never have to pay the money back."

"There are other ways to be under obligation. You would look at me with those big doe eyes if I flunk out. No—if I didn't achieve up to par, you'd give me that look. I couldn't take that."

"I promise I won't."

"I won't take the chance of letting you down, and I'm not going to promise that I wouldn't."

"You have so much potential. Whatever happened to your painting? You were so good, Jimmy."

"Was—as in has been."

"What happened to the passion I saw in your eyes when you talked about your art?"

"My loving parents crushed it. Just like they did my every other dream of mine."

"You have only yourself to blame for that. You let them do it to you."

"Who cares?" Jimmy's hands shook. Casey wasn't sure if it was out of nerves, anger, or withdrawal. She only knew he was in bad shape.

"I care and I think deep down you do as well," Casey said.

"No, I don't."

"Yes, you do. Now where do you keep your painting supplies?"

"I pawned them a couple years ago to buy beer."

"I'm getting you new ones after I come over and clean up this pigsty." She indicated his apartment. "I'm going to set up your easel right in the middle of your living room so you have to look at it every day. I want you to paint a portrait of me, and I'm going to bug you until you get it done."

He laughed. "What're you trying to do, West, get me to follow my bliss?"

"Your love for painting may be buried deep, but it's still there. For me, it's working with disturbed individuals, but it was never about that for you, Jimmy. Your parents wanted you to be a doctor, but your passion was elsewhere, and you need to embrace it."

"It's too late for that, West. My talent, if I had any, is dead."

"Nonsense, true talent never dies, Jimmy. You might be a little rusty, but all you need is some practice."

"Can't I get it through that thick head of yours that I don't want to do anything with my life?" he mumbled.

"I don't believe that for a minute. I've witnessed that passion. I could just beat you when you talk like that. How long are you going to wallow in self-pity when there are people out there who would kill for your potential? When're you going to stop blaming your parents for everything that happens to you? Not all parents love and nurture their offspring. I'm one who should know. My real parents gave me away. I never really bonded with my adoptive parents. You don't see me going around wallowing in self-pity. Do you think I never feel alone?"

Jimmy embraced her. "I'm a selfish bastard. I always thought you got on well with the West's."

"Oh, there were no outward problems, but we weren't close. I'm wondering if there is ever that closeness with the people who raise you."

"It does make you wonder, doesn't it?" Jimmy said wishfully.

"The Wests never approved of us being friends."

"So I was part of your problem."

"You were only a small part of the contention between us," she said. "They didn't want me to be a psychologist."

"No shit! I thought that was a noble profession."

"I'm going to have to go," she said, "but I'm buying some art supplies. Will you promise to use them?"

"I promise," He made the gesture of crossing his heart. "I'll use them."

"Now about the beer…"

"I don't know about giving up the beer. I might need it for inspiration." On seeing the look on her face, he added, "You know about the tortured-artist syndrome."

"I will torture you, Jimmy, if you don't straighten out your life."

"West?" Jimmy's eyes asked her a question.

"Yes?"

"Be careful. It scares the crap out of me, the chance of something happening to you."

"I will."

"I think you're in real danger. I don't like the idea of that cop using you to help his investigation."

"I insisted, Jimmy. Detective Larkin didn't like the idea either. And I'm being careful."

He laughed. "I know. I saw an example of how cautious you are today." Then his mood changed to serious. "I wouldn't get over it, if something happened to you," he told her.

"I have to do this, Jimmy. It's for my own flesh and blood. Trudy was my friend, and she's dead because she was trying to help me."

"So you're doing this because you feel guilty?"

"No, I'm doing it because I need to find out what all of this has to do with my sister and my nephew. Of course, some of it is because of Trudy, but my sister and her son; I'm all that they have. I need to fight for their rights."

Jimmy gazed into the distance.

"I'm also your family, Jimmy," she assured him.

"You're the only one I have," he said, "and I damn sure don't want to lose you."

"You're not going to."

"I hope not, West, but I think you're meddling in dangerous territory."

She shivered. She had just felt a goose walk over her grave again.

Chapter 26

The weekend arrived before Casey knew it. Life at Lakeview continued on smoothly without Kathryn and Sam. Jerry hired someone to take Sam's place—someone normal, who didn't sleep in the hospital vestibule. Since Marcus had taken over the care of Arron, Casey had less than ever to keep her busy.

Casey had Friday morning off so she did some shopping with her sister in mind. She was excited about seeing Jimmy that afternoon. She had also shopped for art supplies. She hoped Jimmy wouldn't be drinking when she visited him on Saturday.

Casey arrived early Saturday morning. She knocked, and a clear-eyed Jimmy opened the door. He was clean-shaven and sported a new haircut. Casey's jaw dropped. "Who are you and what have you done with my friend?" she asked, then giggled as he gave her a big hug that lifted her off the floor. The apartment behind him was immaculate, save for the cases of beer stacked by the kitchen sink.

"I haven't had a drink since you were here. I just wanted you to see that it was all there," he explained. "Will you do me the honor of helping me pour it out?"

Sensing his need for approval, she told him. "Jimmy, I'm very proud of you, but if you had told me you'd poured the beer out, I would have believed you."

The huge smile he gave her let her know her praise hit the mark.

"Your supplies are in the car, and I need help bringing them in. You know you clean up very well," she said, causing his smile to beam bigger.

"Actually, I've accumulated a few things already," Jimmy confided.

"I didn't think you had any money."

"I didn't, but I got in touch with Professor Clarke, and he said that he had given up painting. He only teaches two students now, so he doesn't need as many supplies. He was so excited to hear that I was painting again that he gave me enough supplies to get me started. He even threw in an old easel. I have to watch, or the thing collapses at the most inconvenient times."

Casey laughed. "You know, Jimmy, it's great to hear excitement in your voice again."

"Come here—I have something to show you," he said as he pulled her toward a covered canvas. "Voila!" he said and yanked off the sheet that covered it.

Her mouth dropped open. "I can't believe it, Jimmy! You couldn't have done that in this amount of time." She walked around the work, examining the picture.

"You don't like it," he accused.

"I know it is me, but did I ever look so…"

"Naive, so vulnerable," Jimmy finished her sentence for her. Defensiveness crept into his voice.

They both stared at her portrait as she shook her head.

"Was I ever that innocent, Jimmy?"

"This was my first glance of you, all those years ago."

"I remember this now! Where on earth did you find it? I thought you got rid of it long ago." She walked around it once more, studying it from every angle.

"Robert Clarke, my old art professor, kept it."

"You're kidding."

"I was as shocked as you are."

"Did he tell you why he kept it?"

"He said because I had captured you completely. He says that is very rare for a beginning artist."

"There you go, Jimmy. Didn't I always tell you how good you were?"

"It seems I let more than just you down when I quit," he said, walking over to a chair and slumping into it. "Professor Clarke was so disappointed when I dropped out of classes, but I was in such a mess at the time. I didn't give a shit. For some reason, he never could part with this unfinished painting. He says it's my best work."

"I'm glad he didn't throw it away. Don't you see? This picture has evidently rekindled your desire. It's brought you back to what you love. It makes no difference if your parents never wanted you to be an artist. It's what you want that matters."

"But do I still want it?" He hung his head.

"Jimmy, I saw the way your eyes lit up when I talked about your painting."

Casey squatted in front of him. She lifted his chin to force him to look at her. "You're just afraid of failing, Jimmy. It's only natural."

"If this doesn't work out, I have no place to go but down."

"It'll work out, Jimmy. If the professor thinks your work was good enough to keep all of these years, then it will work out."

"He's having a show in the fall of next year, and he has invited me to add as many pieces as I can finish to the collection."

"That's great news!" She squeezed his shoulder. "Let's get out there and get your other supplies out of the car."

"Do you have an easel out there that doesn't collapse when you touch it?" Jimmy asked. His eyes lit up like a bowler watching his ball head straight toward a strike.

"I hope it doesn't after what I paid for it."

"Thank you so much for everything." Jimmy gazed into her eyes. Sincerity flooded his face. I just don't know how I'm going to support myself before I'm able to sell a few pieces."

"Don't worry about that. I will keep you supplied in groceries, and help you pay your rent. I could do what I used to do, go down to the subway and do character drawings of people for money. I made enough I could probably make it now that I'm not supporting a drug habit."

"Just show everyone else what I know is true. Show your parents how wrong they were for not supporting you in your art."

"You know, West. This is the first time it isn't about them. I don't give a damn if they care or not. This is my life, and I will live it the way I damn well please. "You know, I think my little boy has finally grown up," she said, kissing him on the cheek. She had never heard him talk like this before. "Now let's unload my car."

"Don't leave. Have dinner with me. Please," he pleaded. "I'd forgotten how much I missed you."

"I really need to get in touch with Detective Larkin and let him know what's happening at Lakeview."

"I'll rent a movie."

"What kind of movie?"

"Porn—what other kind is there?" He laughed.

"Be serious."

"How about a horror flick?"

"You know I don't like blood, guts, and gore."

"How about an adventure or a good murder mystery?"

"I feel like I'm living the murder mystery now. Oh, go ahead and rent a mystery, it might be appropriate."

"You want me to cook?"

"You?" she chuckled.

"I make a mean spaghetti and meatballs."

"I'll order a pizza," she said reaching for her checkbook. "I'll write you a check and then run to the police station and talk to Larkin while you pick up dinner and rent a movie."

"Don't stand me up, West Girl. You know how fragile I am right now." He was half joking, but she knew there was an element of truth in his statement.

"Thanks, Jimmy," she said at last.

"For what… I should be thanking you."

"For that whole crazy escapade the other day, and for listening to my problems and not thinking I was crazy."

"I know you, baby. You're not a hysterical woman. You're the most down-to-earth broad I know. If you say there's something weird going on there, I know it's true." He paused. "Besides, don't you think it's payback time for all the scrapes you've seen me through?"

"I guess," she replied. "And Jimmy, I'm so glad you've finally decided to do something with your life."

Chapter 27

That morning, Larkin was surprised to find Jerry Connors staring at him when he glanced up from the work on his desk. Cramer was out on assignment, and Larkin was busy sifting through his notes to prepare to testify in court.

"Dr. Connors," Larkin acknowledged. "What can I do for you?"

"I'm here on official business," he said. "May I sit down?"

Larkin indicated the chair in front of his desk, and Jerry made himself comfortable.

"Has there been another murder at Lakeview?" Larkin couldn't resist the jab.

"No, no. Nothing like that. At least I don't think so."

Larkin noticed that he didn't sound at all convincing.

"Then why are you here?"

"I came in to file a missing person's report on Sam Talbot and Kathryn Bailey. It's been days, and neither of them has returned to work. Kathryn hasn't been home. I've kept checking."

"Missing Persons is down the hall."

"I've filed a report already."

"What made you stop by here?" Larkin asked bluntly.

"I just wanted to apologize for not going along with your theory about Sam Talbot killing the nurse at Lakeview."

"Do you have evidence that was the case?"

Jerry Connors shifted his position.

"I don't know if you're aware that Mr. Talbot had a drug problem."

"Yes, I did actually. We picked him up recently on drug-related charges." Larkin noticed that he used past tense speaking of Sam.

"Well, I don't suppose you're aware that he lost his apartment and I allowed him to sleep in the vestibule at Lakeview until he was able to get back on his feet."

Larkin knew everything because Casey kept him informed, but he wasn't going to let Connors know that.

"That was nice of you."

"Oh, it wasn't totally unselfish of me. For security reasons, it was good to have him close by. There were times the patients would act up, and he was there to take care of the problem."

"I see—and what does that have to do with my department?"

"If you're wondering why I stopped by homicide, it's because I've had some doubts about Sam myself. Maybe he did have something to do with that girl's death."

Larkin came to full attention. "What makes you think that?"

"I began to question his involvement in the girl's death right after he was picked up for drugs the last time. He wanted Kathryn to talk to me. They were involved, you know?" He studied Larkin for a reaction.

"You mean romantically?"

"Sexually, actually, if the rumors are to be believed," Jerry said.

"Go on." Larkin wasn't surprised Connors was ready to throw Sam under the bus.

"Anyway, Mrs. Bailey said that your office had questioned Sam about that girl's death again, and she wanted me to use my connections to make you back off."

Larkin bristled each time Jerry referred to Trudy as "that girl."

"Is that right?"

"Yes. You can see why it made me suspicious, and now," he spread his hands, "that they have run off together, I'm thinking that your interviewing him might have scared them."

"So you believe that he and Kathryn Bailey are together?"

"Yes—I hate to say it, but I think she went willingly."

Larkin digested what Jerry had to say. This man was definitely a smooth operator and while what he said may be true, was he trying to shift the blame for what was going on at Lakeview to the two people who weren't there to defend themselves? Did he know they weren't coming back, and was he responsible for that?

"You're saying that a woman who has been with Lakeview for years and is getting close to retirement age would just take off with a young loser like Sam?"

"I know it's hard to believe, but not many people knew that Kathryn had her problems, too."

"What kind of problems?"

"This is kind of embarrassing," he said as he squirmed in his seat. "Kathryn and I started a... relationship a while back. Needless to say, it was sexual. Kathryn was obsessive in that area."

"She was hard to satisfy?" Larkin asked.

"Well, maybe it was me who had the problem. I'm not as young as I use to be, and I couldn't keep her content. That's when she turned to Sam as well."

"So it was only sex that made her turn to Sam?"

"That, and Sam was supplying her with drugs. She and I had an argument about it the day before she disappeared. I told her to stop the drugs. I told her I was planning to fire Sam and if she didn't give up the drugs, I planned to fire them both."

"So you confronted Kathryn about the sex and drugs?"

"Then I fired Sam. I think that's the reason they decided to leave. That, and the fact that they may have had something to do with that nurse's death."

Both Larkin's and Jerry's faces were schooled into blank pages; neither yielding to the other's gaze. Larkin wondered if the man he was talking to was a psychopath or a martyr. His gut told him that Jerry Connors was a cold-blooded killer.

"Why did you wait so long to report them missing?"

"I'm an optimist, Detective Larkin. I guess I just figured they'd be back. When I'm wrong, I'm man enough to say so."

"And you think you were wrong about Sam and Kathryn Bailey?"

Connors nodded. "What do you plan on doing about what I told you?"

"I'll get a court order to search Kathryn's apartment. And I need to search her office as well."

"You'll have my full cooperation."

Larkin knew that any incriminating evidence was long gone from either site, but there was hope that Connors had missed something important.

"I have a key to Kathryn's house, of course. I can give you that now if it will save you some time." He shifted, pulling a key from his pants pocket, and handed it to Larkin. "If you have a pen and paper, I'll give you her address."

"That's not necessary if you have given it to Missing Persons. I can get it from them."

"Well, if that's all you need, I'll be running along. We're extra busy since the two of them took off."

"Thanks," Larkin said. He placed the key inside of a folder which was clearly marked "Trudy Madison."

"I just wanted to stop by and let you know my take on things. I hope I've been some help." Jerry stood up from his chair as if preparing to leave. "If I can be of further assistance, please feel free to call me."

"I appreciate that, Dr. Connors, and I'm sure that I will."

"As I said, I've changed my mind about what might have happened to the nurse." Maybe Sam and that dead girl were doing drugs together, and he was afraid she would tell on him. Who knows?"

Larkin's jaws tightened at the insinuation about Trudy. "Do you have any idea where Sam Talbot and Kathryn Bailey are right now, Dr. Connors?"

"What?" The blunt question shocked him.

"Kathryn and Sam—do you have any idea where they might have gone?"

"All I know is Kathryn has a sister who lives somewhere in the woods in West Virginia. I didn't really pay much attention when Kathryn complained about her sister living like Grizzly Adams."

"Do you have that address?"

"Somewhere in the files, I'm sure. I'll look it up for you. I doubt it'll do much good though. Kathryn hated the place where her sister lived. She said it was back in the sticks so far, they had to pipe in sunlight. I doubt she went there."

"Maybe her sister has heard from her…"

"Maybe…I'll look for the address as soon as I get back to the office. Sam only has a grandmother and she's living in a nursing home. She has Alzheimer's. I'll have what information I have on them when you come to search Kathryn's office."

"Thanks for coming by, Dr. Connors."

Jerry held out his hand, and reluctantly, Larkin shook it. "Sorry, I couldn't be more help."

"You giving me her key hand your pledge of cooperation helps a lot."

"You'll find I'm very protective of Lakeview, Detective Larkin. My wife passed away last year, and my work is all I have left. Treating my patients has been my whole life."

"It probably feels like you own the place by now." Larkin's comment was casual, but Larkin saw Jerry flinch.

"It almost seems like it—yes."

"Who is the owner, if you don't mind me asking?"

"Who knows? It's really a bunch of investors in some big conglomerate. I don't really worry about it as long as I get my paycheck."

Larkin would like to know how large his paycheck was, but he knew better than to get too personal right off the bat. At least the man was beginning to offer some assistance.

"I suppose you'll start your investigation at Lakeview right away?"

"Does this mean you've called off the watchdogs in high places?" Larkin retorted.

"You, Detective Larkin, are a very blunt man. Yes, I won't obstruct your investigation at Lakeview or anywhere else."

The two men sized one another up. If Connors thought there was evidence left, Larkin knew he wouldn't have offered to let him search Bailey's office. He hoped Jerry hadn't been as careful as he thought, and with the right clue he would break the case.

"I suppose you'll begin looking for the missing pair right away?"

"You can be assured that we will. I'll have the department put out an APB immediately."

The police had been looking for the missing pair's vehicles unofficially since Casey had told Larkin about their disappearance, but he couldn't tell Jerry that. "We wouldn't normally put out an APB on them, because an adult has a right to leave whenever he or she wants. It's a different story if someone is suspected of a murder."

Jerry smiled. "I do hope you find them, Detective."

"I'll have forensics search Kathryn's apartment later today. Unless they find evidence of a murder, there isn't a lot we can do unless we can link either of them to a crime. Like I said, It's not against the law for an adult to leave. Sam is facing drug related charges, but I doubt that law enforcement will pursue him. I'll need a photo of both of them to put in the newspaper."

"I never thought of that," Jerry said. "There's a picture in their personnel file. A photographer comes in every five years for an update. I'll give those to you."

"Good. That means we'll have a relatively recent copy."

"Don't you intend to pursue a murder charge against Sam?" Won't the police go after him for that?"

"Can you offer proof of a homicide?"

"No, not positive proof, but you're not going to give up on that poor girl's murder case, are you?"

Larkin stared at the man. He wondered why all of a sudden he was so interested in finding Trudy's killer.

"I did go to Kathryn's apartment recently," Connors admitted. "Everything looks clean and in order."

Jerry and Kathryn's relationship gave him an excuse for being in her apartment. It only made sense that he would check on her when she disappeared. Jerry also had time to sweep it for incriminating evidence.

"Will you keep me updated on your investigation?" Jerry asked.

Larkin stared at him for a minute. "You do understand that even if we find them, we won't be able to make them return unless we can prove something criminal against them."

"Oh, I understand that. I just would like to know if they are all right." Jerry said. "When is Sam going to court for the drug charges?"

"Next week, but I doubt he shows. If he and Bailey did run off together like you believe," Larkin said, "then I don't expect either of them back. He was only caught with a little pot, which isn't that serious. The police aren't really going to do much."

"I do have reason to believe he was supplying Kathryn with cocaine."

"That may be the case, but when we picked him up, all he had on him was a little marijuana."

"Was it a ruse to question him about the girl's murder?"

Larkin studied him for a time. The man in front of him was intelligent, very cunning, and he had a gut feeling, he was also dangerous. Why did he all of a sudden want to place the blame for Trudy's murder on the missing pair?"

"So—what you're saying is, you won't do anything to find them?"

"We will try, but we have greater priorities in my department, than hunting someone down for possession of a little pot," Larkin replied.

"You're the one who believed that Sam had something to do with that girl's death," Jerry accused.

Larkin stared at him a time before he spoke. "I don't think he acted alone. That's the avenue I'm looking at right now. What I think and what I can prove are two different things." Larkin stood up, effectively ending the conversation. "We'll probably be at Lakeview later today to do a search of Bailey's office."

"That's fine. I plan to be there all day. I have to hire someone to take Kathryn's place. I need to fill her position right away. The same goes for Sam. I'll also have hers and Sam's personnel file for you when you get there. Just come on out when you're ready."

"What if they come back?"

"Oh, trust me. They will never come back to Lakeview," he vowed.

Chapter 28

For the two weeks since Sam and Kathryn vanished, Jerry walked around Lakeview with a worried frown on his face. Casey felt sorry for him. Unrequited love was tough, she guessed. It had to be worse when someone left you for scum like Sam Talbot.

That evening, Casey studied her patients' files at her desk, waiting patiently for the other employees to leave.

For the last week, she had been staying late in her office, then she'd grab the key and sneak into her sister's room after the day shift left.

Every moment with Ruth was bittersweet. She was convinced more than ever that this woman was her sister. Casey gained her trust slowly, wooing her like she was a wounded lioness. Yesterday Ruth actually smiled at Casey as if she was happy to see her. Ruth allowed Casey to clip and file her talon-like nails, bathe her, then dress her in the new flannel gown she had purchased especially for her. She had also bought her a soft, warm blanket, sheets, and a new pillow. Casey had taken the filthy bedding outside before she left for home and disposed of it in a trash receptacle behind the building. She wished she could do more for Ruth, but she had to move slowly.

Casey arose from her desk, stretched, and pressed her fingers to her temples. She peered out the window at another raging storm. Her sinuses ached. She knew a full-blown headache wasn't far behind. The weather was crazy this year. The two tornadoes that ripped through the area in the last few weeks had left a couple of people dead and many more injured.

Casey rubbed the tension from her neck and walked to the reception hall doors. The lightening zigzagged in the distance followed by a rumble of thunder. She wondered if Ruth was afraid of the storm?

She strolled by Marcus's office and sighed. A sliver of light shone from underneath his door. The late nights were taking its toll on her; she needed a good night's sleep. Marcus usually didn't stay this late. Why did he pick this week to stay past eleven o'clock? Was he watching her? Could he be part of the scheme she believed that was going on here?

Casey walked back to her office, turned off the light, locked the door, and then sank down in a chair. Maybe if Marcus thought she had gone, he would leave also.

She closed her eyes and lay her head back against the chair. She didn't trust the man, but somehow she felt a dark attraction to him. It was her body's way of betraying her, she guessed.

She must have dosed off because a boom of thunder shook her room, causing her to start and become wide-awake. She jumped to her feet convinced she had slept for hours. It was so quiet in the hospital, when the thunder let up, she could hear her own heartbeat.

Easing her door open, she looked for the light under Marcus's door. All was dark. She breathed a sigh of relief.

She took the keys from pegboard and hurried directly to Ruth's room. She had the hairbrush she had bought for Ruth in her pocket. She had never allowed Casey to brush her hair, but Casey knew it was just a matter of patience. Ruth would allow it in due time.

Casey hadn't even told Larkin about her late nights with Ruth. He would say it was too dangerous. She didn't want anyone trying to stop her.

Ruth sat rocking back and forth in her usual spot on the bed. Casey joined her and said, "Hello, Ruth. I'm sorry I'm late. I missed you."

Casey slipped her arm around her shoulders and gave her a hug. A lump caught in her throat when Ruth, seeking comfort, laid her head on Casey's shoulder. Casey remained still for a few moments, and then slipped her hand into her pocket, removing the brush. With long strokes, she brushed her sister's matted mane. Sister or not, this woman needed love and attention.

Click! Creak!

She heard the doors at the end of the hall open. Then, footsteps echoed moving down the hall.

Ruth tensed beneath Casey's hands.

Casey's first thought was Sam Talbot!

"Ruth, stay here," she whispered. Casey moved quickly away from the bed, and flattened herself against the wall on the same side as the door.

She held her breath and waited. The footsteps stopped outside.

Casey's mind backtracked through her movements. She hadn't turned on any lights. She had parked her car in a secluded area behind the hospital this morning. How did anyone know she was here? Her heart skipped a beat. Did she lock Ruth's door? She couldn't remember. The only way to unlock a patient's door was with the key she had in her pocket. You could lock it from the inside, but anyone with a set of keys could get in. Sam Talbot had a key, of course, and that's what frightened her. Oh please, don't let whoever it was try the door.

The doorknob rattled. Horror restricted her throat. Trudy must have suffered the same terror.

Casey slid along the wall and removed the nightlight from the socket, plunging the room into total darkness. Ruth gasped. A crash of thunder almost stopped Casey's heart. A whining noise came from Ruth's direction.

Casey was afraid to draw a breath as she heard the door click unlocked, open, and then closed again. The intruder was in the room. She jammed a fist to her mouth to keep from crying out.

Chapter 29

Through the blackness of the room, she inched her way toward the door. She reached out and slowly turned the knob. Locked! Whoever had come in had cut off her means of escape. She knew the noise of her unlocking it would start the chase. She had to think. Larkin believed Trudy had met her fate by trying to outrun her attacker.

Casey remained still. She knew her visitor was letting his eyes adjust to the darkness. Her eyes darted around the room. There was no place to hide.

She moved into the middle of the room, hoping to keep him away from her. Oh no! She had taken her eyes off the shadowy figure for just a second to look at Ruth, and now she had no idea where he was. She stood perfectly still, hoping to catch a movement. She never heard a sound, or saw any motion, but suddenly a wall of hard muscle crashed into her back and her stalker grabbed her in a bear hug. She kicked backward as hard as she could with her right high-heel connecting with the intruder's shin.

The brute cursed her, but he also let her go. A cigarette lighter blazed to life. Marcus held it with one hand while he rubbed his leg with the other.

"Casey—what the hell?"

She ran to the door trying the doorknob again. It was definitely locked.

She tried to scream, but Marcus clasped his hand over her mouth to stop her. "Do you want to scare the patient to death?" he snapped.

He limped to the light switch and flipped it on.

Guilt and shame washed through her as she looked toward Ruth. How could she have forgotten how frightened Ruth must be?

Ruth huddled on her bed, rocking back and forth, her eyes filled with sheer terror. Casey started toward her, only to have Marcus grab her and pull her back.

"Can't you get it through your thick head that these people are dangerous? What the hell are you doing back here anyway? Do you want to wind up like your friend, Trudy?"

Casey shook loose from him. "Are you here to murder me?" she snapped. "You're far more dangerous than she is." She pointed to Ruth.

She ran to the frightened woman, holding her in her arms. In a soothing voice, she rocked back and forth calming Ruth. To her surprise, Marcus plugged in the nightlight, and waited until Ruth had stopped trembling.

"You do know we're locked in here?" he said as last.

"I— I didn't lock it." Casey accused.

He looked at her as if she were retarded. "The storm must have caused a glitch in the automatic locking system."

"I didn't even know there was an automatic locking system," she said."

"It's in case of emergency. If there's a problem, we can lock down the whole institution with a touch of a button. Maybe you should spend more time finding out about the running of this place than sneaking around in the middle of the night visiting dangerous patients."

"These people are treated like animals," she said.

"As I understand it, this woman wouldn't let anyone near her to do any personal hygiene."

"I was close enough to cut her nails, Dr. Wise Guy."

"I knew you were up to something. That's why I came back. That and the fact that I found your car hidden behind the building."

"Why are you watching me?"

"Because you need a keeper. You were so involved with the boy, and he gave you some crazy idea that this woman was his mother. I just put two and two together and figured out where you would be."

"Well, genius. What do you suggest we do now?"

"There's nothing we can do until tomorrow when someone lets us out."

"Oh God! Can you imagine what gossip this is going to generate?"

A deep belly laugh erupted from Marcus. Seeing his face, she had to chuckle also.

Ruth's whimper sobered them both. "It's all right, Ruth," Casey soothed.

"Are you out of your mind engaging a violent patient like that?" Marcus kept his voice even. "And why are you calling her Ruth? I'm sure the woman in this room is named Dana Collins."

Casey decided not to respond to the statement. She had to be more careful in her thoughts and actions.

"You're pushing my patience to the limit—stopping people's medication, sneaking around to violent patient's rooms, interacting with them as though they're normal. You insist on taking chances with your own safety as well as your patients. Sometimes, I think you might be crazy."

Marcus's statement hit home. Having studied her mother's disease, she was afraid she would wind up the same way her mother had.

"Maybe I am crazy, but I hate how the people on this floor are cared for…" Tears formed as his insinuation touched on her biggest fear. "You should have seen this woman before I started caring for her," she snapped. She was careful not to use her sister's name again.

"She's not your responsibility. Why would you let yourself get so involved with a patient? It goes against all of your training."

"I—I think she's my sister," she blurted, before she could stop herself.

"Now, I know you're crazy," he said.

"Just back off and don't scare her—please."

"Don't scare her…We're the ones locked in a room with a dangerous mental patient."

"Just shut up," Casey ordered….

Marcus threw up his hands. "All right, I'm going over and sit by the door. I need to get off this leg. It's beginning to throb."

"There are a couple of blankets in the drawers next to you. It would give you a softer place to sit."

"Thanks," he said, limping over and removing one of the covers. He hobbled back to the door, trying the knob once more, and found it still locked. He doubled the blanket and sat down. "Do you come here every night after everyone leaves?" he asked as he watched Casey hold and rock Ruth on the bed.

"Shhhh," Casey cautioned, indicating that Ruth was falling asleep.

Casey gently rocked back and forth until she was sure that the other woman was out, and then she eased her down on the nice fluffy pillow. Casey waited until the woman's breathing became even, still sitting on Ruth's bed. She covered Ruth with one of the blankets she brought her.

"You may as well join me," Marcus said, patting the blanket beside him. "We're going to be here a while."

She sighed. Well, at least she wasn't in this room alone if Sam returned. There was no way Sam would kill her in front of Marcus, she hoped. Then another troubling thought assaulted her mind. Maybe they were working together. She dismissed the thought quickly. If Marcus meant her harm, he could have killed her already.

Once more, Marcus patted the blanket.

Casey shook her head, but it did look inviting. She didn't trust him, but she was definitely attracted to the man. She had been fighting it for some time, but he looked so handsome in the subdued light. She sighed and joined him on the blanket.

"You want to tell me what's going on here?"

"What do you mean?" Casey evaded.

"You said you believed that this patient is your sister."

"And like you said—I'm crazy."

"Bull shit. You're an intelligent woman. You graduated in the top of your class—I know that. I also feel there is something not quite right going on at Lakeview. Right now I want to know why you think this woman is your sister."

His intent look cut through the dim light. Casey knew she had revealed too much.

"I told you, you need to trust me," he said gruffly.

"I don't know if I can do that. What have you been looking for in Kathryn's office and her apartment?"

"I ask you—why do you believe this woman is your sister?" He ignored her question.

"It's just a crazy hunch." Casey looked away, not knowing how much to reveal. For some reason she was tempted to share her burden with him. But how could she do that without knowing whose side he was on.

"I'm not going to let up until I know the answer," he said

"I'm sure Jerry has told you I was adopted."

"He mentioned it."

It didn't surprise her that Jerry had told him.

"My adoptive parents were killed in a traffic accident. What he didn't tell you is at the time of their deaths, I found a folder that had mine and my sister's birth certificates in it. It also had a picture of my sister Ruth. That picture was of this woman, I'm sure of it."

"She looks nothing like you!"

"I hired a private detective to search for my real family. I found that my mother had mental problems and was unable to care for my sister and me. My father felt that he wasn't able to cope with us alone, so we were given up for adoption."

"I've explained all of this to the detective investigating the murder here at Lakeview."

"And the detective thinks this woman is your sister?"

"Not exactly." she said, wishing he would be satisfied with this much of her story.

"I was the lucky one. Jerry, was able to help my parents place me with a rich family. My guess is that Ruth was already showing signs of schizophrenia, so my adoptive parents refused to take her. She spent years going from home to home, and then she was finally institutionalized here at Lakeview."

"Wow!"

"I studied her file, and at the beginning she was doing better. It was about the time that the outpatient program began. She even married and had a child. Then she started having problems again and had to be put back into the hospital."

Marcus slipped his arm around her shoulders. "You still haven't told me how you know that this woman is your sister." He spoke so close to her ear that she felt his warm breath.

In spite of herself, Casey's body reacted, and she found herself relating the whole story about finding the picture and about Trudy taking a snapshot of the woman in this room. She even told him of visiting the woman the hospital released as Ruth Thompson and finding out she was a fake. She spoke about Arron recognizing the woman in this room as his mother.

"You think Arron is your nephew?" He was finally becoming clear on why she felt so close to the boy.

"I'm sure of it." She nodded.

"This explains a lot."

"What do you mean?"

"Why you're ignoring your training."

"Gee. Thanks a lot."

"You have to admit that you're not following procedure. You're too personally involved with these people."

She pushed away from him. "These people are my family."

"Are you a hundred percent certain?"

"I would bet my life on it."

"If what you believe is true about your friend's death, I'd say you're doing just that."

"You don't believe me, do you?"

"I didn't say that," he said, shaking his head. "It all just seems too incredible." "Look, I can understand wanting to find your family, but I'm sure this obsession you have with these two patients is unhealthy."

"Like you said, maybe I am crazy as well."

"I didn't mean it that way," he said gently. "I just wished you would be more objective. There is no real proof that these people are related to you."

"I'm sorry, but I happen to think there is."

"But the woman in this room is named Dana Collins. Lakeview released Ruth Thompson a few months back. I studied all the patient's files."

"I found a file on Ruth Thompson as well. It was written by a doctor when she first entered Lakeview."

"A doctor recorded her progress up until Jerry took over her case." She was doing so well that Jerry released her. I'm sure you have read the same file," he said

"I'm telling you, I went to see that woman, and she is not the same person as the one in my adoptive father's folder. Trudy took a picture of my sister," she said, pointing to the woman asleep on the bed. "She's the person whom Arron claims is his mother. That is good enough for me."

"If that's the case, then the people who work here are lying about her identity. Why would they do that?"

"I wish I knew."

"It just doesn't make any sense." He frowned.

"You don't believe a word I'm telling you, do you?"

"I just need to analyze some things."

"You asked me to trust you," she said at last. "How about you trust me?"

"I'm trying to, but it all seems so preposterous."

"Admit it. You think I'm as disturbed as the rest of my patients."

"I'll admit there are things that have been bothering me," he replied.

"What...?"

"I'm wondering why you were at Kathryn Bailey's house the day after she disappeared, and why did you and your boyfriend take the files Jerry sent me to get." Casey stared at him. He was accusing her and Jimmy of taking the documents.

"I'll admit we were there, but the files weren't in the safe. What I'm wondering is why Jerry sent you to get them?" It was slowly dawning on her that Jerry had been the man talking to Kathryn that day. Sending Marcus to get the evidence of a crime proved he was either guilty of something or just protecting his mistress. Either way, she knew now why Larkin told her not to trust Jerry.

"Jerry gave me the combination to Kathryn's safe and the key to her house and asked me to pick up the file. He said Bailey had taken some papers he needed. When I heard all the commotion from the bedroom, I ran to the window to see who was leaving. I saw you and your friend running to your car. The safe was wide open with nothing inside. If you didn't take the files, then who did?"

"I could ask you the same question?" she said.

"I had an excuse for being there."

"And what makes you think you had a better reason than I did?" she said.

"My boss asked to go there."

"So you say."

"Surely, you can understand why I would be reluctant to trust you. It makes me wonder if you're stable, breaking into a woman's home and stealing property belonging to your employer."

"I didn't take them, but I believe there's evidence in them that will incriminate someone. Maybe more than one person," she said, staring at him.

"I found the safe wide open and empty just as you said you did," Marcus related.

"When Trudy was murdered, the forensic people believed she was killed in the file room, and her body was dumped in that patient's room. Jerry has friends in high places and Detective Larkin was ordered to stop gathering evidence."

"And that makes you suspicious of files that Mrs. Bailey had in her safe?" He shifted his position and stretched his legs out. "This floor gets hard after a time," he said, leaning back against the wall.

Casey ignored his discomfort. "Right after the police left that day, I overheard Kathryn and some man talking about moving the files to her safe because the police might get a warrant to search Lakeview."

"Whom was she talking to?"

"I couldn't tell. The man's voice was much lower than hers, and he was trying to be quiet. I do know that she didn't want to keep the papers in her safe."

"Could it have been Sam's voice you heard?"

"Sure, I suppose. She and Sam were involved in a lot of commotion that day. All I know is there was something incriminating in those papers. Something they didn't want the police to find."

Marcus elaborated on his errand at the Bailey residence. "The day after Kathryn disappeared, Jerry told me, for security reasons, he needed me to pick up everything in her safe. He asked me to bring it all to him. It made sense to me, since I was driving right by there on my way home. I had a half day off from work, so I agreed to do it."

Casey studied him through the illumination from the night-light, wondering if he was telling her the truth, or if he was involved up to his handsome neck.

It surprised her when he reached forward and pulled her head down on his shoulder. He smelled like soap and after-shave, and it was doing a number on her senses. She gave a contented sigh and took comfort in the strong arm he placed around her. It surprised her even more when he bent and rested his head against hers. She felt safe wrapped in his embrace, and she was beginning to relax even though she didn't completely trust him. Men usually wanted one thing from her, and she was tired of fighting off their advances. She rarely dated anymore and up until this point, she had thrown herself into her work.

"Why didn't you call the police on Jimmy and me?" She asked after a time.

"I don't know...I just find you so exasperating. The truth is, I guess I just didn't want to get you in trouble."

"Did you tell Jerry we were there that day?"

"No, I told him that Kathryn must have taken the papers with her."

"And he was okay with that?" She moved out of his arms and turned to look at him.

"He gave me a hard stare when I told him, but he didn't say anything. It makes me wonder if he thought I took the damn things," Marcus said.

His statement caused Casey concern. If Jerry thought Marcus had the files he might consider him a threat, and it surprised her to feel her heart beat faster to think Marcus could be in danger.

"Do you think I took them?" she asked

"Either you took them, or Kathryn did."

"If you thought I took the files; why didn't you tell Jerry?" she asked.

"I don't really know," he said shaking his head. "I think it would be nice if you were as loving to me as you are with her." He pointed to Ruth.

His lips were inches from hers before she saw the kiss coming. It was soft as a gentle breeze. He caressed and tasted her mouth. She leaned into him intensifying the sensations. Her hands slipped inside his shirt, feeling the smooth skin and hard muscles. She slowly moved her hand upward to touch the pulse beating in his throat. Marcus deepened the kiss, allowing his mouth to work its magic. His tongue sought entrance to her mouth. Parting her lips, she allowed him inside. He pushed her down on the blanket almost lying on top of her. She matched him kiss for kiss and tongue for tongue. He was breathing hard, but suddenly he pulled back from her and pulled her up straight. "Whoa, he said holding her away from him. "Like I said. You never cease to amaze me."

"I'm sorry." She lowered her head, embarrassed to have reacted to his kiss the way she did. When it came to men, she usually held back.

"Don't be." A grin played around his lips. "I rather enjoyed it myself. You should let yourself go more often."

"I guess now you think I'm a promiscuous little hussy." For the first time since she met him, she cared what he believed.

He gave a deep belly laugh. Casey liked the sound.

"I know there are a lot of guys after you, but I've never seen you give any of them the time of day. You're beautiful, you know."

"I'm really not…"

"As for the other, I think you're a passionate, caring human being, and I certainly can't fault you for that." His voice softened and he was trying to study her in the dim light.

"Jimmy is just a good friend," she said. "We attended college together. He's more like a brother than anything else." For some reason she didn't want Marcus to think she was attached.

"Is Jimmy your breaking and entering partner?"

She chuckled. "He's the one. It would take too long for me to explain Jimmy to you."

"We' have all night unless that automatic lock decides to open," he said. "Although I could think of other things we could do to occupy our time," he said with a twinkle in his eye.

"I'm afraid that making out on a blanket in my sister's room is not my idea of a good time."

"It's not mine either," he chuckled. "I was kidding."

"I know… But the way I acted…I just don't want you to get the wrong idea."

"I want out first time to be on a bed sprinkled with rose petals," he said, nuzzling her neck.

"What makes you think there'll be another time?" She moved her neck out of reach.

"Because, I think you're as attracted to me as I am to you. Do you deny it?"

She couldn't. Her response to his kiss spoke volumes.

"I know you think I've dreamed up some wild conspiracy." She studied his face trying to read him.

He paused. "It's hard to reason it out, but there are some things I'm concerned about."

"What are you questioning?"

"It's about the boy."

"You mean Arron?" She had some hope for the first time that he might believe her.

"I think you're right about him. There's only one thing that bothers me, and that is he still insists that the woman in this room is his mother. I'm wondering if you've projected your perception to him."

"I told you, he was the one who saw the photo and said it was his mother. This was the first session we had. I have never told him who I thought she was."

"Are you sure you've never told him what you believe?"

"You think he's normal. You just said so."

"I didn't say that. You know mental patients have times when they appear normal. Then something will trigger an episode."

"You stopped his medication, didn't you?"

"I'm monitoring him closely."

"You think he's normal. Why don't you have the guts just to say so?"

"He may be. I need to give it some time."

"Then why can't you believe Ruth is his mother?" Casey replied, pointing to the peacefully sleeping woman.

"If this is true, then I have to believe Jerry Connors is a liar. Have you thought about that?"

"You don't think it hurts me realize that the man I've known all my life is a monster involved in murder. And there's Kathryn and Sam's disappearance. I just can't see Bailey running away with a loser like Sam."

"Whoa! Are you accusing Connors of doing away with those two? I happen to admire the man. It's hard for me to believe he would lie about a patient's condition, and do the things you're accusing him of."

"What do you think about me? I've known him all of my life. I've loved him as a trusted friend. I wouldn't have this job if it weren't for him, but things aren't adding up. You saw for yourself how luxuriously Kathryn Bailey's home is decorated. Do you think she would run away with a bum like Sam Talbot?"

She could tell she had given him pause for thought. "You've known the man longer than I have. Do you honestly believe him capable of that?"

"I know it sounds preposterous…"

"I just can't believe Jerry's doing something wrong."

"Maybe Kathryn deceived him. Maybe he didn't know what was going on with the boy," Casey said. "What worries me, though, is he was the one who sent you after the files. Doesn't it make sense that if he knew where they were, he was the one who I overheard talking to Kathryn that day?"

As she reasoned things out in her own mind it was becoming clearer to Casey all the time. Jerry had to be involved in whatever was going on at Lakeview. That was unless Marcus had lied about Jerry sending him after the files. Could it be that Marcus was the one she heard talking to Kathryn that day?

"It could be as simple as him wanting me to protect his patient's privacy."

"Maybe," Casey agreed.

"Maybe Sam and Kathryn were into something illegal, and Jerry was trying to protect the woman he loves."

"That must be it!" Casey exclaimed. "Something in those files incriminated Kathryn, so he sent you to her house to get them. He's protecting her."

Casey stared at him long and hard. Maybe she was trusting a killer?

"It's simple…Kathryn took all incriminating evidence with her because she knew there would be an investigation if she disappeared," Casey said. "Maybe she left her safe open to send Jerry a message."

"I don't understand."

"Maybe she plans to blackmail him. If they were into something illegal and she was planning to run away with Sam, maybe she took the evidence to assure Jerry wouldn't cause her any trouble," Casey reasoned. "I don't know." All this thinking was giving her a headache.

"Your assumptions are just so thin. All this drama about the files, what has it got to do with the woman and her son you feel are your relatives?"

"There's a clue in those papers somewhere. Why else would Sam have murdered Trudy?"

"You're assuming an awful lot don't you think? What if the girl was really killed by a patient, like the management claims?"

"I'm going by what the police believed happened."

"Don't you think the police could be wrong?"

"All I know is, I trust Detective Larkin and his team. They say it happened in the file room and I feel in my gut that's exactly what happened. Something else I've been wondering about. Why do you think Jerry sent you to get the contents of Bailey's safe? Was it because he thought the police were watching her place and he was planning to let you take the fall?"

Casey could see him frown in the semi darkness.

"Why do you try to make a conspiracy out of everything?" he said, shaking his head.

"You would have been the perfect patsy."

His frown deepened. "What do you mean?" It was clear, he hated her thinking of himself in that light.

"If you'd been caught, he could have denied knowing anything about what was in those files. He could have accused you of plotting with Kathryn and Sam."

"Whoa, you don't trust anyone do you?" Marcus exclaimed.

"I've gotten a wake-up call in the last year. I found out that my real parents didn't want me. Then I found out that the couple who called themselves my parents weren't that at all. No one saw fit to tell me the truth. It really isn't a stretch to believe the man who gave me my first job and claims to be my friend isn't what he seems to be either."

"I think the death of your adoptive parents caused a great shock. I think instead of dealing with it, you've transferred your feelings to this woman and her son without having any proof they're even related to you. Look, I know how badly you want a family, but I have to agree with Jerry on this."

She withdrew from his embrace. He could see her shutting down. He had crossed the line when he gave her his analysis.

"You've discussed my situation with Jerry?" she asked.

"He's very worried about you."

"I'll just bet he is." She scooted farther away from him. "I should have recognized where you'd gotten your spiel from. Are those the very words he used, or did you paraphrase?"

"Look... Does it make sense he would have sent me after the files, if he thought there was something incriminating in them? Wouldn't he be afraid I would read them?"

"It would make more sense if you're in it with him," she accused, but deep down she hoped Jerry was duping him just as he did her at first.

Marcus shook his head. There was just no reasoning with her. Maybe she had some psychological problems. It was in her family history. He knew he was getting too involved with her. She was a beautiful woman and he was attracted to her right from the start. He fought hard to suppress it, but it kept resurfacing every time they were close.

"I'm telling you, there is something in those files Jerry doesn't want the police to see, whether it's to protect himself or Kathryn Bailey." Casey was insistent.

"Let's face it, Casey. People in love do crazy things." His eyes bored into hers Was he trying to tell her he was in love with her? All she knew is, the statement and the way he was staring at her did crazy things to her insides. She found herself wanting it to be true. She had a burning need to have someone in her life who wanted more than sex from her.

Determined to put these concerns out of her mind, Casey yawned in exhaustion. She'd lost too much sleep waiting for everyone to leave Lakeview so she could tend to her sister. Then there was the thought that a lifelong friend had betrayed her. All of it together had sapped her energy. She hoped she was wrong about Jerry, but she had only a slim hope he wasn't involved. On the other hand, Marcus thought Jerry was a saint.

"You're worn out. Why don't you put your head back on my shoulder and try to get some rest. I have a wide one," he said, smiling at her.

Yes, he did have a broad chest and it did look inviting. She gave a sigh and came close to him again, using his shoulder as a pillow. She knew Marcus was only humoring her, but she was so tired and he was impossible for her to resist.

His arm curled around her, pulling her close. She let herself relax against him, realizing that being in his arms was the best she'd felt in ages.

"How is Arron doing?" she asked, after he believed she was sleep.

"The kid seems normal, like you said." He didn't tell her, however, that he couldn't dissuade the boy from claiming that his mother was the woman in this very room. The kid seemed intelligent. He couldn't help but believe Casey might have aided him in that belief. He wasn't going to bring it up. It felt too good to hold her the way he was doing now.

"Can I see him?"

"I don't think it's a good idea at this time."

"You think I'll add to his delusion."

"I didn't say that. I just don't think it would be wise at this point. If what you think about Jerry is true, he will be watching you to see if you're getting too close."

"I guess you're right. Did you discontinue his meds?"

"You know I can't discuss that with you."

"Why not? It's not like I'm an outsider. We're colleagues, aren't we?"

He chuckled. "You just won't leave this alone, will you?" He stopped her from lifting her head once again. "If you must know, I saw no need to put him back on his medication until I tested your theory."

"You mean you believed me when I accused Kathryn of giving him LSD?"

He shifted around on the blanket. "Not exactly, but I thought that I would allow him to have another psychotic episode to convince you."

"Gee…Thanks a lot."

"It seemed so far-fetched. I just can't get a handle on someone doing what you suggested"

They lapsed into silence for a time, where the only noise was from the soft snoring of their patient. "Thank you," Casey said.

"For what?"

"For not putting, Arron back on the medication."

"It was the least I could do considering all the trouble you went to taking it away," he chuckled softly. His breath in her ear gave her the chills.

"I just wish you had done it because you believed me."

"Okay, so, I didn't do it because I believed you. It has still had the same outcome. He has continued to get better the longer he is off the medicine," he admitted.

"Thank God for that!" she exclaimed, "even if I didn't exactly get your vote of confidence."

"Give me a break, woman. I had an inexperienced doctor, just out of school, claiming that a well-known hospital with a spotless reputation was sabotaging a child's efforts to get better."

"I can see your point. It made more sense to believe that I was crazy."

"Not crazy. Just impressionable," he said. "Not everyone is cut out for this kind of work. Now that I know the whole story, it sheds a new light on everything."

"Are you admitting that I'm right about Arron and Ruth being my family?"

"I didn't say that. I know you believe it."

"I'm planning on proving it once we get out of here," she said.

"How are you going to do that?"

"I took fingernail clippings from when I cut Ruth's nails, and I have hair I pulled out of her hairbrush. She patted her pocket. "I plan on giving it to Detective Larkin to test her DNA against mine."

"I can't believe that man would put you in danger like this," he snapped.

"No. No, you have it all wrong. Larkin doesn't know anything about me doing this. I'm planning on surprising him."

"When are you going to give it to him?"

"Tomorrow, I'll call him. I have Larkin's number on speed dial."

Marcus felt a stab of jealousy course through him. He was allowing his feelings for her to get out of hand, when she might be more disturbed than the woman she insisted on calling Ruth. The same woman who snored softly in her bed.

"What happens if you find out you aren't related to her?" he asked, after a time.

"That's not going to happen. I know she's my sister." She pointed to Ruth." I feel it right here, in my gut."

"I just want you to realize it's not a sure thing," he said, as he gave her a squeeze. He was afraid that if she was wrong, she couldn't cope and maybe she would become unhinged.

"I'm prepared to accept it if it turns out I'm wrong," she said after a time.

"Are you sure?"

"I'm positive," she assured him.

Chapter 30

Casey awoke with a start. There were people milling around on the main floor. She had slept with her head on Marcus's shoulder as the drool on his jacket revealed. She peered at his face in the morning light. He looked as innocent as a boy when he slept. She gazed at him for a moment before shaking him awake.

"Good morning." She caressed the roughness of his beard against her cheek by rubbing her face against his. "Someone will be here soon to check on Ruth, I suspect."

Marcus stirred and blinked himself awake. Reaching up, he rubbed at the kink in his neck. Suddenly he became wide-awake. He struggled to his feet and pulled her along with him.

"Damn," he said, still rubbing his neck. "I'm too old to sleep like that."

"You must be all of what? Thirty-five?" Casey quipped.

"Thirty-six, actually. A baby like you couldn't possibly know what damage it does to an old man."

"I'm twenty-nine, almost thirty."

"I know how old you are. I studied your personnel file."

She looked at him quickly and opened her mouth, but she heard other voices coming near them distracted her.

"Quick! Stand over by the door and let me handle this," Marcus ordered.

"All right." She flashed him a knowing look and complied.

The male aid who had taken Sam's place was surprised when he unlocked the door and Marcus stepped out into the hallway.

"Dr. Kelly? What are you doing here?" he exclaimed. He shot a look to the other male nurse that followed closely on his heels.

"I had to stop for some papers last night when it was storming. The patient was agitated, so I went in to see if I could calm her down. The lightning must have struck the automatic lockdown system because I couldn't get out."

Casey was amazed at how easily the lie came to him.

"I noticed the other set of keys were gone," the man said. "I have Sam's." He showed them to Marcus. "He gave them to me because I agreed to cover for him the night he disappeared."

"Well, it's wonderful that you are so observant. What are your names?" Marcus led them down the hall as they spoke.

"My name is Vince, and this is Carter. He's new and I'm showing him the ropes."

"Well, you two are right on your toes, and I plan to tell Dr. Connors so. You both can run along and take care of your other duties. I'll make sure the key gets back on the pegboard."

"We need to give this patient her meds."

"She's sleeping right now. She had a rough night because of the storm. Could you see to everyone else first and come back later?"

"I guess so," Vince said reluctantly. He had developed a routine since taking Sam's place. He glanced toward his co-worker who shrugged his shoulders. After all, the doctor was their boss and they needed to do as he asked.

"We can get all of the medicine ready to pass out and then come back," Carter said.

"Just please make sure you put the keys back where they belong," Vince said. "We'll get in real trouble if Dr. Connor's finds them missing."

"Sure thing...about the keys. I'll remember to do that," he called after them as the two disappeared down the hall.

Remembering that she still had the keys, Casey reached into her pocket then gasped. The keys were there, but the baggie with her sister's hair and nail clippings wasn't. She held the keys in one hand and checked both her pockets again. Her proof was gone.

Furious, she came flying out of the room to confront Marcus. She didn't give a damn if the pope was in the hallway.

"You bastard!" she spat, flinging herself at Marcus. "Where is it?"

"What?"

"My evidence," she hissed. "You stole it from me while I slept. "All that sweet talk was to get me to trust you."

"Be quiet. You're going to draw attention to us."

"I'll cause a scene like no one in this hospital has ever seen before if you don't hand it over," she threatened.

Marcus sighed and slowly removed the evidence from his pocket and handed it to her. "I just didn't want you to be disappointed if it didn't pan out."

Casey jerked it from his hand. "You're all heart," she snapped. Clasping the precious evidence to her chest, she sprinted to her office, not caring if she ran into the devil himself. Hitting one button on her phone, she dialed Larkin.

Chapter 31

Casey couldn't believe she had trusted Marcus enough to sleep on his shoulder. She patted her pocket. She had come to close to losing her precious evidence. Marcus, with all his pretending to understand, couldn't be trusted. It made her sick thinking of all the information he'd tricked her into revealing. Most of all, she had let Detective Larkin down.

Casey went straight to the police station after leaving work that evening. She barged into Larkin's office, swept past Cramer who was slumped in a chair, and dropped the bag that held the hair and nail clippings onto Larkin's desk.

"Here is the evidence you need to prove Ruth is my sister."

Larkin smiled. "I'm not even going to ask how you obtained this." He held the clear bag up to the light. "These are nails? They look more like claws." He was sorry the minute he said it. There was such pain evident on Casey's lovely face.

He patted her shoulder. "You look worn out," he said. "Did you get any sleep last night?"

"The storm caused a glitch in the automatic shutdown system and I got locked in Ruth's room last night," she explained.

"Do you think it's wise to go to a patient's room?" Larkin asked.

"She's not just any patient, she's my sister. She isn't violent either. I've been going there ever since Sam Talbot disappeared," she said. "Marcus

Kelly took over my nephew's care, and I had to do something to help them."

Larkin sighed. He wished she knew how worried he was about her without sounding patronizing. There was really nothing he could say when he saw the determination on her face.

"How did…?"

"Like I said, Ruth is not violent, but she is frightened. She's been treated like an animal. I was gentle with her, and getting her hair and nail clippings was easy."

"I just want you to be very careful," he said, as he put on gloves and transferred the hair and nails to another evidence bag. He wrote Casey's name on it.

"You know we won't be able to use it as evidence in court." Larkin told her. "We didn't have a warrant to obtain it and Connors's lawyer will protest it."

"I'm not interested in proving it in court, Detective Larkin. I know who she is. I'm interested in proving it to others," Casey said.

"Like who? You have me convinced," he said.

"I need to convince…"

"Your boss," Larkin interrupted, shaking his head.

"I need to prove to him that I'm not crazy."

"You're a gutsy broad," Cramer burst out. He had been sitting back listening to their conversation.

Casey glared at him.

"No offense," he blurted.

"Call David for me, will you?" Larkin turned toward Cramer.

Cramer took his cell out of his pocket and dialed. "He said that he can't leave right now," Cramer told Larkin.

"Tell him that's okay. I will catch him later."

"We don't want to press our luck," Larkin said, looking at Casey. "We don't have a court order for the evidence. It might take a little persuasion on my part to have it examined. Can you come back later?"

Casey thought for a second. "Sure, I need to go home and freshen up."

Larkin looked her over. She looked fine to him, just a little tired. "Why don't you come back this afternoon? I should have an answer by then."

"I'm expecting to have an answer today." Casey said, as she turned to leave.

Larkin smiled. Again he realized how much they were alike.

Deep in thought Larkin stood up and paced the floor. He and his team had searched Kathryn's apartment and never found any evidence. It looked like the woman had left for the day, fully planning to return, and then just disappeared. The apartment was spotless; her expensive clothing was still in the closet. She even left a steak rotting in the sink. Evidently Kathryn was planning to have it for dinner.

The only thing he couldn't explain was why her safe was wide open and empty. There were no fingerprints on it other than hers. Larkin had compared the prints found on her safe to the ones in her employee file. With Jerry's blessing, he'd also checked the fingerprints of every employee at Lakeview. Larkin was surprised that Connors even insisted they test his as well. The only employee with a record was Sam. The DNA that Casey had collected from the woman in room 14 might prove to be the only evidence in this elusive case. Now, he had to get David to test it.

"I'll be back in a while, Cramer. Hold down the fort."

"Give my regards to David," Cramer crooned, for he knew where Larkin was headed.

Larkin hurried downstairs to Forensics. David looked up from his work as Larkin opened the door.

"Oh no..." David groaned.

"Is that any way to treat a guest?" Larkin quipped.

"Any time I look up and see you Larkin, I know I have a big job ahead of me."

"Do you remember the Trudy Madison case?"

"Yes, I remember it," David replied. His jaw tightened as he spoke. David hated someone foiling his investigation as much as Larkin did.

"I told you a little bit about what was going on. Casey West is convinced that the woman they're passing off as her sister is a fake."

"Yes, I remember that."

"Well, Casey has come up with a way to determine the truth."

"I'm afraid to ask, but how?"

"She believes the woman in room 14 at Lakeview is her sister."

"And she wants us to test the woman's DNA against hers?" David sounded harassed.

"No wonder I like you so much; you're so quick on your feet," Larkin said as he held up the evidence bag of clippings.

"You're kidding," David said as he handed it to him. "There's no way that Jerry Connor's attorney will allow you to use it as evidence"

"I know that, David," Larkin agreed. "But Casey needs proof that the woman is her sister. Frankly, I need to know as well. I have a gut feeling that Trudy Madison was murdered because she found evidence of a crime in that file room, and it has something to do with the woman Casey believes is her sister."

"You always pick the busiest times, my man."

"Is that a no?"

"Hell no! I hate that Jerry Connors. I would like nothing better than to put his ass in jail."

"So is that a yes?"

"Get the woman down here. I'll do a swab on her and compare it to the DNA of the nails and hair you gave me."

Larkin took another baggie out of his pocket that had Casey's name on it and handed it to David. "I thought I would save us some time." He grinned. "I took a swab from her while she was here."

"Of course you did." David took the offering from him.

"I'm swamped right now, but I'll do the test as soon as possible."

"Thanks, David." Larkin breathed a sigh of relief and slapped him on the shoulder. "You're a good man."

"And you're a master manipulator."

"What do you mean?" Larkin asked.

"You knew I would do it the minute you brought up Jerry Connors."

Larkin laughed. "In my business, you soon learn to use whatever it takes to get the job done."

"Just be patient. I'm so far behind now that I think I'm ahead. And I'm not getting anything done standing here talking to you."

"I'll go. I can take a hint."

"Rumor has it the lady is not bad to look at," David said. "Maybe I'll give her the results in person."

Larkin stopped at the door of the lab.

"When she shows up, just remember you're married."

David laughed, waved him on, and went back to his microscope.

"By the way, what are we going to call our mystery lady?" David called out before Larkin could leave. "I have to give her a label, you know."

"For now, let's call her Ruth Thompson," Larkin said. "That's who Casey is convinced she is."

David nodded at him as Larkin left the room.

Larkin went back to work. Cramer left at five while Larkin stayed late as usual. It was after hours and he was surprised to find Casey knocking on his door.

"I actually stopped to see your forensic man," she said, "but he said you wanted to talk to me about an urgent matter."

Larkin smiled. He knew David's tactics for getting rid of him when he kept hounding him for DNA results. He also figured out that Casey would be as persistent as he was.

"What did you want to talk to me about, Detective?" Casey asked, sitting down.

"I don't like the idea of you taking so many chances," he began. "Frankly, I have grown quite fond of you, and I'd never forgive myself if something happened to you."

Casey smiled. "I feel the same way about you, Detective."

Larkin threw Trudy Madison's folder on the desk in frustration. "I hate a case where my hands are tied. It's sad when the only evidence you obtain is supplied by a novice."

Casey hung her head. "I'm afraid I've let you down, Detective. I'm sick about it, but I made a real error in judgment. I confided in Marcus and I know you told me not to trust anyone."

"Tell me you never talked to Jerry Connors about any of this!"

"No—no… I told you I've been sneaking to Ruth's room after everyone left at night."

"Yes, that's why I want you to be careful. If you remember right, it's what got your friend murdered."

"It was storming last night, and the lightning did something to the automatic lockdown system. Marcus Kelly followed me to Ruth's room. When I first heard him, I thought that Sam Talbot had come back. I was petrified. Then I found out I was locked in Ruth's room with Marcus."

"Did he threaten you in any way?"

"No, he used other tactics." She felt herself blush. "To make a long story short… The worm gained my confidence, and I told him everything about my sister and her son."

"Do you think you can trust him?"

"At first I thought so, but that's what I'm trying to tell you. I don't think that I can. I'm so sorry, Detective Larkin."

"Do you think he believed you?"

"I don't really know." She hung her head. "All I know is that he betrayed me."

"In what way?" Larkin asked.

"I told him about collecting Ruth's DNA to test against mine. He wanted to know where it was. I told him I had it in my pocket. Then, the creep stole it from me."

"How did he get close enough to take the evidence from your pocket?"

"When we found out we were locked in, we shared a blanket that we'd doubled up and placed on the floor." Casey didn't feel the need to tell Larkin she had slept the night on Marcus's shoulder. "He removed the hair and nails while I slept—the rat."

Larkin's face fell.

"He insisted on knowing why I was so interested in Ruth and Arron, and I had to tell him something. I was sleep-deprived. I've been up late every night. I know it's no excuse, but it's all I've got."

Larkin patted her arm. "It's not your fault. I should never have put you in this position."

"Don't blame yourself, Detective. I would have been doing the same thing on my own. It's not like you told me to go to a patient's room."

"You said he took the clippings and hair from your pocket while you slept. How did you get it back?"

"I told him I would cause a scene that no one would forget if he didn't give it back," she said.

Larkin laughed. He knew she would have done it, too. "So did he hand it over?"

She smiled and nodded her head. "He hasn't talked to me since, but he gave me back my evidence."

"Did you ask him why he had taken it?" Larkin asked.

"He gave me some lame excuse about not wanting me to be disappointed when I found out I was wrong."

Larkin thought it over. He believed the guy cared for her. It was easy to see how thoroughly convinced she was that these people were her family. She was now calling the woman in room 14 Ruth. Maybe Marcus did just want to protect her.

"I'm sorry," she said at last, breaking the silence. "I know I screwed up."

"That's okay. It's my fault. I should never have put you into this dangerous situation."

"But I let you down. I should have had more control over my emotions," she said, hanging her head.

"You have feelings for Marcus Kelly, don't you?"

"I hate him."

"I think the lady doth protest too much."

"He had me fooled. I thought he really believed me. I know now he only wanted information. I even told him about..." She stopped, knowing that she had said too much.

"What else did you tell him?" Larkin demanded.

She paused for only a second. "I might as well tell you the rest. The rumor around Lakeview was that Sam and Kathryn had run away together, and they weren't coming back. Knowing Kathryn was gone, I got my friend Jimmy to help break into her place. I wanted Jimmy to open her safe so I could get the files. Before you say anything, I know I broke the law."

"Did you get them?" He asked. He was on the edge of his seat. The police had searched Bailey's apartment but found absolutely nothing.

"No... We found her safe with the door wide open and empty."

That's the way the police found it also.

"Do you have any idea who took the files?"

"No, but while we were there, Marcus showed up and almost caught us. He told me last night that Jerry had sent him after them."

"What do you think?"

"I don't know if he's lying or not. He said Jerry gave him the combination to Bailey's safe and asked him to pick up what was inside."

"Do you think he's the one who stole the evidence?"

"I know he didn't open the safe or take anything out, because he came after we did."

"What do you think happened to the files?"

"My guess is that Kathryn took them with her."

"There is something that bothers me about the whole thing," Larkin said. "Why would she leave a closet full of expensive clothes, all her bills and personal papers, and just take off like that? She even left a steak out to defrost. Why would a woman who was planning on leaving for good do that?"

"There is so many things about this mess that just doesn't make sense," Casey volunteered.

"Jerry Connors turned over Kathryn's personnel file to me yesterday. I called her sister's number, and the woman who answered, said she hadn't seen Kathryn in years. That agrees with what Jerry Connors told me. He said the sisters were estranged. Some feud over their home place being willed to her older sister."

"How is the trace on their cars going?" Casey asked.

"I have an APB out all over the country. It's as if both their cars vanished with them. Connors gave me their pictures and the news story is supposed to come out in the local paper this evening along with their photographs. We're appealing to anyone who has seen either of them to come forward."

"It sounds like Jerry is cooperating."

"It does seem so, doesn't it?" Larkin commented.

"But you don't think so, do you?"

"I still say don't let him fool you," Larkin said. "I've dealt with a lot of criminals in my career, and I'm a very good judge of character. I just don't trust him."

"What is your next step?" Casey asked.

"I'll check to see if Sam has extended family, but his grandmother is supposed to be his only living relative."

"The police spend a lot of time on wild goose chases, don't they?"

"That's true," Larkin agreed. "But it's sure a thrill when things start falling into place."

"Do you think it will ever happen with this case?"

"Something else I've learned in my career is, never to give up. Sometimes it may take years, but the break you need will come through eventually," Larkin reassured her.

"When Jerry came to see me he said he believed I was right about Sam being involved in Trudy's murder. He thinks that's why he and Kathryn ran."

"It does make sense. They left just after you questioned Sam again about the murder."

"I think he was coerced into killing Trudy."

"I know you don't care for Uncle Jerry, but I still can't believe he is capable of murder. It sounds like he's ready to cooperate."

"We'll see," Larkin answered. "Right now, young lady, I want you to stop taking dangerous chances."

"You're limited as to what you can do, Detective. I'm not! I'll do what I have to do to save my family."

Larkin was quiet. He would do the same in her position.

She got up from her chair and headed for the door.

"You wanted to know what I was going to do. Now I want to know what you're planning," Larkin asked.

"I'm planning on keeping a low profile while waiting for the results of the DNA test."

"And I am concentrating on finding our two suspects," Larkin said. "I never found a computer when I searched Bailey's place. Most everyone has one these days. I was wondering if someone might have taken hers. I asked Connors about it and he said Kathryn didn't own one."

"That's a lie." Casey bristled. "She carried a laptop with her to work every day. Why would he lie about something like that?"

"I don't know." Larkin gave her a hard look. "The forensic team didn't find one when they searched her office."

"Take my word for it. Wherever she is, she carried it with her. The two things she was most protective of were her PC and the keys to the South Wing."

"She had to take the contents of that safe with her. I told you I heard her and some unknown man discussing what to do with the files. She finally agreed to take them home with her and keep them in her safe," Casey said.

"If Jerry sent Marcus after them, that means he knew the files were in her house," Larkin said

"I wasn't sure who she was talking to that day," Casey said. Marcus could have lied and just said Jerry sent him after the files." Casey wasn't ready to believe Jerry was the one doing these horrible things. I only know that Jimmy and I found the safe empty."

"You said Marcus came after you and your friend did," Larkin said.

"Yes…So that leaves only Kathryn who could have taken the evidence with her."

"What worries me is, there has been no activity on her credit cards or money withdrawn from her bank accounts since she disappeared. There's no record of Sam ever having an account. By questioning his friends, we found out he spent his whole pay check on drugs. I don't see him financing their trip."

"Neither do I," Casey agreed.

Larkin was amazed that he and Casey were so good at brainstorming. He and Cramer did it all the time and it helped them solve their cases.

"Are you going to arrest me for breaking into Kathryn's house?"

"The district attorney took me off the case, remember? If Deets knew I was investigating on my own, he would see to it that I was fired. It makes no difference if Connors did give me the okay. We found nothing incriminating. That means if there was ever any evidence at Lakeview, someone disposed of it."

"Are you and Cramer investigating Kathryn and Sam's disappearance?"

"Not officially; that isn't our department, but I just showed up while a team was looking through Bailey's place. They allowed me the run of the house and answered all my questions."

"You're a sly fox, aren't you? Do you believe their disappearance has anything to do with Trudy's murder and what's going on at Lakeview?" Casey asked.

"What do you think?"

"I really hadn't thought about it," Casey confessed. "All I've been thinking about is their leaving left me free to look after my sister."

"Maybe Jerry wasn't part of the plot against my family. Maybe it was all Sam and Kathryn, working with Marcus." For some reason she didn't want to believe it was Marcus, but if it wasn't, it had to be her lifelong friend.

"I'm worried about you," he said. "You're taking too many dangerous chances. Not only that. You don't believe that Jerry Connors is involved other than protecting the woman he loves. Promise me you won't trust him enough to give him any information."

"I promise. I won't tell him anything, but what about Marcus? He'll probably tell Jerry about Jimmy and me breaking into Kathryn's house. If Jerry's dangerous, he probable thinks I'm the one who has the files."

"That's exactly what I would think, Larkin said. "It would have to be you, or Marcus."

"That means if Jerry is behind the plot, Marcus is in danger also."

"That's right."

"Maybe not…He might think Kathryn took the files with her. That would be the obvious thinking, wouldn't it?"

"Unless he knew Kathryn wasn't coming back."

"What are you implying, Detective?"

"He might know Kathryn and Sam are dead."

"Or it could have been Marcus who killed Kathryn and Sam because they knew too much." She couldn't believe the man who had gone on vacations and boat rides with her family, who came to their house for dinner, was a cold-blooded murderer. "There's no proof that they're dead."

Larkin wanted to assure her that Marcus could be trusted, but stopped himself in time. His gut said the man was in love with Casey and Larkin didn't believe he would harm her. He also believed that if Marcus had told Connors about catching Casey at Bailey's house that day, Jerry would have murdered her already.

Larkin was leaning towards the view, that Sam and Kathryn were dead. An all-points bulletin had gone out for them and their vehicles. He couldn't believe that neither car had turned up. There were no hits on either of Kathryn's credit cards. Kathryn hadn't taken money out of her checking or her savings.

"I know you think that it's Jerry who is behind all of this, but why?" she asked, shaking her head.

"I don't know why, but weren't all these things going on before Marcus came?"

"Yes, but he could have been working behind the scenes. There might be a reason he chose Lakeview other than what he claims. I wasn't aware that he'd ever applied for a job, and then all at once he was there in our meeting," she said.

Larkin was worried. Casey didn't believe that Connors was behind everything because she thought she knew him. He had been in the business of murder for long enough to know a person never really knew anyone. More than likely, the villain was someone people thought would never do such a crime. Casey was getting in way too deep and he felt instinctively that something was about to blow. He just hoped that Casey wasn't in harm's way when it did.

Chapter 32

Casey returned home to find Marcus parked in her driveway. "Oh no," she moaned as she slid out of her car. She quickened her pace, but he was out of his vehicle before she made it to the door.

He still wore the same clothes he had on last night with a ten-o'clock shadow darkening his jaw. This was the first time she'd seen him other than clean-shaven. It made him look dark, mysterious, and dangerous.

"What are you doing here?" she asked, abruptly, as he approached her. "Didn't I give you enough information last night?"

"I didn't want to leave it strained between us. I tried to call, but you weren't home."

"I was home," she snapped, I just didn't want to talk to you."

"Look…I told you I didn't want you to get hurt."

"It's so nice of you to be concerned," she said.

He reached out and caught her arm in a vise-like grip. "I am concerned about you, damn it. I'm busting my ass trying to watch out for you."

"Don't bother," she said, jerking her arm away.

"Jerry told me that Arron had convinced you the woman in room 14 was his mother. He's concerned that you might go there and be harmed."

"I told you, I can take care of myself. Now get out of here. I need to take a shower and change my clothes. Obviously, you need to do the same," she said, wrinkling her nose. The truth was, he smelled a little musty, but it wasn't a turn off at all.

"I'm still wearing your perfume." He smiled, sniffing his lapel. "Nice." He offered her a smile, but she gave him a mean look in return.

He followed her to her front door.

"Look, I need to be alone and do some thinking," she said.

"That's what I dropped by to tell you. You can take tomorrow and the next day off."

"I need to work," she insisted, glaring at him.

"And I don't want you going to patient's rooms in the middle of the night anymore. I'm sleep deprived, trying to keep you safe."

"You're just trying to keep me away from my sister."

"You're obsessed with people you only believe are related to you."

"I have no doubt they're my family."

"Just so you know. I'm keeping the keys to the South Wing in my pocket from now on."

"Why are you doing this to me?" Her eyes pleaded with him to understand her need to help her family.

"I'm doing it for your own good, and for my peace of mind."

"I think you're involved in the cover-up."

"Oh, yes! The great conspiracy," he said.

It frustrated her like hell because he didn't believe her, but standing so close to him she couldn't stop her body from responding to his magnetism and remembering his lips on hers.

"I'm only doing what I think is right," his voice was husky. "Did you turn in the patient's DNA yet?"

"Screw you, Marcus. I'll tell you exactly what you tell me, nothing."

He had the nerve to look hurt. "I'm doing this for your safety, whether you believe it or not."

"I was never in any danger from Ruth."

"Look, we're not getting anywhere like this," Marcus said. "I know you've turned in the patient's DNA. Can you agree to just stay away from her at least until the results are back."

"Her name is Ruth, Marcus, and she's a person, not an animal."

"These patients are dangerous. Why can't you see that? Anyway, I've studied her file, and it says her name is Dana Collins."

There was no use trying to convince him of what she believed. She felt the real Dana had been released as Ruth Thompson, but she had no way of proving it until the DNA sample came back. "Did you tell Jerry about me collecting Ruth's sample?"

"I'm not answering any questions."

"Go home and take a shower, Marcus," she snapped. "You stink." She slipped inside and slammed the door in his face.

She slumped into the chair at her desk, put her head down, and cried it all out. Everyone at Lakeview was determined to keep her away from her family. She was bone-tired from all the late nights with Ruth and she needed a good night's sleep. Maybe it was best she did take a few days off from work. She certainly didn't feel like seeing other patients when she wasn't allowed to go anywhere near her own sister. After all, she had gotten a set of sheets, a clean flannel gown, and a couple of warm fuzzy blankets for Ruth's bed. She had changed her clothes before Marcus began stalking her last night. She knew Ruth wouldn't get changed again until she went back to work, but at least she was better off than before Casey started caring for her.

Chapter 33

Larkin sat at his desk lost in thought. Yesterday, Kathryn Bailey's and Sam Talbot's pictures appeared in the local paper. Usually a story like this brought out a dozen crazies at least, but not one person had called concerning their disappearance. No one had reported seeing Sam's 1999 Cutlass or Kathryn's brand-new BMW. It was as if no one cared that they were missing. In snooping around Lakeview and asking questions, Larkin found the other workers didn't care much for Sam. They all accused him of being bossy, even though, he had no more authority than they did. The same went for Bailey. They agreed the woman was hateful and mean. Casey had even talked Larkin into letting her offer a reward for anyone who had information as to their whereabouts.

Could Kathryn have made up with her sister and she and her lover be holed up in the hills of West Virginia? In these kinds of cases you followed the money, but there was still no activity on any of Kathryn Bailey's accounts. Casey had made a statement that Larkin was considering more and more. She'd made the remark that maybe Kathryn had cash stashed away in her safe and they were living on that. His people had checked all public transportation and there was no record of them leaving Springfield together. They could have used assumed names, but what in the world did they do with their vehicles? Earlier, an upset Casey West had called him. Marcus had told her not to return to work until Monday, effectively stopping her from visiting her sister. She wanted to know if Larkin could do anything to help her. He felt bad for her, but maybe Marcus had done her a favor. Larkin was concerned himself about the chances she was taking. With Casey away from Lakeview, he would have more time to really work on her case without having to worry that she was in danger.

Larkin jumped when the phone rang. It was Taylor in Missing Persons. "We have a couple here you might be interested in talking to," he said.

"Tell me it's not another murder case?"

"They claim to have seen Kathryn Bailey around the time she disappeared."

"Direct them to my office immediately," Larkin ordered. Could this be the break he'd been hoping for?

A few minutes later, a tall, scruffy man and a plain, petite woman appeared at his door. Larkin directed them to come in and sit down. The couple kept glancing at each other as if wondering what they had gotten themselves into.

"Could I have both of your names?" Larkin pulled out some forms and took his pen from his pocket. The woman glanced at the man.

"Is it absolutely necessary that we give our names?" the man asked. "I was under the impression; we could remain anonymous."

"James, we have to do this," the woman whispered. "It's the right thing to do."

"I know, baby," he said gently.

"We're both married, Detective Larkin, but not to each other," the woman spoke softly. "That's why James doesn't want to give you our names."

"I do need them. I'll be as discreet as I can, but I may need to ask you some questions at a later time."

"I told you it was a mistake to come here," James said.

"Now, James," she urged. "It's our civic duty to tell what we know about that woman."

"I thought that we vowed we would forget the incident ever happened," he said, breathing in a sigh.

"We don't love our spouses, Detective, but a divorce would mess up our children's lives," the woman explained.

"If we become involved in a scandal, the cops don't care what happens to our kids." James snapped.

"It's not my intention to hurt your families," Larkin said. "I promise, if I need to contact you, I will get in touch with you at work."

James sighed again. "My name is James Schrader, and she is Molly Kincaid." James rattled off his work numbers. "If you need to contact us, will you call me at work, and I'll get in touch with Molly."

"Taylor, in Missing Persons, tells me, you think you saw Kathryn Bailey on the night she disappeared?" Larkin said.

"We did see the woman you're looking for," James said, nodding and looking at his girlfriend. It was the date the paper mentioned that she disappeared.

"Why are you so positive about the date?"

"We were celebrating our anniversary," Molly spoke up.

"Excuse me?" Larkin said.

"We met a year ago on March 5th. We celebrate on that date every year." He gazed lovingly at Molly, and she smiled at him in return. .

"The date fits," Larkin agreed. "Kathryn didn't come to work on March 6th. What makes you so sure it was the same woman?"

"She was wearing the same clothes as in the picture in the paper," Molly answered.

"It was a black-and-white picture."

"She had on a checked jacket and I remember I liked the way the suit was cut," Molly explained. "It's something a woman pays attention to."

"All I remember is the blood," James shivered.

"Blood," Larkin asked.

"She was a mess," Molly said. "Her whole front was soaked in blood." She indicated an area from her shoulders to her waist. "Her legs were all scratched, her stockings torn, and her nails were all broken and bleeding."

Larkin snapped to attention. "She looked like she had been in a struggle?"

"It looked more like a war," James exaggerated. "She told us she'd been in an automobile accident."

"Where exactly did you see her?"

"We were about a quarter of a mile past the old quarry, heading back toward town," James said. "I almost hit her."

"I will never forget how she looked," Molly shivered. "Her hair was all wild, and she was soaking wet, the rain mixing with the blood." She shivered again.

"And you stopped for her?"

"I had to stop or hit her," James volunteered. "She ran right out into the road. We offered to take her to the hospital."

"Did she go to the hospital?" Excitement rose in Larkin. Maybe he could find out some information from the emergency room.

"No, she insisted we drive her home," James said.

"Did you take her home?"

"Yes, she was shaking so badly, and I had the heater going full blast. Her teeth were chattering so that I was afraid she was suffering from hypothermia."

"Was there anyone with her?"

The couple looked at each other and both of them shook their head.

"Was there anyone at her house?"

"If there was, I didn't see them." James replied.

"Did she ask you to come inside?"

"I stopped just inside the door…It was pouring rain, and I didn't want to mess up her carpet. She offered to pay me, but I told her she didn't owe me anything. She insisted, saying she owed me big time. She disappeared into a back room and came back with a hundred-dollar bill."

That was another clue. It proved Kathryn had money in her safe.

"I told her it was too much, but she insisted I take it. I was running late getting home, and I did need gas money, so I took it,"

"Is that the last time you saw her?"

"Yes…Until yesterday when I picked up my news-paper. Molly saw it also, but it took a while for her to talk me into coming here."

"We swore we would never tell anyone what happened that night," Molly explained. "I knew something was wrong with her story at the time, but in our situation we didn't need publicity."

"I understand," Larkin said. It certainly wasn't his place to judge them.

"She claimed the accident happened just down the road, but we never saw her car. When I passed back by that area after taking her and Molly home, I never spotted her vehicle."

"We'll do a search of the area where you say you picked her up. It's a wooded area and it was possible her car wouldn't have been seen from the highway."

"I guess," James said, but Larkin knew the man wasn't convinced.

"I think that's all I need right now, and I want to thank you both for coming in," Larkin said.

"There's a reward, isn't there, for us coming forward? I don't want any money for myself, but Molly could sure use it," James said.

"I don't want any reward just for doing the right thing," Molly said as if appalled.

"That's why I love you so much," he said.

The two of them stood to their feet. Larkin and James shook hands then Larkin assorted them to the door.

"If either of you think of anything else, you can give us a call." Larkin handed James his card.

"Please try to keep this from our families." James shifted from one foot to the other, clearly afraid of what Larkin would do with the information they supplied.

"I do appreciate you coming forward," Larkin said, "and I will do everything I can to keep this confidential. I'm sure the young lady who offered the reward will gladly give it to you if this information helps close the investigation."

James looked as though he doubted it and Molly just looked worried.

"We didn't come forward just for the money. I want you to know that," Molly said.

Larkin was on the phone to Cramer before the couple left the parking lot.

"What's up," Cramer answered on the second ring. He was on his way back from a drug related homicide.

"I just interviewed a couple who saw Kathryn Bailey the night she disappeared." Larkin waited for his reaction.

"Are you sure it was her?" Cramer sounded excited waiting for Larkin to continue.

"They're sure of the date because they're having an extra-marital affair, and it was the anniversary of their first meeting." Larkin allowed his message to sink in.

"Isn't that quaint? An affair anniversary. I wonder if Hallmark has a card for that.

I think I'll start working on my submissions now," Cramer said, his voice drenched in sarcasm.

"Still having trouble at home, huh?"

"I'm thinking about letting my wife move in with my mother. That way they can run each other nuts. Don't ask," he said, hearing the question on Larkin's mind.

"So getting back to our love-birds…They saw Kathryn Bailey, huh?"

"The thing they remember the most was that she was soaking wet and covered with blood."

"I wonder whose!" Cramer exclaimed.

"They don't know. It might have been hers from the way they said she looked."

"Or, maybe old Sam's," Cramer volunteered.

"I thought about that," Larkin admitted.

"Where did you say this sighting took place?"

"They claimed to have seen her close to the old gravel pit. She told them she had been in an accident."

"Are you sure the couple didn't have too much wine during their celebration?"

"I believe them. The man took Bailey home, and he described the area where she lives. He even told me the right address. It was her all right."

"What do you make of it?" Cramer asked.

"I have no idea what she's up to, but I can't imagine why we haven't found her car. There was no traffic accident reported. The couple never saw a disabled vehicle that night either."

"It's just another hole in a case that's riddled with them." Cramer sighed.

"We know three things; we didn't know before."

"And what is that?"

"Kathryn Bailey is alive, she had cash in her safe, and she took the elusive files that Casey told us about." Larkin volunteered.

"That's a Rodger," Cramer answered.

"Would you like to meet me out by the old quarry?"

"I thought you'd never ask," Cramer quipped, turning his car around.

"How did you make out on tracing the owner of Lakeview?" Larkin asked, Clinton Cummings their PC geek.

"It's owned by some overseas conglomerate. There are about ten different stockholders; Jerry Connors and a Franklin guy are both on the list. I have no idea if it's the Franklin you're looking for. Does Casey West know what her Father's first name and middle initial is? Franklin is a common name."

"I don't know, but I'll ask her."

Wow!... Larkin was excited. There were two names he recognized. He had no proof, but he would bet money that one of them was Casey's biological father. He needed to know who would receive Franklin's share of Lakeview, now that he was deceased. With that information, Trudy's clue to Casey made more sense. If he was right, Casey had another inheritance coming.

"It's been like I'm chasing my tail," Clinton said. I think you need to find someone way beyond my geek level."

"David says there is none better," Larkin said, patting him on the shoulder. "Just keep at it, and let me know the minute you find something."

"Will do," he said.

"Thanks for doing this for me. And I need to thank David for letting me borrow you."

"Hold off on that. I didn't tell him I was working on this. Cramer came over and said that Larkin needed me, so I left."

"Maybe I can smooth it over with your boss later," Larkin said.

"If we crack this case, he might forgive me."

If it's any consolation, my gut says we're darn close," Larkin said.

Larkin sat in his office lost in thought. His gut said Jerry was after the Franklin children's share of Lakeview. How he was going to prove it was another story.

Chapter 34

Kathryn sat on her sister's porch, listening to the soft chirping of the birds, and sipping her morning coffee. She breathed in the fresh mountain air. It would soon be time for her next move. At this point, she hadn't decided what she was going to do.

She felt safe here in the thick backwoods, twenty-five miles from civilization, but she was also smart enough to know it was just an illusion. Jerry knew her sister's address and soon he would figure out she was still alive, and he would send a hit man to kill her. She felt a twinge of conscience when she realized she was not only putting herself in danger, but her sister also. It was short-lived, however. Staying here would give her some time to regroup. She wished now she hadn't left her safe open. It was just too tempting to send Jerry a message. Now he would know she was still alive and that she had the evidence to hang his ass.

Kathryn sighed, got up and walked inside, carrying her coffee cup. Beth Ann sat at the table with a bowl of oatmeal and a novel, beside her on the table.

"Beth, would you to make a call for me when you're finished with breakfast?"

Beth eyed her suspiciously. "I don't think so. You're not weaving me into your web of deception. It's bad enough that I'm harboring a fugitive. I'm not getting any more involved."

"You won't be getting involved…"

"That's what I said. I'm not getting involved," Beth vowed.

"Fine. I'll do it myself." Beth was a mean bitch, and she never would have allowed her to stay if she hadn't shelled out five hundred dollars and promised her she would get out before the month was over. She knew now why she and her sister never had gotten along. Beth had always been a sniveling coward. She was glad at this point that she'd kept the card Larkin had given her.

"Detective Larkin, Homicide." There was silence on the phone for a second.

"You need to listen carefully, and you might want to write this down," a woman's voice that he recognized said into the phone. It was Kathryn Bailey.

"Who is this?" he asked anyway, just to make sure. There was a rustling sound over the phone. "You don't need to waste time trying to trace this call. This is Kathryn Bailey and I have information that you need about a couple of murders and another attempted murder. I'm interested in making a deal."

Larkin's breath caught. "What murders are we talking about?"

"Trudy Madison's and Sam Talbot's," she said. "I have enough evidence right in front of me to fry Jerry Connors."

"We need to get together and discuss this in person," Larkin sit up at full attention. He motioned for Cramer to set up the taping equipment.

"I'm not ready to come in just yet."

"Can you tell me some of this evidence? I'll need a few more details before I can offer any deals," Larkin told her.

"Have some divers go out to the old quarry. I think you'll find something very interesting. You also need to talk to a lawyer named Perish about Gary Franklin's will. He has an office on High Street there in town. I have to go now, but I'll call you back later."

"No, don't go. I need to know more," Larkin begged, but it was too late. The phone went dead.

Somehow she knew that Larkin wasn't the one to offer her a deal. Maybe the district attorney would be more willing to cooperate with her. Jerry had mentioned being friends with Deets, and going through Information on her phone, she was soon in touch with his office.

* * * *

"We need to keep this as quiet as we can," Larkin told Ted Cramer when he hung up the phone. "Let's get some divers out to the old quarry and see if there's anything there. I know we said we'd wait to investigate that couple's story until tomorrow, but this can't wait. This case is finally coming together. While the divers are out there, we're going to be looking up a lawyer named Parish."

"I have it right here," Cramer had heard Larkin mention the attorney's name, and he'd looked up the name as Larkin spoke to Bailey. "Here you go," he said, handing Larkin the phone book with John Parish's name and address underlined.

Chapter 35

Larkin and Cramer were almost out the door when District Attorney Deets caught them. "Where are you two going?" he asked.

"To chase down a lead," Cramer grumbled.

"I need you to step into my office first," Deets said.

"What the hell is going on, Deets?" Larkin snapped, as he entered his office and noticed him with a handful of papers.

"Kathryn Bailey is turning state's evidence about a couple of murders," he explained.

"What are you saying? You've made a deal with the devil?" Larkin asked. "What did you offer her, considering she's in it up to her neck?"

"We're offering her five years' probation."

"You have got to be kidding. You're letting her get away with murder."

"I thought you would be happy to wrap this thing up," Deets said.

"You didn't believe there was a case when Trudy Madison was murdered. Now you are interested in investigating Kathryn Bailey's allegations. How can you let her get away with this?"

"You know how the system works, Larkin," Deets smirked. "Sometimes we have to let the not-so-guilty walk in order to convict the monsters. If she can prove all of her allegations against Connors, he's about as bad as they come. Your job is to find out if what she's saying about him is true. He's an important man in this town and I want to make sure we have the evidence against him before he's arrested. She's supposed to be in town Sunday to deliver the rest of her evidence, and if it pans out, we can pick him up first thing Monday morning."

"I can't believe you're letting her get away with this." Disgust oozed from Larkin's voice.

"She says she went along because she was frightened of him. The man did try to murder her, for heaven's sakes."

"If he did, that's the only reason she's telling on him," Larkin snapped.

"You're just upset that she came to me after going to you first," Deets accused.

"I believe in justice, and she knows I would have put her butt in jail."

"Don't you understand? She threatened to leave the country if we didn't let her turn state's evidence." Deets whined.

"Would it be too much to ask you to keep this out of the press until we actually have enough evidence to put Connors away forever?" Larkin's voice dripped sarcasm.

"Do you think I want to take the chance of this getting out and then finding it's just a hoax? I'm going to make sure we have an airtight case before the press gets wind of it. You need to keep me abreast of what's happening every minute. Don't try keeping me in the dark like you usually do. Is that understood?"

Larkin gave him a dirty look before taking his keys out of his pocket and motioning Cramer toward the door.

"Where are you going, now?" Deets called after him.

"We're going to see a lawyer," Larkin supplied.

On the way, Larkin filled Cramer in on the phone call from Kathryn.

"It's funny she mentioned Casey West's father, because David Blake's PC geek tracked it down until he found out Franklin, who I think, is Casey's father, was once a shareholder in Lakeview."

Cramer said, as they rode along. "Cummings told me that most of the owners sold out to one person. He's not sure, yet, who that person is."

"My guess is Gary Franklin?" Larkin replied.

"How did you know?" Cramer exclaimed.

I keep going back to the clue Trudy left Casey about Franklin and owner. My guess is that Casey's father was the one who finally wound up owning the place."

"But Franklin is dead," Cramer said.

"Dead people leave wills, right?"

"And we're on our way to find out what is in Franklin's," Cramer said. He gave Larkin a high-five, almost wrecking their police car.

"I haven't made out my will yet," Larkin told him, how about being a little more careful."

* * * *

Larkin and Cramer were in John Parish's office only about thirty minutes before they had all of the answers that had eluded Casey West. Larkin didn't know how he would contain himself until Monday.

Chapter 36

Larkin and Cramer pulled behind Jerry Connors's car in the parking lot at Lakeview on that fateful Monday morning. Jerry got out of his BMW and looked toward the two policemen who were following him toward the main entrance.

"You have everything we need," Larkin asked his partner.

"Yes, I have the warrant, my handcuffs, and gun." Cramer patted his pocket. I can't wait to put the bracelets on that sick son-of-a bitch."

"Make sure you read him his rights."

"Don't worry, boss, I've got this."

"You have your cell phone?"

"It's just like American Express. I don't leave home without it."

"Here's Casey's number. Call and make sure she's on her way. She deserves to be a part of this."

Cramer quickly connected with Casey and she assured him she was already on her way to work. He exited the conversation and gave Larkin a big smile. Larkin returned it. He knew Cramer lived for these moments.

Jerry stopped and waited for them at the front doors, a frown on his face as he watched Cramer make a hurried phone call. The two detectives had hung around Lakeview far more than Jerry cared for, but today it seemed different somehow. He was sure he'd left no evidence at the facility that they could use against him. The only thing that concerned him was the files that Kathryn kept in her safe. He would feel a lot better if he knew who had them. Marcus said he found her safe empty, but Jerry was suspicious. Maybe he read the files and turned them over to the police.

"You're out early this morning, Detective," Jerry said as the two cops approached him.

"I have some things I need to talk to you about," Larkin said.

"Certainly, but I'll need to unlock everything first. We can meet in my office in five minutes."

"We can go with you while you do all of that," Larkin said.

"This must be serious; why don't we step inside my office now," Jerry invited, as he unlocked his office door. Cramer stepped inside as well.

"Won't you both have a seat," Jerry offered, going to a closet and hanging up his top-coat."

Cramer remained standing but took out a small tape recorder and placed it on Jerry's desk.

"Would you like to tell me what this is all about?' Jerry looked worried for the first time since they knew him. Surely his new partner hadn't ratted him out. He hadn't told her too much so they couldn't have a lot on him. The only one who knew everything, hopefully, drowned at the bottom of the quarry.

"What can I help you with, Detectives? I do need to get to work."

"You could start by confessing to a couple of murders," Cramer said.

A knock at the door interrupted them, and Jerry looked shocked. Were these two just fishing or had someone gave them evidence against him?

"Excuse me, gentlemen," Jerry grumbled, getting up from his desk and going to answer the door. "This seems to be Grand Central this morning."

"Casey! I have company, dear. Could you come back later?" he asked.

"Oh, I asked her to stop by," Larkin interrupted. "You don't mind, do you?"

Jerry bowed and waved her into the room. Casey looked confused. She had no idea why she was here.

"I hate to rush this," Jerry said, returning to his chair behind a sturdy mahogany desk, "but I do have a hospital to run."

"It shouldn't take very long," Larkin said, toying with his prey.

Both Casey and Jerry looked toward Larkin, waiting for an explanation. Just then the office door burst open, and Connors went a deadly pale.

Casey exclaimed, "Mrs. Bailey!"

Larkin was shocked also. This wasn't part of the plan. But by Jerry's expression, Larkin was anxious to see it play out.

In her arm she carried a folder as she stepped up to Connors's desk.

"What's the matter, Jerry? You look like you've seen a ghost," Kathryn said.

One look at Jerry's face and Larkin knew he recognized the folder she carried.

"Kathryn, we've been so worried," Jerry recovered quickly.

"Oh, shut up, Jerry," Kathryn snapped. "You should have used one of your precious bullets on me like you did on old Sam."

"You shot Sam!" Casey gasped, looking at Jerry.

Kathryn smirked. "The police are probably fishing him out of the quarry as we speak. If you turn on the TV, you might catch a newscast about what they found."

"Shut up, Kathryn. I'll get us a good lawyer, a whole team of them if I have to," Jerry spouted. Remember, when they find the gun, it will have your prints on it, not mine."

"You made me clasp it in my hand, but I was careful not to touch the trigger.

"It's too late for an attorney, Jerry," she said, walking around him. "You shouldn't have pushed me into that quarry. When you did, you sealed your fate. You thought you were so damned smart," she said, "but the truth is I've been one step ahead of you from the start. It's sad when two people have been involved in a relationship as long as we have, and you know nothing about me." Kathryn sneered. "You see, I know everything about you, Jerry. Like what a psychopath you really are. You used me, Jerry, and then you tried to murder me."

Cramer started to handcuff Jerry, but Larkin caught his arm to stop him. He was anxious for Casey to hear everything.

"What are you rambling about, Kathryn?" Jerry finally asked.

"I'm sure you would've done things differently had you known that I was once head of a swim team. I was this close to making the Olympics," she said, snapping her fingers. "I was number one on the women's team in college. I'm sure if you'd known that, you would have put a bullet in my head before pushing me into the quarry."

"Shut up, Kathryn, you're in this as deep as I am."

"I rolled down the window to beg for my life. I knew the only chance I had was getting through that opening and being able to swim. It's surprising how it all comes back to you when you're trying to save your life."

"Shut up, Kathryn. We'll hire the best lawyer's money can buy."

"Thanks, love," she grinned as she moved her face close to his. "But I'm not going to need one." She tossed her head toward Larkin. "I've decided to cooperate with the detective here and turn state's evidence. I also talked to your old friend, Deets. He's the one who told me about the detectives' little party. I wouldn't have missed it for the world. It's amazing how fast the district attorney turned on you when he found out how putting your ass in jail will boost his career. Because of my helpfulness, I only get a few years' probation."

Casey gasped, causing Larkin to look at her. "Believe me, it wasn't my idea," he said.

"You, bitch!" Jerry arose from his chair and lunged at Kathryn, but Larkin intervened.

"Sit back down, Connors," he ordered. "The party is just getting started.

"I think we'll let Kathryn continue. I just wanted you and everyone else to know how much we have against you, and how useless it is for you to keep on lying."

"What have you told them?" Connors's eyes hardened into chips of ice as he stared at Kathryn.

"I told them who really owns this place." Kathryn smiled.

"The deal you made with Franklin and the signed documents which were once in this folder. It holds useless pieces of papers at this point. But you ought to have seen your face when you recognized the folder." She laughed. "I've already given all the evidence to the prosecuting attorney. You should have listened when I said you ought to destroy them."

"Franklin's lawyer has a copy of them, but no one was ever supposed to know about him," Kathryn said.

"Who does own this place?" Casey asked.

Kathryn turned toward the younger woman. "Oh, I guess that would be you, dear," she said.

"Me?" Casey gasped. "How can that be?"

"Would you like to tell her, Jerry, or shall I?"

Connors glared at Kathryn as if he'd like to cut her throat.

"It's a long story," Bailey said, "but I'll try to give you a short version." She looked at Jerry then back to Casey. "Your father and several investors bought this place. Your father used his inheritance from his mother's estate. He did it because your mother had mental problems, and he wanted a place for her to get the treatment she needed."

"Half of that money he inherited should have been mine," Jerry interrupted.

Kathryn turned back to him. "I'm telling the story, Jerry," she said. "We gave you a chance, but you clammed up."

"I'd like to hear the story from him, if you don't mind." Casey walked up to his desk, so she could look him eye to eye.

"What do you want to know?" he asked, seeming to realize he was defeated.

"For starters, I want to know why you think you should have half of my father's inheritance," she said.

"The truth is, honey, there is a lot you don't understand," Kathryn interrupted. "You see, Uncle Jerry here is really your uncle…Well, sort of."

"How can that be, when my real father's name was Franklin and his is Connors?"

"Your dad and I were stepbrothers." Jerry took over and began to talk. "My mother had me before she married, Henry Franklin, my stepfather," Jerry explained. "It was his intention to adopt me and raise Gary and me as brothers, but his mother wouldn't hear of it. She hated my mother and me, and she told Henry if he adopted me, she would exclude him from her will. We weren't good enough to have the Franklin name," he spat. "I think the Franklins did pretty well by you," Kathryn snapped. "Henry's mother did pay for your fancy education… Isn't that right? I think you mentioned that to me one time."

"She only did it so I wouldn't be an embarrassment to her and the rest of the Franklin clan," he said.

"For whatever reason, you should have been grateful," Kathryn asserted.

"So the old bat turned loose enough money to educate me. I worked my ass off to be the best psychiatrist around. I made a name for myself, but instead of being proud of me, she left everything to Gary. He was the one with the precious Franklin name. Instead of doing the right thing and giving me half, your dad kept the whole inheritance," he said bitterly.

"What I want to know is where my sister and nephew fit into all of this?" Casey asked, pacing back and forth in front of his desk.

"When your mother started showing signs of psychosis, your father and a group of investors bought Lakeview. Your father asked me to treat your mother, and if I would, my name would be considered as one of the investors. When his mother died and left all her money to him, he bought out the other investors. He was a very weak man, Casey. He wanted someone else to take care of his problems. He always passed his responsibilities off to someone else, usually me. That's why he put you and your sister up for adoption. He said that if I took care of your mother and any of his family who inherited the sickness…" he made quotes with his fingers. "That is what he called it, he would leave Lakeview to me. You see, he had just found out he was suffering from terminal cancer and didn't have long to live."

Casey shook her head in disbelief.

"After his death, I finally felt I was going to get what I deserved, and then his lawyer contacted me. He told me that Gary had put all of these restrictions in his will. He wanted me to find his children, and if they had mental problems like his wife, I was to take care of them here at Lakeview. The only way that I could inherit this place is if one of you signed it over to me. The catch was that you girls had to be competent enough to know what you were doing. I convinced the attorney handling his estate that I would find you both, so the lawyer stopped looking."

"Don't let him kid you, honey," Kathryn spat. "He knew where you were all the time. He made a bundle by placing you with the Wests."

"You sold me to the Wests?" She looked toward Jerry for confirmation.

Jerry shrugged his shoulders. "I did you both a favor. They couldn't have kids, and you were placed in a wealthy family. I monitored you as you grew up. I had nothing to worry about from you. I knew your adoptive parents left you well provided for, and they vowed not to tell you anything about the adoption. I contacted Gary's lawyer and explained your situation and Ruth's. He said he would have to do some investigating on his own. He did some research and found out that I told him the truth about your adoptive parents leaving you well off. I convinced him that we shouldn't bother you, that we should respect the Wests' wishes about you not learning you were adopted. He finally saw it my way, but that left only Ruth. He said that I was going to have to wait six months and then he would talk to Ruth and determine if she still wanted to sign the place over to me. I knew she was as crazy as they come, but I insisted she was in her right mind and capable of signing. I knew in six months the woman would be worse. It was then I decided on the fake Ruth. That way I could show that she had been released and living on her own, so therefore she was well enough to sign the papers.

Casey gasped. "You come up with this scheme, just to steal our inheritance?"

"Now you're getting smart, Kathryn said. Then to Jerry, "You were that close to having it all, and you blew it by trying to murder me."

Jerry turned to Casey. "I took care of your crazy mother, then your sister for all these years. The place should have been mine," he whined.

Kathryn broke in, "He had until April 1st to settle things with you both."

Casey shivered. The first of April was next week. "So, you were planning this since day one," she accused.

"Your sister was married to a piece of white trash and had a kid. I gave her old man a few thousand bucks and he gladly let me bring her to Lakeview. He realized she was crazy and he was glad to get rid of her and the kid. Especially since I told him insanity ran in the family, and the boy would turn out just like her. I convinced him that I was concerned about them because they were family."

"So you brought my sister here and decided to treat her like an animal. To—to drug my nephew…" Casey spluttered through her rage. "And you did it all for this place?"

"Don't judge me," he said. "I took care of your mother, almost all of her married life. Your father was spoiled and weak like his old man. He handed all of his problems over to me. Don't you see? He owed me this place."

"What about my sister and her son?" Casey hissed.

"As for your sister, she was nuts anyway," Jerry excused.

Casey's hand came out in a resounding slap against Jerry's cheek. "And what about me, Jerry? What was your plan for me? Was I going to conveniently lose my mind as well. Was I to be incapacitated by drugs? Was I going to wind up living in the South Wing along with my sister? Or, were you going to murder me like you did my friend, Trudy?"

Jerry cowered behind his desk, rubbing his red cheek. "If the couple I gave you to had never died, you would never have known you were adopted. After the fake Ruth signed the papers. I thought maybe you and I might get together. Some women like older men."

Kathryn gave a belly laugh at the look of revulsion on Casey's face.

"You, have really got to be kidding!" Casey exclaimed. "After the way you treated my sister and nephew, I wouldn't spit on you," she said.

"Don't you see? We would have had it made if we'd gotten together. Do you have any idea what this place is worth?"

"You're more disturbed than my mother and sister," Casey said through clenched teeth.

"I'm not crazy. I just didn't expect the Wests to die and for you to ask me for a job. I thought it over and decided it would be best if you were here, so I could watch you. All I had to do was bade my time until the fake Ruth signed the papers. Everything would have gone as planned if that crazy nurse hadn't started snooping around the South Wing, taking pictures. Kathryn and I were afraid she had discovered something. We had to kill her don't you see?"

"You murdered her because she discovered the truth."

"Actually, Sam murdered her for Kathryn." He stared at the woman in question.

"I did it because you wanted it done," Kathryn countered.

"But I didn't get laid for executing the order," Jerry snapped.

Casey stared at the man she had always love and respected. "What kind of sick fantasy world do you live in?" she spat.

Kathryn smiled as she swept her gaze from Jerry to Casey. "Well, I'm glad I helped shed some light on a few things for you, dear."

"You're worse than he is for going along with this scheme." Casey whirled on her. "If I had my way, you'd be going to prison right along with him." Casey turned to Larkin. "I need you to get them both out of here, so I can breathe some clean air. I'm the owner of this place, right?"

Larkin nodded. "You will be the first of April."

"Why, your ungrateful little bitch!" Kathryn moved toward Casey, but Larkin stepped between them and took hold of Kathryn.

"Cramer, cuff Connors and take him down to the station."

Jerry got to his feet and Cramer spin him around to put on the cuffs, at the same time beginning to recite his Miranda rights.

Larkin then told Kathryn, "The deal you took was strictly Deets's idea." he assured her. "I agree with Casey a hundred percent. If I had my way, you both would be going to jail. Just know that I'll be watching you. If you violate your parole just one little bit, you'll find yourself in prison right along with Connors."

Kathryn's countenance changed. "I know you probably won't believe this, Detective, but I didn't do it for the money. I was in love with the bastard. I would have done anything for him. I did do everything for him until he tried to murder me. You may find it hard to believe me, but I have become quite fond of the simple life. It's beautiful in the mountains and peaceful. I've saved enough that I can live a comfortable life there. My sister and her daughter need me, and I'll be able to help them out as well. I've changed, whether you know it or not. I've been given a second chance, and I'll use it wisely, you can rest assured of that. I'm thinking of getting me a mountain man and living happily ever after."

"Just be here for his trial. The deal is off if you're not here to testify."

"I wouldn't miss it for the world," she said. She gave Jerry a defiant look.

"Let's go downtown, shall we, Connors?" Cramer said.

"I demand to see my attorney!" Jerry shouted as Cramer marched him out of the office.

'Can you come to the police station so we can sort this out?" Larkin asked Casey.

She started to answer when Marcus Kelly barged into the office.

"What the hell is going on?" He observed Jerry in handcuffs and Casey and the two detectives starting to leave.

"And what part did you play in the mess?" Casey asked.

"Actually, he's been helping me keep an eye on you." Larkin smiled.

"Don't tell me you're really a cop instead of a doctor," she snapped.

"No, nothing like that." Larkin laughed. "He came to see me the day after the big storm that locked you two in together. He stampeded into my office irate over the way I was using you in my investigation."

"And trying to watch you was a full-time job," Marcus said irritably.

"I didn't ask you to watch out for me," she snapped.

"No, but Detective Larkin did," he replied. "I love you, damn it, or haven't you figured that out yet?"

Tears filled her eyes as she threw herself into his arms. "I love you, too, but I was so afraid you were involved with what was happening to Ruth and Arron." Marcus was kissing and caressed her.

Larkin smiled. Casey deserved some love in her life. He recognized that prickly evolvement they had going on and knew from the start they were attracted to each other.

"Arron, where are you, buddy?" Marcus called.

The door burst open again and Arron flew into the room at full-speed, throwing himself at Casey. She gathered him in her arms, squeezing him with all her might. "It's going to be okay from now on. I promise you," she told the boy. "By the way... I'm your Aunt Casey."

"I know," Arron said, pushing away from her slightly. "Marcus has already told me."

"How did you know?" she asked, looking over Arron's head.

"I kept some of Ruth's sample, Marcus said. "I paid to have it analyzed. I needed to have the proof for myself."

"How did you get my DNA?"

"I got your saliva from my jacket where you slept on my shoulder."

"How...?"

"They cut a piece out of the jacket."

"You ruined your beautiful suit." Casey was embarrassed about drooling on his shoulder. "Why didn't you tell me what you planned to do?" she asked.

"I know you didn't trust me, and I knew if you found out for sure Ruth was your sister, you would try to take matters into your own hands. I was afraid you would confront Jerry and he wouldn't hesitate to kill you. I didn't want anything to go wrong before there was enough evidence in place to arrest him," Marcus confessed.

"I hate to break up this happy occasion, but I need to allow Larkin to read the paper Deets and I signed, before I head back to the hills." Kathryn stepped up and handed Larkin the document in question. Everyone had forgotten the woman was still there.

"Deets has the contracts that Jerry and Franklin signed. Everything was put together by, John Perish, the Franklin's family, attorney. All she will have to do," she nodded toward Casey, "Is go to his office, sign papers and take possession of this place." She shivered. Believe me, she's welcome to it." Kathryn said.

"Let me see that," Larkin said.

She handed him the paper and waited while he read.

Larkin shook his head and handed it back to her. "Here's to seeing you one last time in court." His voice dripped sarcasm.

"The feeling is mutual, Detective," she said taking back her pardon and walking out of the building for the last time. She would look for a man from the hills and learn to live quietly like her sister.

Chapter 37

Later that month, Casey answered her doorbell and found Larkin holding a beautifully wrapped gift. She threw herself into his arms and gave him a big hug.

"I'm so glad you stopped by," she said, inviting him into the living room. "I've missed you."

"I've missed you as well," he said.

"This is for you." He held the box out to her.

"What is this?" she asked.

"It's a little gift for a job well done," he said with a smile.

She placed the gift on the table. "Do you have time for a cup of coffee?"

"Sure, why not." He said, taking the seat she offered him.

"I stopped by to see how things were going with you now that the trial is over."

She called to him from her kitchen. "I only have instant coffee; will that be okay?"

"That's fine," he assured her. She returned with a steaming mug and a can of diet soda for herself. "Two spoons of creamer, right?"

"Do you have a coaster?"

She waved as if it didn't matter.

Larkin smiled. The woman would never be little Susie homemaker. Like him, she lived her job.

Casey sat down on the love seat next to him. "I made Marcus an equal partner in Lakeview," she said, then took a sip of her diet soda. "Do you think I did the right thing?"

"It doesn't matter what I think. What do you think?" Larkin asked.

"He has such amazing ideas for Lakeview," she said. Her eyes shone when she talked about Marcus. "Actually, we both do."

"How so?" Larkin took a drink of coffee, grimaced, and forced himself to swallow.

"Too strong?" she asked.

"How many spoons of coffee did you put in this cup?"

"Six. Was that too many?" she asked. "Hold on, I'll make you another."

He shook his head. "I can't stay that long. I just wanted to know how things were going for you."

"Marcus has asked me to marry him, and I said yes," she said. "As soon as we're married, we're going to start the proceedings to adopt Arron. He'll be living with us."

"That's great news!" Larkin exclaimed. "I'm happy for all of you. What about your sister? How is she doing?"

"She has suffered such trauma, Larkin. I don't think she will ever be able to leave a controlled environment like Lakeview. She does have a regular room now with plenty of windows where she can see the sunshine. We painted her room a soothing blue. It is a color known to calm patients. We allow Arron to visit her every day and most days, she recognizes him. It's good for them both."

"Does the boy understand about his mother?"

"Absolutely. He knows the truth about her condition. He's an intelligent boy who loves his mother."

"You're a remarkable young woman," Larkin said. "If Marcus hadn't beaten me to it, I would be making a play for you myself."

"You can't kid me. You're married to your job, Larkin. It takes one to know one. I believe it'll work between Marcus and I because we're both obsessed with helping the disturbed."

"The first thing I decided to do at Lakeview was eliminate the South Wing. We've moved the violent patients to another facility. There were only a couple, when Marcus and I evaluated them. The others we plan to place in cheerful rooms and work with them. We've started renovations to transform the South Wing into a modern apartment for us to live in."

"Wow! You two have been busy," Larkin said.

"You need to stop by, Detective," she said. "You wouldn't recognize the place."

"I'll do that," he promised. "It sounds as though you're changing the atmosphere of the place."

"That's the plan anyway," she said smiling. "I'm taking care of my sister and her son for the rest of their lives. I think that's what my father had in mind when he drew up his will."

"What I don't understand is why he allowed a snake like Jerry Connors to be in charge of finding his children and running Lakeview?" Larkin said.

"In my father's defense, Jerry Connors fooled many people, including me. He and my dad were raised as brothers. Why wouldn't my father trust him?"

"What do you think about the outcome of the trial?"

"I think two consecutive life terms was appropriate, don't you?" she asked.

"I was satisfied with it," Larkin agreed.

"I think Kathryn was shocked when the judge put her on probation for the rest of her life," Casey smiled.

"I think so, too," Larkin agreed. "I think the judge felt the same way we did about her."

"What about the woman who Jerry was going to pass off as Ruth Thompson? Did you ever find her?"

"Yes, we traced her to a cabin that Jerry owns beside a nearby park. She had to be hospitalized; she was in such poor condition when we found her," Larkin said.

He stood to his feet. "I hope, now that you're marrying Marcus, he won't stop me from visiting."

"I will divorce him if he tries," she vowed. "I was afraid I'd never see you again, now that this is all over."

"Someone has to teach you to make a decent cup of coffee," he grinned.

"It's good to see you have your priorities straight," she laughed.

"How about opening your present so I can go," Larkin said.

"You really shouldn't have," she said, as she unwrapped the package.

"I had no idea what to get a rich woman who has everything to show my appreciation?" Larkin quipped. "All I could think of was this. Something you would never buy for yourself. I couldn't have solved this case without you, you know."

"I was highly motivated," she said.

She took the piece of red cloth out of the box and shook it out. "It's—It's a cape," she said.

"Read the back of it," Larkin directed.

The bold black writing made her laugh. "Crusader of Lost Causes," she read aloud. "I love it!" she exclaimed, kissing him on the cheek.

"You earned it!" He nodded his head. "I wish you and Marcus the best."

"As I do you as well." She hugged him once more. "The cape will be one of my proudest processions, I assure you. When I look at it I will think of Trudy. I think this really belongs to her."

Larkin nodded. "If you ever need anything, just call," he said. "I mean that."

"Thanks, Detective. The same goes for you."

He kissed her on the cheek, and then headed to his car. It never hurt to have a wealthy friend, and he couldn't ask for a better one than Casey West. He would always think of her as his partner and a fellow crusader of lost causes.

Now that Jerry's trial was over, she could concentrate on helping her friend Jimmy who was trying desperately, for the first time, to get his life in order. He was painting again, attacking it with such passion that Casey believed he would go the distance this time. His old art instructor had come out of retirement to work with Jimmy, his prize student. Casey knew that Robert Clarke had many connections in the art world, and he had already set up a couple of showings for Jimmy. As she thought about her friend, she began to smile. Her sister and nephew were thriving, and Jimmy was doing so well, she would have to look around for another lost cause.

www.ingramcontent.com/pod-product-compliance
Lightning Source LLC
LaVergne TN
LVHW011931070526
838202LV00054B/4580